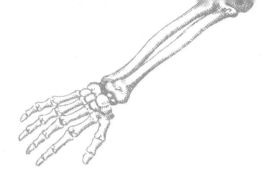

Doggone Bones

A Sarah Booth Delaney Mystery

CAROLYN HAINES

MINOTAUR BOOKS
NEW YORK

First published in the United States by Minotaur Books, an imprint of St. Martin's Publishing Group.

DOGGONE BONES. Copyright © 2025 by Carolyn Haines. All rights reserved. Printed in the United States of America. For information, address St. Martin's Publishing Group, 120 Broadway, New York, NY 10271.

www.minotaurbooks.com

The Library of Congress Cataloging-in-Publication Data is available upon request.

ISBN 978-1-250-37765-4 (hardcover)
ISBN 978-1-250-37766-1 (ebook)

Our books may be purchased in bulk for promotional, educational, or business use. Please contact your local bookseller or the Macmillan Corporate and Premium Sales Department at 1-800-221-7945, extension 5442, or by email at MacmillanSpecialMarkets@macmillan.com.

First Edition: 2025

1   3   5   7   9   10   8   6   4   2

In memory of Pat Sellers, a fearless worker for animals her entire life and a bang-up journalist to boot.
I miss her every day.

1

Heat blasts from the oven as I crack the door open and peek at the baking sheet of heart-shaped cookies. Almost done! I have just enough dough for one more batch.

"Well, look at you, Miss Betty Crocker!"

I didn't need to turn around. Jitty is standing behind me, literally breathing down my neck. The sudden appearance of the resident haint of Dahlia House no longer startles me. Most of the time. The truth is, while I complain about Jitty, I also love that she is with me. Most of the time.

"What's shaking, Jitty?" I resist turning around to look at her. She always shows up in the craziest personas. Greek goddesses, ancient warriors—Jitty has centuries of options.

"Sweets for the sweet," she says in that sly voice that lets me know that back in the day, Jitty was very likely a romantic wrecking ball when she chose to be. She loved her husband, Coker, but she knew how to sashay and flirt.

"Valentine's Day is around the corner and, yes, I am baking

Toll House cookies for Coleman. I'll take some cookies to the deputies, too."

My romantic partner, Coleman Peters, happens to be sheriff of Sunflower County, Mississippi. DeWayne and Budgie are his two deputies. They are good law officers and friends.

"What about Tinkie? Are she and Oscar and Maylin going to get some cookies?"

Now Jitty is just deviling me. "Of course. I wouldn't leave my business partner and her family out of a sweet treat."

"Good news. Something tells me you're going to need Tinkie's help soon. Very soon."

Jitty has a lot of mysterious powers. Sometimes she implies she can see the future. Sometimes she delivers brief messages to me from my parents, who died when I was twelve. As a ghost, Jitty moves between the past, present, and future with ease.

"Am I about to get a new case?" I ask her.

"Seems to me your time would be better spent figuring out how to fertilize one of those dying eggs clinging to life in those sad Delaney ovaries." Jitty pulls no punches. From the minute I returned to Zinnia from New York City and became aware of Jitty in my family home, I also learned Jitty's primary goal was for me to get pregnant so she would have a Delaney heir to haunt. I am the last of the Delaneys, a fact that troubles Jitty, since she's been with my family for nearly two hundred years.

"I have no desire to be pregnant right now." Jitty and I have been over this ground many times before. "I need a new case. Coleman found a contractor to paint Dahlia House, but I need the cash to pay them."

Maintenance on a place like Dahlia House is expensive.

Worth every penny, but still costly. Jitty loves Dahlia House, but that doesn't mean she'll cooperate.

"You need a baby. Your mama was almost as stubborn as you are, but she finally got pregnant. With you!"

I pull the pan of cookies from the oven and put them on a cooling rack. I arrange the last of the cookie dough on another pan and slide the cookies in to bake. Another fifteen minutes and my chore will be finished. Clever little tin cannisters are open on the counter, waiting to be filled with cookies for Valentine's Day delivery.

When I stand up and turn around, a woman is only inches from my face. "Damn!" I step back. "Who are you?" I know it is Jitty, but this incarnation is incredibly beautiful—slender, with a bouffant do. I know the face, but I can't place it.

"You can call me Brigitte," she says with a slight accent. French? And then I know exactly who she is.

"Brigitte Bardot." I can't help it; I'm in awe. She was a goddess of the silver screen admired by both of my parents. Not just for her acting, but for her outspoken activism on behalf of animals. At the tender age of thirty-eight, she walked away from a big film career and started a foundation to help those without a voice. I take in the low-cut evening gown, the perfect makeup and hair. She is so beautiful. "What are you doing in Zinnia?"

Even her smile is tender. "Remember, sometimes it only takes one person to stand up and make a difference."

"Okay." My parents often said the very same thing.

I hear the loud, resounding bay of Sweetie Pie Delaney, my big hound. She rushes into the kitchen, toenails scrabbling on the floor. Sweetie is excited to see Ms. Bardot and makes it plain. I'm curious to explore the evidence that even though

Ms. Bardot is Jitty—a ghost—it would seem Sweetie Pie adores being petted by her. Go figure.

"What brings you to Mississippi?" I ask the French film star and activist.

"You'll know soon enough. Remember, those who are bonded by their love of animals are people you can count on."

For some reason, her advice, though spoken with a melancholy smile, sends a tremor down my spine. "Is someone going to try to harm Sweetie Pie? Or the horses? Or Pluto?" Sweetie Pie the hound dog, Pluto the cat, and the three horses were the family I'd built since moving home.

"Be careful, Sarah Booth. Your parents taught you to take a stand. Some people will try to run you down. Be smart. Don't put yourself in a place to get hurt."

"I promise."

Ms. Bardot's smile widens. "Good girl." As she speaks, she begins to fade and is replaced by Jitty, my everyday haint, wearing my barn clothes instead of a glamorous gown.

Then there is the sound of loud knocking at my front door, and just as I put the oven mitt and dish towel on the counter, Jitty evaporates with tiny little cartoon hearts popping all around her. So much for a dignified withdrawal.

"Sarah Booth! Help! You have to find Jezebel!" Tammy Odom, known professionally around Sunflower County as Madame Tomeeka, psychic medium, pushed through the swinging door between the dining room and kitchen. She hurried into the room, stopped to sniff, and then closed her eyes. "Chocolate chip cookies!"

"Help yourself." I'd made plenty.

Tammy took a cooled cookie and bit into it. "I didn't know you could bake!"

"I can bake some cookies. Jeez. You make it sound like I'm a terrible cook."

"You aren't?" Tammy looked confused. "You never cook. Tinkie is worse than you are, but I've heard stories about your cooking. Or lack thereof." Admittedly, my lack of culinary skills is well-known, but I have a few tricks up my sleeve.

"Exactly. I am not a *bad* cook, I am just not a practicing cook."

"But you had to make some Valentine cookies for Coleman, right?"

I nodded. "I wanted to make him something good. And cookies for others, too."

Tammy helped herself to another. "These are really good."

"You can't go wrong with chocolate chip. So, what brings you here?" I loved that Tammy dropped by to visit, but she wouldn't have done so without a good reason on this cold February day.

"Jezebel!" Tammy's eyes widened back to attention. "You have to find her. Tilly Lawson is beside herself."

I knew the name. Tilly Lawson was one of Sunflower County's very active senior citizens. She was a mover and shaker in getting things done in the small town of Nixville, just on the eastern edge of Sunflower County.

"Someone stole Tilly's chow chow/spitz–mix pup. They cut the lock on the gate and took the dog from Tilly's backyard. There's a dog thief on the loose in Sunflower County."

"Did Tilly report this to the local police chief in Nixville?"

"She did. He wasn't helpful, so I told her I'd get you to help. Will you?"

I thought of Brigitte Bardot and her unexpected appearance in my kitchen. Maybe Jitty had actually been giving me a hint about the future. "Of course. I'll ask some questions and see what I can find out."

"Great. Nixville just installed CCTV cameras. Maybe you can get something from those."

Tammy whipped out her phone and pulled up a photo of a fuzzy white dog with dark brown eyes.

"She's beautiful."

"She's a great dog. Kind. She gets along with everyone and everything. Tilly is beside herself."

I didn't think a missing pooch was a case complicated enough to charge for, but I'd do my best to help Tilly out. "Does Tilly have an enemy who might steal her dog?"

"Tilly has some enemies. She's a spitfire and attends all the city council, supervisor, and school board meetings. She writes articles for the *Zinnia Dispatch* sometimes."

I was well aware of her articles. She kept a fire under the feet of all the local elected officials. "Any personal enemies? Stealing a dog sounds very personal to me. Like they want to upset Tilly." Even as I said it, I hoped this was just a cruel prank pulled by someone trying to get under Tilly's skin. A prank that would result in Jezebel being returned unharmed to Tilly's yard.

"She's divorced. But that was a long time ago. No children. No relatives in this area, as far as I know."

"What do you think happened to Jezebel?" Tammy was a psychic medium. Maybe she intuited something useful.

Tammy's brow furrowed. "I'm worried, Sarah Booth. Jezebel is Tilly's family. That dog is just like her child. And Jezebel is so sweet. I know folks steal dogs for bait dogs for fighting or to sell to labs for medical experiments. I would never mention any of this to Tilly, but whoever took the dog cut a lock. They left Jezebel's collar on the sidewalk in front of the house."

It was definitely a deliberate act. Was it malicious or for profit? "I'll check the CCTV footage." Nixville was only about twenty minutes away. I'd never met the police chief or law enforcement officers of the small town, but I could check with Coleman about their reputation. Hopefully they were competent and would take the dog theft seriously. So many people acted like animals didn't matter.

"Can I tell Tilly you're taking the case?" Tammy asked.

I hesitated. "Look, I don't want to charge her to find her dog. Just tell her I'm going to look for her pup, but it isn't right to charge for something like this."

Tammy put a hand on my shoulder. "Thank you."

"Thank me when we find Jezebel and get her home safely."

2

Tilly Lawson lived in a bungalow several blocks off Main Street. The cottage was neatly landscaped and even sported a LAWN OF THE MONTH sign near her steps. Though it was February, Tilly had daffodils and paperwhites blooming in several beds. A Japanese flowering cherry was a cloud of fuchsia at one corner of the house. There was also a privacy fence with a hasp where a padlock had once secured the fence. Only the hasp remained.

Tilly stepped out on the porch. "Are you Sarah Booth Delaney?"

"I am."

She came down the steps, spry for someone who I guessed to be in her seventies. She gathered me into a big embrace. "Thank you. Thank you. I can't go on without Jezebel."

I understood how she felt. I'd left Sweetie Pie and Pluto at Dahlia House. They often helped me with my cases, but I knew Tilly would be hurting and I didn't want to have my dog safe and sound with me while hers was missing. It would be bruise-mashing, in my opinion. If I felt Sweetie Pie could help me, I'd bring her at a later date.

"Where is the lock that was on the gate?" I asked, walking over to look.

"Let me get it." Tilly disappeared into the house and returned quickly with a big padlock in her hand. "They used bolt cutters." She handed it over to me.

The lock had been cleanly cut with bolt cutters, as she said. It would have taken some strength to do that. "Do you have a toolshed or something in the backyard that the thieves might have been interested in?"

"Yes, but nothing was taken."

"Just the dog." I was musing aloud. "Tilly, is there anyone who would do this to upset you?"

She sighed. "I aggravate people because I stand up for what's right. I upset all the politicians and a lot of business leaders. Progress, to me, isn't constantly building and growing and destroying the good farmland for development. Progress is a city that takes care of each citizen. I'm kind of a thorn to some people."

That would be a mild understatement, from my assessment of how some people were. "Would Jezebel go with anyone who called to her?"

"No. She wouldn't leave the yard without me."

So, whoever cut the lock had to have physically taken her. "I'm going to check the CCTV footage. Have you seen it?"

"Police Chief Garwool hates me. He won't show it to me. I have some suspicions about his social activities that might involve white robes. I've been trying to get him fired."

Oh, baby. The police chief would certainly hate her guts.

"No worries, I'll handle Garwool." I said it with assurance. Coleman could help me out if Garwool proved to be the boulder in my path. "When was she taken?"

"Sometime after I let her out," Tilly said. A tear escaped her eye, and she angrily brushed it off her cheek. "I didn't hear anything. She didn't even bark. She likes to be outside in this cool weather, and I didn't check on her like I should have."

"Blaming yourself is a waste of energy. I'll talk with Garwool. If you have social media, please post Jezebel's photo and offer a reward for her safe return. Make it a good reward, and don't accuse anyone of stealing her. Just get her photo out and see what happens."

"Good plan." She squeezed my shoulder. "Madame Tomeeka said you could find her. I know you will."

That was too much pressure. "I will try, Tilly. I can't promise anything."

"How much do I owe you? I can write a check."

I shook my head. "Let me look for her. Maybe we can find her quickly and I won't need to be paid."

Tilly stepped back and really looked at me. "I knew your parents. I met you, too, when you were a little thing, following your daddy around like he was a god from Mount Olympus. He was a good man who stood up for right and against wrong. Your mother was the same. The day they died, Mississippi lost far more than anyone knew."

I swallowed a lump. Sometimes the sense of loss was like a scream stuck in the back of my throat. Tilly brought up a flood of memories that I had to rise above or I would blubber. "I miss them, too." I pulled my car keys from the pocket of my jeans. "Now let me get after this. The quicker we act, the better."

"I hope the chief is helpful. He may be, since he knows

you're best friends with Cece Dee Falcon, that reporter. Garwool hates bad publicity. Which is one reason he dislikes me."

"He may dislike you, but he still has a job to do. A sworn duty." I didn't have a lot of patience for law officers who played favorites.

"You sound just like your mama, Sarah Booth. She believed in holding people to their oaths. But Bill Garwool doesn't listen to anyone. He does as he pleases."

"Maybe. I'll see what I can do with him."

"Do you really believe you can find her?" Tilly's voice broke. "She is the sweetest dog. Her heart is gentle, and she is so loving. I can't stand to think that something bad is happening to her."

I didn't want to put any more dread in her life, so I kept my lips zipped. I knew the horrors that could come to a dog— fighting, being used as bait, injured and left on the side of the road. There were so many bad outcomes. It was best not to say anything except, "I'll do my very best to find her quickly."

"Thank you."

"I'll check in with Garwool and see that CCTV footage. If I have any more questions, I'll be in touch. Just be sure to start posting on social media and ask all your friends to share."

"Will do."

I patted her shoulder as I prepared to take my leave. This wasn't a case I would have sought out, but I owed it to Tammy to try, and I certainly couldn't walk away without doing my best to find Jezebel now.

The police station in Nixville was tiny. There was the chief's private office, then a bigger room with a couple of desks for two officers. The dispatcher, a woman, was in a corner by the front door. Four cells, all empty, completed the jail. Bill Garwool was a tall man, beginning to widen around the middle. He made it clear he was annoyed that I'd asked to speak with him.

"You're trying to find Tilly's lost dog, right?"

"I am." I gave him a smile, which he ignored.

"She's driven us all to the brink of exhaustion. She can't accept that the dog is gone."

"The dog didn't just wander off. Someone cut the lock on her gate and took the dog. I understand there is footage of the theft."

Garwool called to one of the deputies and told him to show me the footage on his monitor. I walked over to take a look. The officer had cued the tape to a slender person in a black jacket with a hood cutting the lock off the gate with bolt cutters. The beautiful white dog made no attempt to leave. The thief used a leash around the dog's neck and pulled her out of the yard. The dog tried to break free, but the thief wrangled it down the sidewalk and out of range of the camera. There was never a clear view of the person's face. Judging from the stature of the person, it could be a small man or a tall woman. I couldn't say for sure.

"This is clearly a theft," I said to Garwool.

He shrugged. "It would seem to be, but dog theft isn't high on my priority list."

My temper hit red hot. What a smug butt the police chief was. "What are you doing to recover Jezebel?"

"We've checked the local pound. The dog isn't there, but there are plenty of dogs available. A person doesn't have to steal a dog in Mississippi. There are thousands of strays looking for a home."

"Which begs the question of why that person on the footage is *stealing* Tilly's pet."

"Tilly should answer that question, not me."

"Thanks for your help, Chief." I had to leave before I broke bad and cussed him out.

"Give my regards to Sheriff Peters."

"Will do. I'm sure he'll be in touch."

"Tell him not to bother. We've got this handled."

"If you get any leads on the dog, please let me know. I'm happy to recover Jezebel if we find out where she is."

"I wouldn't hold my breath, Ms. Delaney. I doubt that dog will ever be found."

I couldn't take it. I had to take a stand. "Do you know something about Jezebel that I don't?" I asked.

"I know that dogs are a dime a dozen here. That dog is nothing special. Not a purebred, just a mutt. That dog is likely on the way to a research lab. Just my personal opinion."

Garwool had a mean streak a mile wide. One of the deputies got up and walked out of the station. The other one buried his head behind his computer monitor and clacked away. I walked outside and headed toward my car. The officer fell in step beside me.

"I'm Tom Terrell. I asked Tilly to make some posters with a reward and a photo. I told her I'd help put them in store windows and on telephone poles." He was probably in his mid-twenties, a good-looking, clean-cut young man. He looked upset.

"Thank you. I told her to do the same on social media."

"That's a good idea. She loves that dog so much. We have to find her."

The deputy's kind brown eyes showed real compassion. It had to be a nightmare for him to work with Garwool. "We'll do our best. Thanks for your concern." I had a thought. "Has anyone else reported a stolen dog?" If folks were stealing dogs to sell to medical labs, surely there would be more than one taken.

"Not that I know of. Garwool doesn't share a lot of things. We're on a need-to-know basis, and most of the time he doesn't think that I need to know. The other deputy, either."

"Charming."

He laughed, and his shoulders lifted. "The only reason he has the job of chief is that he's dating the mayor's daughter."

"Sounds about right."

"Look, I'll keep my ears open and if I hear anything, I'll let you know."

"Thanks, Deputy . . . Tom."

"Glad to help if I can."

"I'm going to ask a few people on the street where Tilly lives if they saw or heard anything."

"It was the middle of the day when Jezebel was stolen," the deputy reminded me.

"Yes. I'm going to check with the local animal shelter, too, and see what I can find out about missing dogs in the area."

"Good plan." He held out his hand and we shook. Then it was time to call my partner and let her know I was working a missing dog case. Tinkie would approve, and wouldn't expect payment, either. We were all dog lovers.

3

Two hours later, I had discovered that no other dogs in town had been reported missing. I'd checked with a dog-training class and five kennels. No one knew a thing about the stolen fur ball. The dog was well-known in Nixville as Tilly's constant companion. She was a striking dog—solid white, with thick fur that Tilly kept sheared, according to the two groomers in town.

The CCTV footage hadn't included the vehicle the dog thief was driving. That would have helped a lot, but after talking to a few local residents, I discovered there was a contingent of folks who hated the CCTV cameras. Their conspiracy theories ran from the notion that one political party was spying on them, to the concept that aliens were watching humans as they prepared to put in place a future plan to harvest the human species as food.

I headed back to Zinnia and Hilltop, the home of Tinkie Bellcase Richmond. That I would get to see Maylin, her adorable baby girl, was sugar on top of the oatmeal.

I pulled into Hilltop and was greeted by Chablis, Tinkie's little dust mop Yorkie. The sun glinted off my partner's coiffed head of blond hair. As I came closer, I was surprised to find she was actually wearing a tinfoil hat!

"What the hell?" I approached with a hand in front of my eyes. She was blinding me.

"What are you doing here?" Tinkie leaned against the post on the front porch.

"Working. What are you doing with tinfoil all over your head?"

"Pauline is giving me a multi-shade dye job."

I blew air softly through my lips. Tinkie was all about looking good. She went to the most expensive salon in Zinnia—and sometimes to Memphis if it was a special occasion. She even took Chablis to a colorist for her sun-glitzed do. I couldn't believe Tinkie would allow an amateur—in this case, Maylin's babysitter—to touch her curls.

"Come on inside, Sarah Booth. I have to get back under the dryer."

I followed her into the kitchen where a bonnet dryer had been set up. Tinkie took a seat and put her head under the hot air. I didn't envy her. The high-pitched whine of the hair dryer made me want to have a fistfight.

"Why are you doing this?" I whispered to her when Pauline went to get fresh towels.

"Maylin is growing up. She'll go to preschool soon. I love Pauline, and her biggest dream is to be a hairdresser, so Oscar and I are sending her to beauty school. She has to have ten photographs of hair color and cuts in her portfolio to be accepted into the Los Angeles School of Beauty, so I volunteered to be a client. She wants to be a hairdresser to the stars, and I want her to have that opportunity."

Tinkie and Oscar were the most generous of employers. And, truthfully, Pauline was more like family now.

While waiting for Tinkie to come out from under the dryer, I drank coffee and chatted with Pauline, who was also an exceptional cook. When Pauline was taking the foil off Tinkie's hair, I told her about Jezebel.

"What kind of a monster steals a dog?" Tinkie was hot under the collar, and it wasn't from the hair dryer.

"I'm hoping it's a malicious prank directed toward Tilly, and that the dog will be returned safe and sound."

"But you fear it is something far worse." Tinkie could read me like an open book.

"There is no reason for me to be such a pessimist," I reminded her. "I just go a little nuts when an animal might be in danger."

"If someone has taken that dog to hurt Tilly, we're going to find them, kill them, and dump the body in the river. Maybe there will be a shark willing to eat it." Tinkie was generally kindhearted, but cruelty to the helpless brought out a vengeful streak.

"We can always figure out a good means of disposal." Being a private investigator came with that kind of know-how.

"Do you know about the online pet detective group?" Tinkie asked.

"No." I was at a loss.

"It's pretty cool. These groups are springing up all over the world. Some of them work to solve human crimes. Others are focused on bringing animal abusers to justice. Or sometimes they just help find lost dogs and cats that have wandered away from home."

"How do they do this?" I was curious.

"They have a network of people. If it's a local matter, they

engage the folks in the area to help find a dog or cat or horse.
Hey, a group around Zinnia helped recover a horse stolen
from West Point. A fancy Friesian that someone stole from
a pasture. Just pulled into the pasture in the dead of night,
loaded the big gelding, and took off."

My gut clenched. If someone took my horses, I wouldn't
recover. "Was the horse found?"

"Oh, yes! That's the best news. This pet detective group—I
think they call themselves Hound Dog Patrol—did tremen-
dous leg work. They not only found Theseus, the Friesian,
but also ten other horses getting ready to be transported to
Mexico for slaughter. The pet detectives arrived on the scene
just as the horses were being loaded onto an eighteen-wheeler.
Dawson Reed, the local pet detective investigating in Zinnia,
pulled the thief out of the truck and beat him so severely he's
still in the hospital."

"Good." I had no remorse for wishing pain and suffering
on a horse thief.

"Why don't we contact Dawson Reed?" Tinkie suggested.

"Great idea. How do we find him?"

"Leave a message with Hound Dog Patrol of Mississippi."
She popped open her laptop and pulled up a website. The only
member of the group with a first and last name listed was
Dawson Reed. And he'd conveniently left an email addy. Tinkie typed out a quick message about Jezebel and sent it. Before
she could even stand up, there was a ding.

Dawson had replied—and with an offer for help. I could
have kissed him.

"We're checking the area and will be in touch," read Dawson's message.

Tinkie and I still had a bit of daylight, so I called Tilly and found out that Jezebel was microchipped. I called the chip company with her ID number—no one had reported that she'd been found.

Pauline did a quick style of Tinkie's impressive mane, snapped her photos, and we were out the door. It was a short drive to Nixville, and we were ready for action. We walked up and down the street Tilly lived on, knocking on doors and showing photos of Jezebel. Every family knew her, but no one had seen her.

"Did you see anything unusual?" I asked a young mother who said she was getting ready to pick up her kids from a school activity.

"There was a black Camry parked right over there earlier today," she told us. "I should have paid more attention, but I was putting a pot roast together for dinner." She pursed her lips. "There were two people in the car." She paused. "I don't know if they got out of the car or not. I'm sorry."

"Did you see them with the dog?"

"No. I went back to the kitchen to finish cutting up the potatoes and carrots."

"Do you remember what time this was?" The theft in broad daylight was bold.

"Just before eleven o'clock. My husband is a postal worker, and that's when he comes home from his route."

That was another possible lead. A postal worker saw a lot of people and events. "Might I have his name and contact number?"

She gave me her husband's cell phone and I gave him a quick call. He was nearby and we met him for a chat.

"I know Jezebel. A sweeter dog has never been born," he said. "I can't stand that this has happened. Tilly is going to be lost. That dog is her child."

I understood that feeling. Sweetie Pie was my baby.

"Does your postal route take you by Tilly's house?"

"It does, but I delivered her mail at about ten o'clock. I dropped a few letters in the slot. I heard Jezebel barking in the backyard, and when I walked by, the padlock was on the gate."

"Is it common for Nixville residents to padlock their backyard gates?" I was curious what he'd say.

"Several months ago, some kids started breaking into toolsheds and taking things. Most of it was mischief, but they also took some valuable tools. I talked Tilly into putting that lock on her gate. Sometimes simply discouraging bad behavior is an effective approach."

"Do you recall seeing anyone lurking around her place?"

He thought about it before he answered. "There's not a lot of foot traffic in the neighborhood these days. Maybe a few kids on bikes. Jezebel got out of the fence last week. She was lying in the front yard just barking at people passing by. She's not aggressive at all. She was just letting everyone know she saw them."

"Did you see anything else out of the norm?" I asked.

"Some man in a blue pickup screamed out the window at Jezebel and said he was going to shoot her if she wasn't confined. He said it was against the law for her not to be on a leash."

"Do you know this man?" I asked.

The postal worker sighed. "Jason Lomus. He's an asshole."

"No doubt. Do you know his address?"

"I know everyone's address," he said with a laugh. "Lomus lives at 1414 East Boulevard. Call the chief and take a deputy with you if you go there. He hits the bottle hard and he is aggressive. He's in and out of trouble all the time."

"Do you think he would hurt Jezebel?" Even asking the

question made my stomach churn. The laws for protecting animals in Mississippi were awful. All Lomus would have to do was claim the dog came at him and whatever action he took as "self-defense" would free him of any legal trouble.

"Lomus likes to get into fistfights at the bar on the outskirts of town. I never considered him to be a man who would harm a dog, but you just never know. If he was tanked up and the dog barked at him . . . he might."

Tinkie, who had been unusually quiet, finally spoke. "If he hurt that dog—"

"We are going to bring him to justice." I didn't want her to make a threat. Especially in front of the postal worker who liked to do a bit of tongue-wagging. It was always better to be cool, as I'd learned the hard way.

I didn't know Nixville well, but it was a smaller town and East Boulevard was a main thoroughfare. I parked the car in front of 1414, a neat bungalow with one of those lawns treated with abundant chemicals. With any luck at all, Lomus would be home and would talk with us.

"Ready?" Tinkie got out of the car. We weren't armed, but she was loaded for bear, nonetheless. She knocked on the door and stepped back. We both were startled when the door was flung open and a big, beefy man stepped out on the stoop. "What do you want?"

"Have you seen this dog?" Tinkie showed a photo on her phone.

"What if I have?"

"We're trying to locate the dog and return her to her owner."

"That dog is a pest and a nuisance. If she never gets back home, that's fine with me."

I put a hand on Tinkie's shoulder. I could feel the anger thrumming through her muscles. "Did you harm that dog?" she demanded.

Jason Lomus laughed at her. Oh, man, he was stupider than he looked. Tinkie could take his head off in an instant.

"What are you going to do to me if I did?" he asked. "It's just a dog."

I tried to stop it but I was too late. Tinkie stepped forward and brought her knee up sharply into his crotch. The air went out of him with a whoof, and he doubled over in pain, unable to catch his breath. Not the smartest move Tinkie had ever made, but on the whole, I couldn't disagree with her action. Lomus deserved much, much worse.

"I'm calling the police on you," Lomus gasped.

"Go ahead," Tinkie said. "Just know I'll be back to see you. And I'm really going to make it hurt."

I cleared my throat. "If you know anything about Jezebel, you'd better tell us now."

"Get off my property." Lomus was breathing a little easier. It was time to split.

Tinkie looked at me, her mouth set in a stubborn line that didn't bode well for Lomus. "Let's go," I said.

"But—" Tinkie wasn't ready to give up.

"We'll find more evidence and come back." I looked at Lomus. "And you'd better pray I don't find out you're involved in this dog's disappearance."

4

On the way back to Zinnia—when I wasn't looking in the rearview mirror to see if the police chief of Nixville might be on our trail to arrest Tinkie for assault—I called Dawson Reed. The online pet detective sounded smart and energized. And he didn't pull any punches.

"When someone cuts a lock off a gate to steal a dog, it's intentional and planned. They had to bring bolt cutters with them. That tells me they really wanted that particular dog," he said. "This isn't just a random case of someone seeing a loose dog and picking it up to keep as a pet. They know this dog belongs to someone and they took it anyway."

He made perfect—if infuriating—sense.

"What can you tell us that might help us find Jezebel?" Tinkie asked. I had the phone on speaker so we could both talk to him.

He asked about doorbell-camera footage, and I made a note. We'd asked the nearest neighbors, but at some of the houses, no one had been home. We'd need to go back after five o'clock, when folks got off work and could check the footage.

We went over the reward Tilly was offering. She wasn't playing around; she'd set the reward at two thousand dollars.

"Let me check the online group and see if there's any chatter about dogs being stolen around the region," Dawson said. "Usually, if that's what's going on, a crew will slip into a town and pick up two or three dozen dogs and then move to another area. Jezebel is a pretty little dog. The best hope is that she was taken to be a pet for someone, not to sell to a medical lab. Or breeder. She is fixed, right?"

"She is." Tilly was an excellent dog parent and she had done everything right, from regular vet visits to a secure backyard and spaying.

"You know about the big dog swap in Ripley, don't you?" Dawson asked.

I'd deliberately tried not to learn about it, but I knew enough. It was hideous and perfectly legal. The first Monday of every month, dogs were staked out at what was essentially a trade-and-swap flea market. Dogs were sold for all different kinds of reasons, and there was no one there to enforce anti-cruelty laws or make sure the dogs had some kind of legal protection. It was a free-for-all of greed. Any dogs that weren't bought were left in a pen to be killed or given to anyone who wanted them—including dogfighters looking for bait dogs.

"That sale is next week," Tinkie said. "Why can't that place be shut down?"

I didn't have an answer, except the obvious one. Some people chose money over compassion. They viewed animals, and sometimes women and children, as property over which they had total control.

"I hope we find Jezebel before then." I did not want to go to

Ripley. I didn't want those images in my brain when I was try-ing to sleep at night. Cruelty, abuse—those things stayed with me and upset me. Tinkie and I couldn't run around Ripley driving our knees into the crotches of the people who allowed such cruelty, but I really wanted to.

"Dawson, do you have any suggestions for where to start looking?" Tinkie asked.

"Take flyers to all the vet clinics and post them. A lot of folks who love their pets will see them there and they are people likely to take the time to help you."

It was a terrific suggestion. "Thanks, Dawson," I said be-fore we hung up.

"I'll make the posters tonight," Tinkie said. "We can take them in the morning."

"Yes." Tinkie had a lot more graphic-design expertise than I did. I texted her the photo of Jezebel that I had on my phone just as we pulled into the drive at Hilltop. I needed to get home to feed the horses and my pets, but I took a moment to visit Maylin. She was growing so fast, and each new expression on her face or verbal offering was an elixir of magic. One day she would learn to say my name. How incredible would that be?

"See you at seven," I told Tinkie after I kissed Maylin goodbye.

"I'll be ready."

The next morning I did all the farm chores and headed to pick up my partner. By nine o'clock, Tinkie and I had hit all eight veterinarian clinics around the Nixville area. The clinic staff in each instance had been helpful and concerned. When I vis-ited Dr. Karl Smith's clinic, I discovered that he was Jezebel's regular vet. He had some interesting insights.

"Something tells me the person who stole Jezebel wants her for a personal pet. She's a beautiful animal with a temperament anyone could love. So, I would keep an eye out close to home. I believe she's still in this area."

"Any idea who would do this?" I asked.

"I see a lot of people, often in emotionally stressful situations. It doesn't happen often, but sometimes someone loses a pet, or a family member, and they want to replace that hole in their lives with something to love. Sometimes that can lead to a situation where a person would act out, do something they normally wouldn't."

Reading between the lines, I could see he had at least one client who might steal a dog. Not out of meanness or greed, but to find something to love. It wasn't an ethical thing to do, but folks in such distress might not be looking at ethics. I could view them with compassion, but stealing another person's beloved family member was obviously not an answer.

"Are you willing to give us a few names?" I asked.

"Yeah. I don't know that Biddie McClain would steal anything. I do know she saw Jezebel here at the clinic a few weeks ago. She fell in love with her, and then five days ago, her pug, Wilbur, died. She was devastated, even though Wilbur was sixteen. Look, I'm not making an accusation. It's just a place to check, okay? I know how much Tilly loves Jezebel. It's a tough situation."

He was right about that. "We'll check with Biddie. And thank you."

We had a handful of leads and we had to get busy.

Biddie McClain answered the door when I knocked. She was a petite woman who graciously invited us into her home. The first thing I noticed were the dozens of photos of a handsome pug. Wilbur. But there was no sign of any other dog in her home. Jezebel wasn't there.

"Biddie, we're looking for Tilly's dog, Jezebel. Do you know who might have taken her?" Tinkie asked gently.

"I would take her if Tilly ever couldn't care for her." She looked out the front window, and I realized she was working hard to gain control of her emotions.

"We were so sorry to learn of Wilbur's passing," Tinkie said. She was the one who knew what to say in hard situations. "Dr. Smith said you loved him greatly."

"He was my four-legged boy," she said, a tear tracing slowly down her cheek. She wiped it away. "Everything we love dies," she said. "I knew that when I got him—that too short a time later, I would be grieving his death."

The bleakness of the statement pulled me up short. In my brief lifetime, the people I loved the most had died. Way too soon. Sweetie Pie, Pluto, and the horses were all young and in great health. But time would march over me, too.

"The remarkable thing about humans is that we know we will suffer, but we continue to love."

She was breaking my heart.

"Tell us about Wilbur," Tinkie said softly.

"Oh, he was remarkable." Biddie chuckled softly. "He could tell time."

I was hooked. "How?"

"I have no idea how he knew, but whenever it was time for *The Equalizer* on TV, he would come whine at me. Sometimes he'd take the hem of my pants and pull me to the room where the TV was. He would get the remote and bring it to me."

"He sounds remarkable." Tinkie moved to sit beside her and put a hand on her back.

"He was the most remarkable little soul. Dr. Smith suggested that I get another dog, but I don't know if I can." A few tears escaped her. "No one could ever replace Wilbur."

"Another dog wouldn't be a replacement," Tinkie said. "It would be a loving home for a pup that has no one to be his or her champion. There are so many desperate animals at the shelters all over the nation. Think how Wilbur would love it that you saved another dog or cat."

Biddie looked up at Tinkie with almost wonder. "You're right. I hadn't thought of that. And I wouldn't be alone anymore."

Tinkie was handling the situation like a cross between a humane officer and a therapist.

"How about we go to the shelter to look at the dogs?" she suggested. "I can pick you up and take you. I know you'll find the perfect pup or kitty to be your friend."

"I can help them, and they can help me."

"Exactly."

They set a time for the trip, and I cleared my throat. It was obvious Biddie had nothing to do with Jezebel's disappearance, but we hadn't plumbed the depths of her knowledge about what might have happened.

"Did you ever hear anyone talking about Jezebel?" I asked.

"She's an incredible dog. Everyone who saw her wanted her."

"But who would act on that desire?"

Biddie looked at me. "You thought I might have stolen her, didn't you?"

I nodded. It was pointless to lie. "I thought maybe you'd taken her because you missed Wilbur so much."

"I love Jezebel, but I could never do that."

I nodded. "I know, Biddie."

"We'll find the perfect dog for you at the shelter," Tinkie assured her. "You'll save a life and make yours so much better. But right now, do you know anyone who might have taken Jezebel?"

Biddie thought for a moment. "I don't like accusing people . . ."

"We aren't looking to get anyone in trouble," Tinkie said softly. "We just want to find Jezebel."

Biddie signaled us into her kitchen, where she put on a pot of coffee. "You know Tilly has done things that are illegal."

This was news to me. "Like what?" I didn't see the gentlewoman as a criminal.

"In the past, she's been involved in stealing dogs."

I looked at Tinkie, who frowned. "What are you saying?" Tinkie asked.

"Tilly Lawson is a dog thief." Biddie pursed her lips and nodded.

I couldn't help it; I laughed. "Are you serious?"

"Dead serious." Biddie wasn't laughing. "Never underestimate a woman with a moral conviction."

"She stole abused pets?" Tinkie asked.

Biddie gave her a thumbs-up. "You got it."

I got it, too, I was just surprised. Tilly didn't just talk the talk; she was walking the walk in an extreme way.

I had to view my client with new respect—and some trepidation.

"Can you tell us about any specific dogs she's rescued?" Tinkie asked.

It was an excellent question, because if someone found out Tilly had taken their dog, they might have decided to return the favor.

"Try Rutherford Mace."

I'd heard the name. He was a retired professional wrestler who was rumored to have contacts with drug runners. Unfortunately, Sunflower County had not escaped the flood of opioids or fentanyl. Although Coleman had tried several times to catch Rutherford Mace in the act of selling or transporting drugs, he hadn't been successful. Yet.

"Where does Mr. Mace live?" I asked.

"Just outside of town. But don't go there without someone to look out for you. Rutherford Mace is violent."

Tinkie and I exchanged glances. We both knew we were going. The only question was whether we'd let Coleman and Oscar know our plans.

5

The Rutherford Mace home was wildly different from my expectations. For a man who was reputed to have connections to a violent criminal empire, his home was low-key and beautifully landscaped, understated and serene. There was even a small meditation circle beside a fountain. Not at all what I'd expected.

"This worries me," Tinkie said under her breath.

"Why?"

"I suspect this guy is very, very good at pretending to be something he isn't. That's always dangerous."

She was right about that. And I had my own concerns. I could hear a dog howling. The sounds reverberated from the back of the house.

"Can you start the interview?" I asked Tink.

"What are you going to do?"

"Check out the howling dog." I couldn't ignore it.

Tinkie clutched my wrist. "Can you look without getting hurt?"

"Maybe." No point lying about it.

"I should come with you."

I shook my head. "Distract Mace. I'll be careful, and I am smart enough to realize I may have to come back here when it's dark to take any necessary action." I wasn't above stealing a dog, myself—if the dog was in danger of being harmed or abused. I just didn't want to get caught. Not by the law and not by Mace and his thugs.

Tinkie nodded as she rang the doorbell and plastered a sweet smile on her face. Tinkie could manipulate almost any man on the planet. She was the iron fist in the velvet glove. I was the calloused palm with a heavy wrench in my hand.

I was headed for the back of the house before anyone could answer the door. I heard the door crack open and Tinkie's voice. "Oh, Mr. Mace. Do you have a minute to talk with me?"

"Please come in," a deep voice said. Tinkie could hold her own—I just had to be certain I could, too.

When I got to the back property, I skirted a beautiful kidney-shaped pool and walked past a row of bottlebrush plants. I followed the sound of crying past two outbuildings, to a clump of trees. The dog was tethered to a plastic doghouse with a chain that weighed more than the little beast did.

The dog started to bark, then tried to get into the doghouse, away from me. The chain caught and the poor thing was trapped. The gray pittie-hound mix cowered on the ground and peed on herself. I could see marks where it looked like she'd been hit with something.

I didn't normally wear a belt, but today I had one. I took it off and looped it through the dog's collar before I tried to get her off the chain. I wasn't leaving without this poor dog. She looked like a sister to my precious Sweetie Pie—a coonhound of one type or another.

"What do you think you're doing?"

The deep male voice came from directly behind me.

"I'm taking this dog to the vet. She's been hurt."

"Get away from her."

I finally turned around. The man who stood behind me was over six feet tall and muscled. He looked like he could be a professional wrestler. And he looked like he really wanted to punch me.

I tightened my grip on the belt and bent to examine the way the chain was fastened around her neck. I would need a damn key to unlock the collar. The poor dog didn't look like she would have the strength to run away if she did manage to get off the chain.

"Is this your dog?" I asked. The man advanced toward me, his hands clenched into fists at his sides. I didn't even have a water pistol for self-defense, and I doubted I could outrun him.

"She's not yours, and this is none of your business. Rutherford Mace don't take kindly to strangers poking into his business."

"I'm making it my business. Get Mr. Mace down here." I whipped out my camera and started taking photos. We were in Sunflower County, and while the county didn't have good laws to protect animals, Coleman could charge an abusive owner with something to make his life complicated.

"Take the dog and get out of here."

I almost did a double take, but I wasn't about to argue. I did want more information, though. "Who are you?"

"I'm Zotto Hammerfist. Now get the dog and leave while you can."

Was that his real name? And was he really going to let me go with the dog? Then again, he could go to a shelter and get another one. Or steal one from a backyard.

"Is this the only dog here?" I looked around. There were outbuildings. I wanted to check them.

"Lady, you should leave."

"Or will you make me?" I pushed my luck hard.

He came toward me, but dropped to one knee and unlocked the dog collar. I thought I was hallucinating when the dog licked his hand. "Take her." He stood up. "Just go now and quickly."

It seemed improbable, but Zotto was helping me liberate the dog. Did he have a soft spot for the pooch?

"What's her name?"

"Avalon," he said.

"For the island in the Arthurian legend?" His answer caught me off guard. I hadn't expected a literary reference.

"Yes." The dog jumped up on his leg and Zotto patted her head. "Just get her out of here. Please."

"Are there any other dogs here?" I couldn't leave without checking for Jezebel.

He shook his head. "Not now. They were going to breed her. Puppies for the fighting ring."

Rage flew over me, but something about Zotto made me realize he wasn't keen on the idea.

"Where did she come from?"

He shrugged. "The guys bring them in, a few at a time. I try to do what I can."

I didn't exactly feel sorry for him, but there was more to him than I'd first seen.

I started to walk toward my car, but the dog dug in her heels and refused to walk. I didn't want to drag her by her neck. She was skinny and poor—likely wormy—but she was large boned, and I didn't think I could carry her all the way to my car.

Zotto took the belt from my hand and started walking. The dog fell in beside him like she'd been trained to heel. I took my place in the rear and followed after them. In a moment he had her loaded into the back seat.

"Thank you."

He shook his head. "Don't tell anyone."

"I won't."

"When they get the dogs here, I try to remove them. Rutherford doesn't care, but some of his posse like the dogfights."

"Would you like to see those fights stopped?" It was a long shot, but one I couldn't pass up trying. The logistics might be complicated, but Zotto was an opportunity I might not get close to again any time soon.

"I would. Very much. These dogs don't stand a chance and they deserve so much better."

"I'll work with you." If we had Zotto on the inside, we might actually be able to break up the dogfighting ring. It was an exciting possibility, and I couldn't wait to tell Coleman. Even though he was going to be upset with me for coming to Mace's place without backup.

"I'll do what I can." He looked up toward the house. "Hurry up and get out of here, please."

He was worried someone was going to come out and catch us. I took my cue from him and started the car. Avalon was so tired she laid right down, sighing.

I checked the time and stepped away to make a phone call to the veterinarian. Dr. Smith could see me as soon as I got there. Avalon was about to get the primo care of a lifetime.

"Go on, get out of here," Zotto said, waving me toward the car door. "You're going to get caught, and then we'll all be in a lot of trouble."

"My partner is inside with Mr. Mace. I can't leave her." I

might want to fly to Dr. Smith's office, but I had to get Tinkie. I pointed at Avalon, who was stretched out flat on the back seat. "I'll hurry. She's being very calm."

"If the guys catch you, they'll kill her right in front of you."

I didn't doubt it for a minute. "Thanks, Zotto. Let me get my partner and we're out of here. If you see Jezebel, or any other dogs, would you contact me?" I gave him a business card.

"Don't come back here by yourself," Zotto said, and it wasn't a threat but a warning.

The sound of voices made him look over his shoulder. "Now, hurry. For the sake of the dog."

I nodded and ran toward the front door. I'd get Tinkie and fly to safety with Avalon.

And then?

I hadn't stopped to consider what would happen after the vet checked Avalon over. Goodness, I didn't need another dog, but I had a feeling I was about to get one.

My knock at the front door was answered by a maid who waved me inside. I heard Tinkie's voice and took off in that direction. The Mace house was big and beautifully decorated, but I had no time to enjoy the muted shades of green paint or the beautiful geometrically designed carpets. Tinkie was the only thing I wanted.

I skidded to a halt in a back parlor where Tinkie sipped coffee in a Haviland China cup while talking with Rutherford Mace.

"Sarah Booth, Rutherford has agreed to donate twenty thousand dollars to a spay-and-neuter initiative in Sunflower County. Isn't that wonderful?"

"It sure is." I couldn't help it that my tone of voice was smart-alecky. I thought it ironic that a man who allowed bait dogs to be bred on his property would care about spaying and neutering.

Tinkie gave me a long look and put her coffee cup on the table. "We should go." She'd picked up instantly on my nerves.

Rutherford Mace rose to his feet. He was a giant of a man, with shoulders that honestly could fill a doorway. His dark hair was cut in a modern mullet, and he gave me a look that let me know he was nobody's fool.

He stuck out a hand. "Pleased to meet you, Ms. Delaney."

I nodded. "We should go," I repeated.

"What's the rush?" Mace asked.

"We have a lot going on." I looked behind me to find the maid was also backtracking toward the front of the house.

"Mr. Mace, have you seen Tilly's dog, Jezebel?" I knew Tinkie had surely explored this topic, but I didn't have a lot of verbal gambits to toss around.

"I've covered this with your delightful partner. And no, I haven't."

"Thanks!" I edged toward the front door. It was time to beat a retreat.

Tinkie frowned, but she came to stand beside me. "Thanks for the hospitality. If you see the dog, would you let us know?" she asked.

"Absolutely."

I couldn't tell if he was lying or not, and I didn't intend to hang around to find out. Avalon was counting on me to get her the hell out of Dodge.

6

"What are you going to do with that poor dog?" Tinkie said as soon as she saw Avalon.

"Vet first. Then . . . I don't know. But I couldn't leave her behind."

I drove straight to Karl Smith's office. He might recognize the dog if she belonged to one of his clients. I wasn't sure where the dog had come from, but it was possible she actually belonged to a Nixville family.

The office was crowded with clients, but Karl signaled me to the very back of the clinic, where he worked on horses. He gave Avalon a thorough inspection. She was wormy, but clear of heartworms. "She's about twelve to eighteen months old," he said. "Pit and hound mix."

"Do you know her?" I held my breath.

"Nope. And I don't want to know where you got her. If I don't know, I can't be asked about it."

Karl had a pretty good idea that I'd stolen the dog, though

technically, I hadn't. He wouldn't turn me in, but he didn't want to know the details.

"She's in pretty good shape," Karl said when he'd finished giving her vaccinations. Once you give her the worm tablets when you get home, she'll start to put on some weight. Now she's going to need to go to the bathroom a good bit . . ."

I nodded. "It's okay. I can take care of her."

"Good." He patted my shoulder. "Your dad would be proud of you."

"My dad? Why?" He'd caught me by surprise.

"Oh, he was very active in working behind the scenes to protect animals. He was a dog lover. When he was the district judge, the animal abusers were put on notice. He didn't have a lot of good laws to work with, but he sometimes called me to consult, and he handed out the harshest punishments he could. James Franklin had no tolerance for anyone who would harm an animal, a child, or a woman."

I knew my dad was a good person, but Karl's kind words made me smile with pride. "Yeah, he was like that."

"What are you going to do with this dog?" he asked.

I shrugged. "Not a lot of options. She's going home with me."

He laughed. "Let's see now. You have the three horses, one dog, one cat, one raven, and one sheriff. Now you're adding another dog?"

"Looks like it."

"Will you be adding another law officer to the menagerie?"

"Oh, I don't think so. That could be trouble."

"She's good to go, Sarah Booth." Karl gave Avalon a pat on her shoulder. She licked his hand in gratitude. "Are you going to try to rehome her?"

"I should." I was on a limited budget, and another animal to care for could prove expensive, but . . . I would do the best thing for Avalon.

Karl gave me a hug. "Take her to the farm. See how she does. If it doesn't work out, I'll try to help find a home."

"You're a good friend."

"And you're a pushover."

I was still laughing when I started the car. Tinkie, who'd done some financial checking on Rutherford Mace while I was with Avalon, was unusually silent. "What's up?" I asked.

"I was thinking about my talk with Mace."

We hadn't really had a chance to talk about what she'd discovered. I'd been too determined to get Avalon to the vet. "How did he strike you?"

"He's smart. And he has a lot of money. He uses the Bank of Zinnia." She grinned. "Harold may prove useful here."

Harold Erkwell, our friend and banker, was a real asset in these situations. "Is Mace dealing drugs?"

She bit her bottom lip and let it pop out in a way that drove men wild. "I don't know. On the one hand, he denied it, but on the other hand, he clearly enjoys being viewed as a bad boy."

Tinkie had terrific intuition. "How did he strike you? Good guy or black hat?"

Tinkie thought about it. "I really can't say. He said there were no dogs on the property, and yet there was Avalon, chained up. He said he didn't know anything about dogfighting or any such activities, but his place could so easily be a location for the fights. We need to explore those outbuildings."

She was right about that. I should have done a more thorough job of looking around, but the truth was, I didn't know if Zotto Hammerfist might have broken bad if I'd tried to snoop around. It was possible he had let me rescue the dog just to get me off the property. "We'll definitely have to go back there."

I drove through Zinnia and out to Hilltop, Tinkie's place. The day was over, and I needed to get home and feed the horses, not to mention feed Coleman and myself. "I'll see you later," I said as Tinkie got out of the car.

Avalon lifted her head from the back seat, looked around, and then collapsed back into a puddle of hound dog. She was so beautiful, so accepting, and so exhausted. She'd been on a chain and now she was riding in a car. She just went along with whatever I put in front of her. There was a lot we could learn from animals.

Tinkie reached in the back window and gave her a pat. Then she looked at me. "Rutherford Mace said something that's really niggling at me."

"What would that be?"

"He said that there was no money in stealing a single dog." She sighed. "But he emphasized that word, *single*, like maybe stealing twelve dogs would be financially beneficial."

Tinkie's comment made the hair on my arms stand on end. "Do you think he was blatantly confessing to stealing dogs?"

"I just don't know. Maybe Coleman can talk to him."

Tinkie was a superb interviewer, but Coleman had something we didn't—a badge and the full weight of the law in his corner. That didn't mean people didn't lie to Coleman, but if they did, there were consequences.

"I'm sure Coleman will talk to him." I didn't want Tinkie worried about it.

"I wish you'd had a chance to talk to Mace," Tinkie said.

"I'll get around to Mace. I was tied up with Zotto." I had to laugh at the name. "He seemed like a decent guy, letting me rescue Avalon and all of that, but it could all be a ploy to manipulate us."

"That's my concern." Tinkie intensely disliked being manipulated, though she was good at doing it to others. "And not the first sign of Jezebel. Something isn't right, Sarah Booth. Someone should have seen something. And whoever stole her cut the lock off the fence."

It didn't bode well for a happy ending, but I wasn't about to say that out loud. Tinkie was already depressed by the events of the day, and I needed to get Avalon home and take her for a walk. Karl had warned me about the wormer. It could make the dog a little sick as it killed the worms. Lovely.

I waved goodbye to Tinkie and headed to Dahlia House, my horses, my critters, my man, and possibly a visit with my ghost. If Jitty put in an appearance, I intended to urge her to help me find this missing pooch. She never helped me with a case, but I knew for a fact that Jitty was a soft touch for dogs. With Jitty, anything was possible.

When I pulled up at Dahlia House, I was glad to see Coleman in the barn. He'd fed the horses and turned them back out into the pasture. The nights were getting brisk, and I went to stand beside him after I brought Avalon out of the car.

"Another dog?" He was amused.

"I couldn't leave her."

He took my hand and together we walked the pup down the driveway, giving her a chance to stretch her legs and go to the bathroom. Walking back to the house, I caught sight of Sweetie Pie and Pluto both looking out the parlor window, watching us with the new dog. Oh, those two would certainly have an opinion about this. As would Poe, the raven who'd taken up with me.

As we walked, I told Coleman what I'd discovered so far.

"You think Rutherford Mace is fighting dogs?"

"I don't know. And neither does Tinkie."

"He stumped you both?" Coleman really was amused.

"He's a cool customer. Is he a good witch or a bad witch?" I asked.

"He's certainly involved with some shady business, but folks can change," Coleman said carefully. "He was a terrific athlete, but he also fell in with a tough crowd. When he started professional wrestling, I thought he'd found the niche where he could save himself."

"And did he?"

Coleman shook his head. "I don't know. But I will find out. Tomorrow. Right now, let's feed the dog and ourselves and go to bed. I'm thinking a nice fire in the bedroom."

While Coleman lit the fire in the bedroom, I made a bowl of stew mixed with dog food for Avalon and Sweetie Pie. I was pleased to see that my big red tic girl was accepting of Avalon. In no time at all, the two hounds would be besties. Pluto might torment the new hound—but in the end, they would all be good buddies.

"Do you have any idea who might have taken Jezebel?" I asked Coleman. I was hoping he'd volunteer to talk to the Nixville police chief on my behalf.

"I don't, Sarah Booth. But I intend to help you figure this out."

I went over all the steps Tinkie and I had taken. "Do you have any suggestions? I'm worried that Jezebel may be long gone. Or worse, dead."

"Don't borrow trouble, Sarah Booth. I know your aunt Loulane told you that often enough."

I had to laugh. He was right.

"So, I'll heat up some stew for us, and we'll snuggle in bed, eat, and love on the critters."

Coleman was definitely a soft touch when it came to the animals. "And I'll drive out to talk to Rutherford tomorrow."

I stood on tiptoe and kissed him softly on the lips. When he kissed me back, I had to push him away or we'd forget about eating.

Coleman chuckled at me as he pulled me against him. "Get the food. I'll take Avalon for another walk around the barn, and then we're going to settle in for the night."

It sounded like the perfect plan to me.

7

Coleman had already left for work the next morning when I came in from feeding the horses to a ringing telephone. Unknown caller. I was tempted to ignore it, but the North Mississippi area code lured me into answering. If it was a telemarketer, I could always play dumb and hang up.

"Hello?"

"Ms. Delaney?"

The masculine voice was vaguely familiar.

"This is she."

"Zotto here. How is Avalon?"

It was curious he'd called to check on the dog, but maybe he had a tender heart after all. "She's good. Wormy but otherwise just fine, and the vet has taken care of that for her." In fact, the dog was sitting beside Sweetie Pie in the kitchen, waiting for me to make them breakfast.

"Excellent."

"Do you have news on Jezebel?" I was suddenly hopeful.

"I'm afraid not."

Dang it. "What can I help you with?"

"It's about Rutherford Mace, my boss."

I was curious now. "What about him?"

"He's missing."

Had I misunderstood? "You mean he's disappeared?"

"He isn't here. No one has seen him since last night. The guys are getting twitchy about it."

Rutherford Mace was a fully grown man, a professional wrestler. He wouldn't be easy to abduct or steal. "Are you worried he's met with foul play?"

Zotto laughed. "Now that's a quaint way of putting it. But yes, that's what I'm concerned about. There's not a trace of him at his home, but his car is still here. Rutherford isn't a man who enjoys walking anywhere. And no one saw a car or visitor at his place."

That didn't sound good. "Call the police chief, and the sheriff. You'll probably get more help from Coleman than Chief Garwool."

"Garwool is a fool."

I didn't know the chief well enough to label him a fool, but I suspected Coleman would be a lot more helpful in this situation. It would also give Coleman the ticket he needed to get in a room with Mace to question him—if he could find him, that is.

"Call Coleman." I rattled off his number.

"I asked around about Jezebel to some of the other men around here."

"And?"

"They said to attend the Ripley dog swap or whatever they call it. Are you familiar?"

"I am. A despicable practice."

"Yes, but the dog may be there."

I'd rather have my fingernails pulled out with pliers than attend the Ripley event, but it looked like I'd be checking there for Jezebel. Tinkie would go with me, but she'd be as upset as I was by the way the dogs were treated.

"I'll check it out." I took note of the time. It was just after eight in the morning. When I got off the horn with Zotto I'd give Dawson Reed a call.

Instead of being in a rush to hang up, Zotto lingered on the phone. "Can I do something else for you?" I asked.

"If I can't find Rutherford, will you look for him, too?"

I was taken aback. "I don't ever double book. It isn't fair to the person who hired me."

Zotto chuckled. "A PI with integrity. Will wonders never cease."

His sarcasm made me laugh. "Look, give Coleman a call. I have some things to do in Zinnia, but I'll be back in Nixville before lunch. If you see or hear anything about Jezebel, please call me. And I'll do the same for you with Rutherford."

"It's a deal."

I ended the call and dialed Dawson Reed. I needed to get the pet detectives on the job for Jezebel. And if Mace was missing, Dawson might have heard something about it.

Tinkie arrived at Dahlia House while I was talking to Dawson. She had a sheaf of papers in her hand. She plopped them on the kitchen table and poured a cup of coffee. She'd brought Chablis with her, and the little dust mop was all over the kitchen, snooping in cabinets and having a blast. Sweetie Pie and Avalon followed Chablis around like she was their mama.

"Dawson, do you have any updates on the missing dog?"

"Ms. Delaney, I did speak with one of the online detectives and they have a lead."

This was terrific news. "Tell me." I put the call on speaker so Tinkie could hear.

"Lois Wimms, one of our best pet detectives, found a link posted online for the sale of a female dog that looks like Jezebel. I'm sending it to your phone."

The ding that followed opened up with a picture of a dog that looked exactly like Jezebel. She was on a bright green lawn, looking into the camera expectantly. "That sure looks like the dog," Tinkie said.

"Where is she?" I asked Dawson.

"That's the problem. Lois instantly took action, but the person who posted it has since taken it down and pretends that she never put it up. Luckily, Lois was smart enough to take a screenshot. We have the name of the woman, Madge Millet, who posted the photo and Lois is going to talk to her. Madge said the dog wandered into her yard. She snapped the photo. But now she doesn't want to talk."

"That's strange. A woman named Madge posted the photo of a dog but now wants to pretend she didn't?" Tinkie was as confused as I was.

"Where is this Madge?" I asked.

"North of Nixville. Lois will send the address. You should stop in and visit her," Dawson suggested. "She may be the last person to have seen Jezebel. If that was, in fact, Jezebel. There are a lot of hairy white dogs, you know."

"I *do* know."

"Check in with me if you learn anything, and I'll do the same," Dawson said before hanging up.

"Let's go," I mouthed to Tinkie.

"What are you going to do with Avalon?" she asked.

I frowned. "I was going to leave her here."

"We might need Sweetie and Chablis. They can follow a scent."

She was right about that. "Then Avalon becomes part of the gang. She's with us."

Just one night of living in Dahlia House—and some good vet care from Karl—had given Avalon a new lease on life. She was frisky and ravenous. I fed them all eggs and bacon before we left Dahlia House. I fed Tinkie, while I was at it.

Tinkie still ate like a field hand after having Maylin, but chasing after the baby was giving her long, lean muscles. I needed to spend some more time with Maylin, too. Maybe I could get that elegant look.

We loaded the dogs into my car and headed to Nixville. Dawson had given me Lois's address, so I knew exactly where I was going. It was a beautiful morning—a bit of a gray sky, but the rich Delta soil stretched to the horizon. The fields were still fallow, but I could smell spring on the way.

"Have you thought about what we're going to do if we can't find the dog?" Tinkie asked me.

"Whew. I don't even want to contemplate that. Tilly will be beside herself if we don't bring Jezebel home."

Tinkie nodded. "I know. We need to be prepared."

The problem was that we couldn't truly be prepared. If the dog wasn't found, Tilly would have a big hole in her heart and nothing we did could prevent it or heal it. "Let's just hunt the dog and not borrow trouble. At least not today."

"You're on!"

Lois Wimm's house was easy to find, and she opened the door, expecting us. "I put on some coffee. Would you like a cup?"

"Please. We both take it black," Tinkie said. "Tell us about the dog you saw."

She settled us at the kitchen table with steaming cups of coffee in front of us before she opened up. "First, let me tell you about Dawson," she said. "He's a real skunk. Don't trust him. I mean it."

That statement rocked me back on my heels. "I don't know him very well, but he seems to do a lot of volunteer work to help find missing pets."

She laughed. "Oh, he does a lot of work, but it isn't missing pets he's interested in. He's looking for grieving women to seduce. They're more vulnerable and easier to take advantage of, especially if a guy is saying he's going to help them find their missing pet. Now, he might help a little old lady or a man look for a pet, but it's the young women he's interested in. Someone your age."

I'd heard of a lot of scams, but not one that involved using grief over a missing pet to get into a woman's pants. That was pretty low. If what she was saying about Dawson was correct, he *was* a skunk. "Is he so ugly he has to scam women?" I realized that, though I'd talked to him, I'd never seen what he looked like.

She laughed. "No, Dawson is quite handsome. And charming. But at heart he's a con man. Just keep that in mind. I don't think he can help himself. And you two are just his type."

Well, Dawson wasn't a friend or even an acquaintance. I didn't have to defend him. "Thanks for the heads-up."

"What about the photo of the dog you saw? Did you talk to this Madge Millet?" Tinkie asked.

"I have her contact information. She clammed up, though.

It was weird. She posted the photo saying the dog had strayed up on her property and someone needed to get the pup right away because she has goats and she was afraid the dog would chase them."

That didn't sound good. Some dogs did kill goats and chickens. It was their nature. But most wouldn't bother them. Jezebel was a pampered indoor dog, though she was big enough to harm a goat. "Do you have an address on Madge?"

"She wouldn't give it to me, but I did a little detective work myself, and got her address from social media."

I took the sheet of paper she handed me with an address. "Thanks, Lois. Do you have any suggestions of where to look for Jezebel?"

"The Ripley event on Monday."

She was the second person to suggest this. I looked at Tinkie, who had gone pale at the idea. "I'll go. You don't have to."

"If you're going, so am I." Tinkie was no slacker, but I also didn't see the need for both of us to witness things that would distress us. Maybe we'd find Jezebel before the dog-swap day. I could hope for that.

"Any other suggestions?" I asked.

"Dawson does have some good sources. And a lot of the people who work with him adore him." She stroked her left eyebrow, smoothing it. "He has found a lot of animals with his group."

That was good to know. "Okay, we'll stay in touch with him."

"But be careful." She knew something and wanted to tell us, but was hesitating.

"What else?" I pressed gently.

"Last year there was a young woman in the group who got

a lead on a missing dog. She went to check for the dog, and she was attacked."

That was concerning news. "That's awful. Did Dawson fail to protect her?"

She frowned. "He should have gone with her once he knew she was going to look for the dog on private property. He should have helped her get protection from the law or something. He's set himself up as the leader of the pet detectives, so he should protect the people who work with him."

"That's true. But this is all volunteer, right?" Tinkie asked.

"Yes, it is volunteer. No one is paid. Not even Dawson."

That was good to know. "Where was this pet detective attacked? Was it in Mississippi?"

"Oh, yes, right here near Nixville. That's why I'm telling you. There are some mean people around."

"Where did this happen?" Tinkie asked.

"Some professional wrestler's house. Rutherford Mace. Ever heard of him?"

"Indeed," I said, feeling a tickle of apprehension. "Is Rutherford Mace considered to be a dog trafficker?"

"Maybe. My friend who went there thought they had a dogfighting ring. She went to look for a little spaniel someone had lost. She was hit on the head and left unconscious. When she came to, the dog was gone and so was everyone on the property. She was lucky she could drive home. She had a slight concussion, but she's okay now. But Dawson should have been with her."

I couldn't disagree. Lois refilled our coffee cups. "There's been talk about Mace for many years, running dogfighting rings and selling drugs. He's got a nice spread just outside town. Bunch of men are always hanging out there."

"We were by there yesterday." I decided not to mention Avalon, who was waiting in my car with Sweetie Pie, Chablis, and Pluto.

"I gather you didn't see anything worth reporting to the sheriff?"

"Nothing criminal. Do you know anything else about Mace?"

"Like what?"

"His habits, where he might be, his routine. Anything like that." For some reason I was reluctant to tell her that he was missing. Zotto might be playing me. It was best just to keep our findings to ourselves.

She shook her head. "I'm not familiar with his habits. Really, I don't know him, only the talk about him, which can be misleading." She sighed. "I try hard not to spread gossip and rumors. In the dog-rescue business, rumors can be dangerous."

"You're right about that," Tinkie said, patting her hand. "If we find anything, we'll let you know. Thanks for the coffee." She stood, indicating it was time to go. And it was. We had our work cut out for us.

8

Madge Millet's empty house shocked neither of us. She'd fled the scene, which, in and of itself, was suspicious. I texted Budgie, Coleman's deputy with high-level computer skills, and asked him to run a check on Madge. He readily agreed and said he'd get back to me.

"You're lucky Coleman helps you with this," Tinkie said.

"Yes, and we're lucky that Harold helps us with the financial issues."

Tinkie texted Harold and asked for a check of Rutherford Mace's finances. "He's missing," Tinkie texted. "So, we have a good reason to ask."

"Stay safe," Harold replied. "If I find anything, I'll let you know."

"What now?" Tinkie asked me.

"Door-to-door canvassing near Tilly's house." There were still households we hadn't talked to. Our best bet was someone who'd seen something and just needed a memory jog or to know a dog was missing.

"What about some lunch? I'm hungry." Tinkie tried to look innocent, but it wasn't working.

My watch indicated we'd eaten only three hours ago, but what the heck. "Got a place in mind?"

"There's a diner five blocks over."

That was a good idea. Diner folks were generally friendly, and we could ask some questions.

"I'm thinking some fried dill pickles," I said.

"If only they served Bloody Marys." Tinkie grinned.

"I agree, but don't get your hopes up."

Since it was only a few blocks and the weather was nice, we walked to Bobbie's Diner. The menu consisted of burgers, barbecue, and home-cooked lunches. But no alcohol. We'd have to wait until we got back to Zinnia for a libation.

We didn't have a particularly dangerous day ahead of us, but day drinking was probably a bad idea anyway.

The smell of grilled burgers and spicy barbecue hit me hard as I walked in the door. I hadn't been hungry, but my mouth was suddenly watering.

The diner was loud—folks talking and laughing, waitresses scooting chairs and tables as they cleaned so the next customers could have a seat. Millie's Café in Zinnia had the finest food in the South, but this place looked like they could serve up a delicious plate.

We found a table in the corner and sat. The waitress whisked by and Tinkie ordered a cheeseburger and fries. I opted for fried dill pickles, fried okra, and potato salad. Our plates came to us piping hot and loaded down. Tinkie's cheeseburger could feed a lumberjack. And my basket of pickle chips—to die for. Crispy fried dill pickles were food of the gods, along with fried okra.

At first we were too busy eating to focus on anything else,

but the conversations around me began to float over. A group of developers at one table was talking about buying a tract of land. At another, younger women were whispering about a neighbor's affair. In another corner, a group of older women spoke softly, but I thought I heard the word *dog*.

When I couldn't cram another pickle down my gullet, I swallowed some sweet tea and wiped my hands on a napkin. "Be right back."

Tinkie nodded, her mouth full of burger.

When I got to the table of women, I introduced myself. "I'm looking for a missing dog. A white spitz mix. Have you ladies seen any dogs wandering around?"

"Oh, you mean Jezebel. Isn't it horrible that she was stolen?" The woman shook her head. "We are all sick for Tilly."

"Do you have any idea who might have done this?"

All of the women looked down at their plates and said nothing.

"Ladies, please. Tilly is beside herself, and if the dog has been taken for nefarious reasons, time is short." The truth was, Jezebel could be across the country by now. But I couldn't think like that. I had to believe she was still within my ability to find her and return her.

"Squatty Adams." The woman who whispered the name wouldn't look at me.

"What about Squatty Adams?" I asked.

"She hates Tilly. And she hates Jezebel and all living creatures other than her hideous grandson."

An interesting lead. I signaled Tinkie, who brought the last bite of her cheeseburger with her.

"Tell us about this Squatty person," Tinkie said, licking a tiny dot of mustard off her upper lip.

"She's mean, so we don't want to talk about her. She hates dogs and cats. And birds. And squirrels. And bees and butterflies. And wildflowers. And children. Boy, does she hate children. Except that evil grandson of hers. No matter what he does, she takes up for him. In fact, I'd check his alibi."

"How old is he?" Tinkie asked.

"Oh, he's nineteen or better. Out of high school. No job. Mooches off Squatty."

"His parents?" I asked.

"Squatty ran her daughter off. She left Nixville about twenty years ago and never came home. She just sent the boy to Squatty. He lived with her through high school, and still does. Hard to rent a place if you don't have an income, and that boy wouldn't hit a lick at a snake."

"Do you know his name?"

"Ellis. Ellis Adams. The mother never married his father, so she retained her maiden name." The woman speaking looked up at me, her eyes sad. "The child never had a chance. Just keep that in mind if you find out he's involved in this."

"You said he was still living at Squatty's?" Tinkie asked.

The woman shook her head. "I can't say for absolute certain, but I suspect he is. Where else would he go?"

And that was the question to ask. "Thanks for your help." I keyed the name *Squatty Adams* into my phone and sent a text to Budgie, asking for her address. Less than a minute later, the phone dinged. Squatty's place was not far at all from Tilly's.

After the large lunch we'd consumed, I was happy to walk around Nixville. The afternoon had grown cooler rather than warmer—typical February weather. A dark bank of clouds massed on the western horizon. At this time of year, the storms

typically moved west to east, some of them filled with lightning, big hailstones, high winds, and rain that could turn a
fallow field into mud so thick and gummy it was called gumbo.

"I don't want to linger at Squatty's too long," I told Tinkie. "The dogs are in the car. And Pluto. Let's get them." The
weather was perfect, and they were in no danger of overheat-
ing, but it made me unhappy to leave them sitting in the car.
Besides, I'd ordered them chicken tenders.

We'd picked up the to-go order for the dogs and we walked
down the street. Nixville was tiny. One main street, a back-
street, and a few cross streets. There was a city hall and two
stoplights. The residential area stretched over a space of several miles, then the land opened up to a few brand-new
subdivisions—cookie-cutter houses built side by side on what
once had been farmland—and the vista of open fields. After
static decades, the Delta was changing.

The dogs wolfed down the chicken tenders. Even Pluto
deigned to snack a little once I pulled apart the tender meat.
And then we were ready to go to Squatty's. I put Avalon on a
leash, just to be on the safe side. Chablis and Sweetie Pie were
trustworthy to stay right with us.

"Do you think Harold and Janet are getting serious?" Tinkie asked as we walked along the shady sidewalk. I buttoned
my jacket before I answered. "Maybe. I hope so. I like Janet
a lot." She was a romance author Harold had taken up with.

"Me, too. She is sizzling, though. Have you read her sex
scenes?" Tinkie used her hand to fan her face.

Still laughing, I gave her a thumbs-up. "Harold is a lucky
man."

"And Janet loves Roscoe, his evil little dog. That's a big
mark in her favor."

"If she didn't, she'd be gone. Roscoe is like Harold's hairy little son."

"Speaking of dogs . . ." I slowed to a stop, with Tinkie at my side. Avalon tugged at her leash, but Sweetie and Chablis took guard positions and even Pluto the cat sat down to wait. A well-dressed woman was coming down the sidewalk with an adorable little fluff ball on a leash.

"Who is that?" Tinkie asked.

I shook my head. "Let's find out."

We went forward and I called out a greeting. "Hi, I'm Sarah Booth and this is Tinkie."

"I know," she said, looking down her nose at me. "Private detectives. Ugh."

Well, that was unexpected. She knew us and she didn't like us. She stooped to pick up her little dog like it might catch something from Sweetie, Chablis, or Avalon.

"Yes, we're looking for Tilly's dog, Jezebel. Have you seen her?"

"That dog is a total menace. She's a dangerous animal. In my opinion, Jezebel needs to be put down, and her owner with her. All of these dogs and cats running wild in Nixville! It is horrible. The only good pet here is my little Cupcake!"

Oh, boy. "Have you seen the dog?" I asked. I sounded a little testy, but I was trying.

"Even if I had seen who took that dog, I wouldn't tell you. Or anyone else. I hope that dog is dead."

Whew! I put a hand on Tinkie's shoulder. She was little, but she was fierce, and I could feel that she wanted to launch herself down the sidewalk and throat punch this woman. That would not serve us well. "And you are Squatty Adams?" I asked.

"How do you know that?" She tried to get in my face, but Sweetie Pie had other notions. She slipped between us and then bared her teeth at Squatty. Sweetie Pie generally loved everyone.

"She's psychic. She also knows you're a stupid twit." Tinkie was wound up.

"When was the last time you saw Jezebel?" I had to get this back on track before I had a catfight on my hands.

"I saw her the day she allegedly went missing."

"Allegedly?"

"Well, how do we know Tilly didn't just get tired of her and have her destroyed?"

Wow. "I believe we can assume that Tilly is sincerely searching for her pet."

"You believe whatever you want. Just clear out of my way." She started to push past me but I stepped in front of her.

"Hear me on this. If you know anything about this dog and withhold it, I'll make certain Tilly knows and sues the pants off you."

Squatty drew back. "She can't sue me."

"Don't be so sure," Tinkie said. "Now, be gone!"

9

We tried to talk to a few more neighbors, but folks were either working or busy. Either way, they didn't answer their doors. Luckily Tom Terrell, the deputy, was able to clue us in. By the time we got back to Zinnia, we had the goods on Squatty Adams. She was an unpleasant woman who made enemies instead of friends. Her one redeeming quality was that most folks agreed that she loved her little dog, Cupcake.

Budgie had been able to take the pulse of Squatty's tenure in Nixville. She'd moved there twenty years ago with her husband, who'd died shortly after they bought the house on Aspen Street. His death sent her into a spiral that she'd never recovered from. I could empathize with that, but dang, twenty years? Squatty definitely needed a new attitude.

Budgie also found the possible reason for the animosity between Squatty and Tilly. It seemed that Jezebel had gone over to Squatty's house three weeks earlier and dug under Squatty's fence, helping Cupcake to escape. The two dogs had run amok in Nixville; Squatty and Tilly had chased them both around town for more than four hours. Just before they were apprehended, Cupcake had almost been hit by a car. Squatty had witnessed the near accident, and it had gutted her.

It was after this event, on top of local tool burglaries, that Tilly put a padlock on her gate.

I picked up my phone. "I'm going to call Tilly." There was more to the Tilly–Squatty rivalry than I'd been told.

Tinkie nodded as she called Harold and peppered him with some questions. She was busy writing down a list of figures as Harold talked.

I had Tilly on the horn in short order. "Yes, someone kept opening my back gate and letting Jezebel out," she said. "I assumed it might be Squatty, but I didn't want to accuse her outright, so I didn't mention it. Normally, Jezebel stayed right in the yard, but that one time she went to Squatty's and helped Cupcake escape. It was almost a real tragedy. That's when I got the padlock."

"Aside from Squatty, who do you think might have let Jezebel out?"

Tilly tsk-tsked me. "I thought it was Squatty. I thought she was letting my dog out in the hopes of getting her in trouble or even harmed. But I couldn't prove it."

"Why would she do that?" I really didn't understand.

"It's a long story, and it doesn't reflect well on Squatty or me."

A hint of embarrassment had crept into her voice. "Spill the beans."

"Squatty got it into her head that her husband and I were having an affair."

The question that popped into my head was "Were you?" but I didn't ask that. Instead, I asked, "Hasn't he been dead twenty years?"

Tilly chuckled. "Yes, that's true. And there was never anything between us except that we both liked to play poker, drink whiskey, and laugh. I knew it drove Squatty up a tree for Lon to come over to play cards and drink. I knew it, and I did it anyway. Because it was so ridiculous. Lon adored her, though I never saw the attraction."

Tilly wasn't one to look for a fight, it seemed. But being accused of cheating with another woman's husband would grow very, very tedious. I didn't really blame Tilly for tormenting Squatty. "If there was nothing between you and Lon, why did Squatty think there was?"

"She was insecure. I realize that now, and I should have been kinder. She was always invited to come over, too. And there were other cardplayers. Squatty thought we all were going to hell for playing cards and drinking. I shouldn't have, but I took pleasure in gigging her."

"Did this ever come to a head? Before Lon died?"

"Yes and no. Oh, I almost can't tell you this. I'm so ashamed of myself."

Now she really had to tell me. "Tilly, we have to hear this. Go."

"Lon and the guys set it up so that Squatty would walk past my house one evening and see what looked like me and Lon kissing. You know, a silhouette in the window. But it wasn't Lon. It was another man wearing Lon's straw hat. It was a juvenile, stupid prank. We'd been drinking a bit and it sounded so funny before we did it."

A straw hat? Lon sounded like a dandy. But that wasn't the takeaway I needed. "What happened?" I almost didn't want to ask.

"Squatty had a hissy fit. She put Lon's clothes out in the yard. When he got home the doors were locked with dead bolts and Squatty wouldn't let him in. It was awful. Lon was so upset. He spent a couple of nights at a friend's place, and he and Squatty were working it out, but not a week later he was dead of a heart attack. I always felt I was partially to blame for his illness and death."

Oh, brother. And I'd be willing to bet that Squatty blamed Tilly, too. The whole dog thing was not really about dogs. It was about a man, a prank, and a tragedy. "So, Squatty really has no bone to pick with Jezebel?"

"I wouldn't go that far. Squatty has hated me for years. Long before she got Cupcake or I got Jez."

But was this connected to whoever was letting Jezebel out, or had stolen her? "Why Jezebel? Why would someone go to this much trouble to steal her?"

"I should have told you sooner."

Oh, I hated conversations that went in this direction. "What?"

"Jezebel used to be a drug-sniffing dog."

"What?" I was repeating myself, but this just came out of left field.

"She was a famous drug-sniffing dog. She was shot in the line of duty, and I got her while she was recuperating. She was responsible for a huge drug bust in Jackson. She was an international celebrity for a time. I volunteered to take her and pay all the vet bills, and they were happy to retire her."

This definitely put a whole new spin on the issue. "The drug bust was in Jackson?" I asked.

Tinkie, who was listening, looked up at me, her eyes round and wide.

"Yes. They didn't want to keep her in the Jackson area, which is how I came to own her. I have a cousin who works for the Jackson police and he made the arrangements. I was reluctant at first, but she was such a sweet and gentle girl."

"You said this was all a year ago? Did anyone in Nixville know about her past?"

Tilly sighed again. "I should have kept it a secret, shouldn't I? I didn't tell many people, and I didn't see the harm. Do you think someone is going to hurt her because she helped the police?"

I couldn't lie. "I hope not." I did have one positive observation. "I would have thought that if there were repercussions from her past, they would have come to pass long before now."

"Should I contact the Jackson Police Department?"

That was a pretty good idea. "Do that. Ask them if anyone has inquired about the dog. We might get a lead."

"I'm on it right now," Tilly said. "I'll call you back."

I hung up and waited for Tinkie to finish her conversation with Harold before I told her all about Tilly's ill-conceived prank. When I did, she was also annoyed at Tilly for withholding pertinent information. But she was also more sympathetic.

"She didn't mean to hurt anyone," Tinkie said. "And, you have to admit, it was a cool prank. Jealous people are fun to poke with a stick."

"Tilly told me they were inspired by that old song by the Rays. They even had the song playing on the record player as she walked up." They had gone whole hog, which was the only way to pull a prank, but it had backfired in the worst kind of way.

"That's bad blood that no amount of Clorox is ever going to clean up," Tinkie said.

"I know. Not to mention Jezebel is a former drug dog that was involved in a big Jackson bust."

"Any chance Tilly was caught up in the Manson Family or mixing the Kool-Aid for Jim Jones?"

Tinkie's sarcasm did make me laugh, and I needed a good chuckle. I zipped my lips when Pauline brought Maylin into the kitchen with us. She was still a baby, but I never liked to talk about distressing stuff in front of her. Childhood was brutally short in the modern world of smartphones and television. I'd protect Maylin's innocence with my life.

"Oscar called and said he was coming home and bringing fried catfish from my church fundraiser," Pauline said. She looked at Sweetie Pie and Pluto, who'd scrambled to their feet at the mention of fried catfish. "He's bringing a plate for Coleman, too, if you want to text him and tell him to come here."

My thumbs had never typed so fast! Coleman and I both loved fried catfish, especially from Pauline's church. That congregation could cook!

"I'll mix some drinks," I said. Tinkie had just stopped breastfeeding, so she could have a libation if she wanted one. "Name your poison."

"Surprise me," Tinkie said. "And once we've finished eating, we need to drive back to Nixville and have a heart-to-heart with Squatty. We can catch her before bedtime."

I couldn't say I was looking forward to it.

10

Squatty's lights were on inside, and I signaled Tinkie to shut the car door softly. If she saw us, she might not answer. This was a sneak attack.

We walked quickly up the sidewalk to her house, aware of the CCTV cameras. Lord, I didn't want to be arrested for trespassing. Tinkie knocked on the door. Then she knocked again.

"Who is it?" Squatty called out.

Tinkie remained silent. She knocked again. Curiosity could sometimes be our best friend.

Squatty opened the door a crack. When she saw us, her face collapsed. She threw the door open and grabbed Tinkie in a bear hug. "Thank god you're here. Come in. Come in." She dragged Tinkie into the house and I followed, glad I wasn't being suffocated.

"What's going on?" I asked. Tinkie's face was pressed into Squatty's bosom and she couldn't breathe or talk.

"Oh, dear. Oh, dear." Squatty let Tinkie loose and sank to the floor squalling.

"What the hell?" I whispered to Tinkie. "Has she flipped out?"

"It's Cupcake!" Squatty wailed. "She's gone."

"What?" I admit, I was a little slow on the uptake. I shouldn't have had that second drink at Tinkie's house. "Maybe she got out of the yard and went for a walk."

"No! She was taken. Come look."

She hustled out the back door with a flashlight, and Tinkie and I were right on her heels. She pointed the flashlight at the privacy fence. An entire section had been knocked down.

"Did you hear anything?" Tinkie asked.

"No, I was listening to my favorite opera. Cupcake hates the soprano. She puts her paws over her ears and shrieks. She wanted to be outside, so I let her out. I was a fool. I'm an awful mother. I don't deserve Cupcake!"

I wasn't a big fan of Squatty, but I felt terrible for her. "Hey, I'm sure she's right around the block. Let's go look."

"You would help me?" She brushed the tears from her cheeks. "Even after I was such a jerk?"

"We would," Tinkie said. "We love dogs and we're going to find her."

"You two head out. I'll follow." I wanted to look at the fence. It was a pine privacy fence that was fairly new. The posts had been sunk into the ground properly. The boards had been screwed, not nailed, to give it more strength. And the reason it was down was because someone had hit it so hard they had broken the support boards that held it together. This wasn't an accident, or the result of an aging fence. This was vandalism or worse—dog thievery.

I texted Coleman photos.

"Be kind to Squatty," was his reply. He knew I didn't like her.

"I don't have to be kind. Tinkie will." I shot back to him.

"Your mama raised you better than that," he replied.

"Bite me."

"Oh, I will, when you get home."

I ended up laughing, then put the phone away to go find Tinkie and Squatty. I could hear them down the street, whispering in the dark.

I called Chief Garwool and asked for the CCTV footage of the camera in the area. He wasn't happy, but he agreed to show me the footage if I came to city hall. I texted Tinkie where I was going and took off. They would continue searching the area on foot while I checked in at city hall.

The chief was waiting for me when I got there, and took me into a small audiovisual room to show me the footage. It was almost a repeat of the video taken at Tilly's house when Jezebel was stolen. A slender figure in black clothes, gloves, and a hoodie was on the sidewalk staring at Squatty's house. They went behind the house and returned half an hour later, presumably after they knocked the fence down, with Cupcake in their arms. They rushed past the camera and got into a car parked two blocks down the street. This was going to be a very long night.

I had no doubt it was the same crew that had taken Jezebel. The MO was exactly the same. With Jezebel they'd come prepared with bolt cutters to destroy the lock, and with Cupcake they'd brought the tools to take the fence down. Cupcake was a small dog—truly a lap dog. Jezebel was larger. But they were both extremely attractive dogs with great personalities. Still, it seemed crazy to steal beloved family pets. This was the thing that kept tripping me up.

There had to be more at work here than I could find on the surface. If this was a dog-theft ring, I couldn't figure out what the financial incentive was—unless they intended to use the dogs for bait or medical experiments. But the risk of stealing dogs didn't make good sense. Adopting from a shelter or off Craigslist would always be far easier than breaking into a person's property.

I'd considered the possibility that Squatty was behind Jezebel's abduction—that she'd meant to torment Tilly. Now I no longer believed that. Squatty loved Cupcake. If she'd known anything about Jezebel, she would have said so by now in the hope it would result in the recovery of her own dog.

When I was at the house, I'd snapped photos of the fence and a set of footprints I found in the grass. They led into the yard from the broken fence and then back out to the sidewalk where I'd seen the thief get into a car and drive away.

"Can you get a license plate number from the CCTV footage?" I asked a police officer who was filling out reports at a desk.

He got up and came over to look. "Maybe." He clicked to zoom in on the footage. Three minutes later, I had a partial plate on the black sedan.

"Can you run it for me?" I asked. Coleman would do it if not, but heck, I was standing right there.

"Sure." He went to his computer and pecked away at the keyboard. It took more time than I anticipated, but he came back to me. "Julian Dickerson."

"Who?"

"Julian Dickerson is a local lawyer."

"What?" Why in thunderation would a lawyer be stealing dogs and destroying private property?

"He's a weirdo. I'm not kidding." The police officer rolled his eyes.

"Is he from Nixville?"

"He is *from* here but he doesn't live here."

"What does that even mean?" I was tired, cranky, and frustrated.

"Julian went to high school at Nixville High. He graduated and left for Ole Miss, where he got his law degree. He has a practice in Jackson and on the Gulf Coast. I can't imagine why he would be in Nixville stealing dogs. It doesn't make any sense."

The officer was right about that. "Does Mr. Dickerson own property in Sunflower County?"

"Not sure," the deputy said. "Not in Nixville. Or at least not in his legal name. Of course, it could be in a sibling's name or a company name."

And that would take someone like Tinkie to check out. She was the financial genius of Delaney Detective Agency. And the best shot. I was the fastest runner and the more devious. We each had a role to fill.

"Can you tell me anything else about Mr. Dickerson?" I asked.

"He's smart. Won a big capital punishment case just a few months ago in Jackson. Guy was set to go to death row at Parchman. No one thought Dickerson could win over the jury, but he did."

"Thanks." It was interesting information. "And where does he live?"

"Jackson, I believe. But he has a beach home in Bay St. Louis."

The deputy nodded toward the door of the police chief's office. A petite person stood on the other side. Tinkie. She'd followed me. The deputy signaled her to come in.

I filled her in on what I'd learned, and mentioned that if we needed to pump Dickerson for information, Janet was a good option. She lived in Bay St. Louis and had the flair to cozy up to a smart lawyer and wring anything out of him. It was good to have friends with talent.

"We need to speak with this lawyer, the sooner the better," Tinkie agreed. She checked her watch. "There's only one motel in town. Let's look there to see if we can find Dickerson's car in the lot."

We left the chief's office and drove to the Moonrise Motel. The black sedan wasn't in the lot and the clerk behind the desk told us that Dickerson wasn't a registered guest. Mr. Dickerson was going to have to wait until we could track him down in person and grill him. A job for another day. Now I simply wanted to go home.

11

Tinkie and I were up with the sun. Coleman fed the horses for me, which allowed me, my partner, the puppers, and Pluto to get on the road before the school buses rolled. Impatient was my middle name when I was driving.

"Relax and enjoy the last gasp of winter," Tinkie said, giving me the side-eye when the speedometer crept over eighty. "Spring is right around the corner. Can you smell it? Can you slow down so that we both live long enough to enjoy the changing of the seasons?"

Indeed I could.

"I want Oscar to plant some wild grapes. I think I want to make wine," Tinkie said as we hit the city limits of Nixville.

"Oh, no, you don't." I had a terrible vision of Tinkie's kitchen blowing up from fermented grapes.

She waved off my worry. "I'll start small. If we put in one arbor this spring, maybe we'll have the wild grapes by next fall. I'll be happy if I can produce half a dozen bottles."

I bit down on my lip to keep quiet. If I tried to convince her otherwise, she'd be determined to do it. If I shut up, she might forget. Where I was impatient, Tinkie was flat-out stubborn.

The phone rang and thankfully pushed that topic of conversation away. "It's that lawyer fellow," I said, looking at caller ID. "I guess someone gave him my number and said I wanted to talk to him."

"Saves us from having to track him down." Tinkie saw the upside.

"Hello, Mr. Dickerson."

"I hear you're looking for me. Why?" He didn't waste any time.

I explained what I needed and let him know Tinkie was in the car with me as I put the phone on speaker.

"You want to know about Dawson, right?"

I looked at Tinkie. Dickerson was taking the conversation in a direction I hadn't anticipated. "Sure. What can you tell us?"

"Dawson is a great guy. You won't find anyone who loves animals more than he does. But . . ." He hesitated.

"But what?"

"But he doesn't have sense enough to pour piss out of a boot."

"Meaning?" I had no clue where this was going.

"Meaning I just got charges of assault, trespassing, and vandalism against him dropped. And it wasn't an easy thing to accomplish."

I had to play like I knew more than I did or Dickerson might clam up. "He does have a temper but, like you say, he's devoted to the animals."

"Which is the only reason I took his case," the lawyer said. "Dawson needs to learn to think before he acts. He did save that dog. And that should count for something, though the animal protection laws in Mississippi are so pathetic that he had no legal cover. Had things played out differently, he could have gone to prison."

"How bad was it?"

"He broke that guy's nose when he punched him. But, in his defense, the man was beating his dog with a two-by-four."

"I'm glad Dawson hit him." The words were out of my mouth before I could stop them. Tinkie rolled her eyes and gave a thumbs-up.

"You and most sensible people feel the same way. But he won't be so lucky twice in a row."

"Are you a part of the online pet detective group?" I asked, playing a hunch.

"I was. I had to drop out."

Something in his voice made Tinkie sit forward. "Why did you leave the group?"

"Look, Dawson is a dedicated guy. But I lost my trust in him. I was afraid he'd lose his temper and do something."

"'Do something'?" Tinkie pressed.

"Assault and battery. Dog theft. Sugar in a gas tank. Revenge in one form or another. Dawson is a little . . . prickly about the fact there's little recourse to punish animal abusers or to protect animals."

"Has he done things like breaking a nose before?" I asked.

"I only represented him in that one case. He was lucky. The guy he attacked decided not to pursue the matter. When it came before the judge, the victim didn't show up and the judge dismissed the case. Dawson was very lucky."

"Where did Dawson assault the person?" I asked.

"Nixville."

I glanced at Tinkie, who arched her eyebrows. "And who did Dawson attack?" I asked.

"Some man. Really more of a kid. Grandson of one of the Nixville society ladies."

"Was it Ellis Adams?" I asked.

"Good to know you're on top of the Nixville criminal record. That's exactly who it was," Dickerson said.

"Why did Dawson attack Ellis?"

"I only know what my client said, but it is a matter of public record."

Meaning I could go to the courthouse and look up the court hearing, but that would take too much time. "What did Dawson say? Please just tell us."

Dickerson sighed. "Dawson said that Adams was hanging out with a local dogfighter, a man named Rutherford Mace. Dawson found him with a dog that he was abusing, so Dawson took action."

"Did Dawson have any evidence that Ellis Adams was involved with Mace and his crew?"

"I don't know," Dickerson said. "Since Ellis didn't show up for the trial, we didn't have to put on any testimony. To be honest, I haven't thought about any of this since the day I walked out of the courthouse and the charges against Dawson were dropped."

So, Dickerson had never pursued Dawson's story. "Thanks, Mr. Dickerson," I said. "I'll ask Dawson what evidence he had. But do you happen to know anything about Rutherford Mace?"

Dickerson hesitated. Then he spoke. "There were rumors. Mostly gossip. That Mace was involved in illegal things. He has a nice spread outside of town. He was a former professional wrestler, and a lot of the retired guys hang out there. It isn't a place you should investigate without a gun." I didn't mention that I already had.

"What do you know about Mace and the rumors of dog-fighting and drug running?"

"Only that I've heard them, too. I don't spend a lot of time north of Jackson anymore, but I have some clients in Nixville. I hear things. Just stay away from Mace."

Was Dickerson being deliberately evasive? "What kind of things?"

"Mace runs a wrestling school where he teaches younger boys to perform the stunts. Some of them are very dangerous. And, apparently, Mace has a terrific program. Some people take the courses and head out to LA to do stunts in the movies."

"Yeah, I've watched some of the wrestling shows. Crazy stuff, like flipping out of the rink and landing on their backs. Why would anyone deliberately do that?"

"Money. And . . ." He stopped himself.

"And?" I pressed.

"I've been told they're high a lot. Loosens inhibitions and, believe it or not, they say they don't get hurt as much if they aren't tense."

This opened a door I very much wanted to walk into. "Is Mace selling drugs? I've heard rumors."

"You have to take that up with Bill Garwool. To my knowledge, he hasn't pressed charges against Mace."

"I get there's been no official action. But what do you know about rumors?"

"Now, Ms. Delaney, I don't like to deal in rumors and gossip. I'm an officer of the court, after all."

I could almost hear the laughter in his voice. He wanted to

flirt. Tinkie should have made this call. She had far superior flirting skills. "Indulge me, Julian. What's the gossip?"

His voice grew lower. "Mace is a bad dude. He's got his finger in a lot of pies, and most of them are illegal."

Human beings did a lot of bad things. Drugs were one of them—when innocent people got hooked and ruined their lives. But my interest was in finding out about stolen dogs and dogfighting. Garwool could fight the battle against drugs—unless that crime dovetailed with dog stealing. Then I was on it like a duck on a june bug.

"Has Mace been involved in dogfighting?"

"Hmmm. I don't know. Never heard that. Not really. But some of the men who live at his place, yeah. They've been in trouble with the law before. I know the FBI busted up a ring in the area four years ago. Mace himself wasn't named, but a few of the guys who lived at his place were arrested and sent to prison."

"At least someone was punished."

"Only because the feds conducted the bust. Garwool would likely have let them all go without charges."

That I didn't doubt. But I did think Deputy Tom Terrell would tell me the truth about this incident if I asked him—away from the police station. He worked for Garwool, but he struck me as an officer with a conscience and a desire to serve the law.

"What do you know about Zotto Hammerfist?" I asked.

"He was the best wrestler on the circuit ten years ago. Hurt his back in a bad fall. Is he still out at Mace's place? I think he teaches some of the stunt classes."

"Yes, he's there. What's his reputation?"

"He was a good guy, as far as I know. But why he stays around Mace and that clown show, I'll never know."

I didn't trust Zotto completely, but he might prove to be my ace in the hole at Mace's training camp. "If he's teaching, it's an income." And if he'd hurt his back, he couldn't wrestle any longer.

"Like I said, Zotto seemed like a good guy the times I talked with him. And just a warning. Watch out for that Adams guy. He's a piece of work and his grandmother thinks he's the best thing since sliced bread."

"Squatty's little dog, Cupcake, is missing. Do you think Ellis could be involved in that?"

"He's a little twit. And he hates that his grandmother holds the purse strings. He made some comments that got back to me. I wouldn't put anything past him."

"Thanks, Julian."

"Yes, Sarah Booth thanks you very much, Julian," Tinkie chimed in. I should have known she was being too quiet. "I mean she *really* appreciates it. Are you free for drinks?"

I glared at my partner, but she was having a good time. "Come up to Zinnia and visit us when you get a chance," Tinkie said sweetly.

"I'd like that," Julian said.

"We have to go." I had to hang up that phone so I could throttle Tinkie. Or else she'd have Julian Dickerson on the front porch of Dahlia House and I somehow didn't think that would sit well with Coleman.

"Talk later," Tinkie said cheerfully before she hit the disconnect button. And we were done. At last, we had a viable suspect in both dog disappearances. Ellis Adams. And it would be a bonus to arrest him if it meant Squatty had to eat a little crow.

12

The next morning over coffee I told Coleman about the setup Tinkie had tried to pull. He was laughing hard when he kissed my cheek and put his hat on to go to work. "If you take up with lawyers, I know it's only because you miss your dad. But tell that partner of yours that payback is hell. I can always introduce Oscar to some pretty ladies."

I hadn't thought of Julian Dickerson in regard to my daddy. And I also didn't think Julian Dickerson could hold a candle to James Franklin Delaney. But there was no point saying that. "My heart belongs to you, Coleman." That was the truth.

"But you can still wrangle information out of people with your beauty and charm."

I glared at him, but he didn't seem to be teasing. "Well, that's sweet."

"Love you, girl." He picked up a to-go coffee and his keys. "Call me and let me know what your plans for the day are."

"I can tell you now. I'm going to Nixville to talk to Ellis

Adams, and then I'm going to find Dawson Reed and talk to him face-to-face."

"Stay away from Rutherford Mace's place, if you can. Heck, if you decide to go there, call the office and I'll meet you."

"I don't want that. You have a job to do. I'll be fine. I won't go without the dogs and Tinkie."

He considered a moment. "Okay. Just be alert. I don't think Mace would attempt anything, but there are guys on his property who might."

"Loud and clear." I did hear him and I would pay attention.

Tinkie and I decided not to alert Ellis to our pending visit. We also left the pooches and Pluto at home. The cat was exhausted. He and Poe, the raven, were having some sibling rivalry. Poe had spent the early morning dive-bombing Pluto, and the cat had had enough. He'd taken refuge in the drawing room window, where he could watch the porch. Poe needed to be careful. Pluto was a master of revenge. He was a fine example of not getting mad but getting even. I could take some lessons from him.

As we were pulling into the city limits of Nixville, Tinkie put her hand on my arm. "Maybe we should park away from Squatty's house."

"We're also looking for Cupcake. That's a good reason to visit her house."

Tinkie nodded. "I know. It's just that I have a feeling Ellis will run if he knows we want to talk to him. Squatty is not going to be happy to think her grandson might be involved in dog stealing. Especially since Cupcake was stolen."

Tinkie was right, of course. "All we have to do is get in the room with Ellis. After that, if you can distract Squatty, I'll pinch Ellis's head until a confession comes out." Tinkie, because she had more control over her emotions at the moment, might be the best interviewer for this young man, but I wanted to twist a knot in his spine.

"Good plan. But park down the street."

I did, and we walked up to Squatty's house with Tinkie in front of me. She rang the bell while I kind of hung back behind a shrub. Which was admittedly silly. Squatty came to the door and invited Tinkie in. When I popped out, she almost closed the door in my face, but I slid past her and into the den where Ellis was stretched out on the sofa, drinking coffee and watching the news. He took one look at me, sat up, and struggled to get his feet in his shoes. He was about to take a runner.

I was faster. I sat beside him and put a restraining hand on his arm. "I need to talk to you, Ellis, and I don't want to upset your granny, but I will if you make me."

He glared at me, but sank back into the sofa.

"Squatty, could I have a glass of water?" Tinkie said, distracting the older woman and easing her into the kitchen so Ellis and I were alone.

The minute his grandmother was gone, Ellis started to get up, but I snatched him back to his seat beside me. "Sit."

"What do you want?"

"The truth. Where is Cupcake?"

He looked at me like I'd grown a second head. "Are you nuts? I don't know. You think I'd do something to my grandmother's dog? Hell, she loves that dog more than she ever loved me or my mother."

"I'd be willing to bet the dog is a lot more lovable than you. And a lot more motivated to create a good life. Where is Cupcake? And don't pretend to be innocent. I know plenty about you."

"You don't know half of what you think," Ellis said. "I like dogs. I would never hurt Cupcake or any other canine."

"Too bad I don't believe you." Something about Ellis set my teeth on edge. Maybe it was the way he jutted out his chin and tried to act tough. Maybe it was the fact that he was a layabout who let his grandmother support him. Or maybe it was because I suspected him of being a dog thief, one of the lower life-forms on the planet.

His phone dinged and he checked the message. Lucky for me, his face recognition kicked in. When he put the phone down on the coffee table he'd nearly destroyed by putting his feet on it, I snatched the phone up, dodging his grasping hands, and was able to see the screen that had opened. There was a message from that creep Jason Lomus. "Meet me out at Mace's house. We need to talk."

And boom! There was the connection between Mace and Ellis I needed. Now I just had to tie them to the disappearance of the dogs.

He realized I'd seen the message—and recognized the implications—and put his phone in his pocket. "You need to get out of my grandmother's house."

"Sorry, I work for her. She's the only person who can put me out."

"I'll make sure she does."

"Ellis, she loves that dog. If I can make her see that you're involved in the disappearance of Cupcake, she is going to disinherit you and do everything in her power to make you suffer. Get ready for the big time."

Ellis pointed his finger in my face. "You want to know who

is going to suffer? It's going to be you. Granny doesn't have good sense anymore. She's as dotty as a bitsy bird. And you and your partner are not above taking her for a ride to the cleaners, paying you to find that stupid dog. Cupcake ran off. That's the whole story."

"All except for the fact that someone tore your grandmother's fence down. Otherwise, the dog would still be in the backyard. And I understand Garwool has found some tire prints in the lawn by the fence. He can match those to the vehicle used to pull that section of fence out. And when he does, you're going to be out of luck."

"He can't prove that."

"Wanna bet?" I knew Garwool could do it. I just didn't know if he would. He didn't seem all that excited about solving the dog case. I had to count on the fact that Ellis didn't know that. And maybe Garwool would surprise me. Maybe he would do the right thing.

Ellis stood up abruptly. "I have to go."

I stood also and walked to the doorway, where I could signal Tinkie. "Ellis is leaving," I told Tinkie and Squatty.

"Where are you going?" Squatty asked him. "I have some things I need your help with."

"They'll keep," Ellis said. "I'll be back later."

He picked up his coat from the floor and slid into it. The man's hair was limp and greasy. I hadn't noticed until he stood up. He needed a good hot shower. And maybe a whop on the butt.

Ellis rushed out the front door, and I waited, counting to twenty. By the time Ellis cleared the sidewalk, I was out the front door and following him, as surreptitiously as I could. When I realized he was headed for his truck, parked down the street, I doubled back to get mine. I'd parked behind some shrubs at a neighbor's house, so I hoped Ellis hadn't noticed my vehicle.

I texted Tinkie to let her know what I was up to and to urge her to put the heat on Squatty. Tinkie, with her society credentials, was far more palatable to Squatty than I would be. Someone knew something about what had happened to those dogs. It was up to me to find the person who held the secrets and make them talk.

Once Ellis was in his truck, I didn't have time to think of anything except staying on his trail. He drove like a maniac, and I didn't have the luxury of doing the same and drawing attention to myself. I had to outsmart him. Once I figured out he was headed to Rutherford Mace's place, I was able to take a few shortcuts. During my earlier visit to the facility, I'd sussed out a good place to stash my car and hide it. I was maybe five minutes ahead of Ellis, so I didn't have time to waffle. I took action and pulled onto the property and into the woodland path that offered lots of camouflage for a car.

I got my gun out of the back of the vehicle and crept through the thick brush to a vantage point where I could see Ellis pulling into the yard. He hadn't wasted any time. He clearly knew where he was going, too. He strode across the property toward one of the outbuildings. Before he could knock on the door, it opened and a man I'd never seen before stepped out on the small porch.

"You shouldn't be here, you idiot. You're going to get all of us caught." The man, who had dark hair and a dark beard, was angry at Ellis. The notorious Jason Lomus.

Ellis was almost whining. "I didn't have a choice. Those private investigators Tilly hired are all over town."

"So what? They don't have anything connecting us to any of it."

"You're wrong about that, Jason. They can track the ruts you left in Grandma's yard when you pulled the fence down. I told you not to bother Cupcake. I told you it wouldn't work. Taking her has only fired everyone up more to find the dog thieves."

The man laughed, clearly enjoying Ellis's frustration. "Sounds like a personal problem to me, Ellis. Maybe you should get your granny to back off, if you can let go of her financial tit long enough to do it."

I expected Ellis to draw back and slug him, but it didn't happen. Instead, Ellis backed up. "I don't have to take this from you."

"Yeah, you do."

"I'm going to talk to Rutherford."

The man only laughed. "Go tattle on me, like the sniveling little boy you are."

Ellis's face grew red and his mouth was a thin line of hatred. "I'll make you pay for all of this."

The man only laughed. "Go home, boy. Go tell Grandma to bake you some cookies."

"Where is Cupcake?" Ellis asked.

I inched closer. This was what I needed to hear.

"That dog is long gone. You'll never get her back. I got a nice price for her, though. Those research labs pay pretty good for small dogs."

"Quit jerking me around and tell me where she is," Ellis demanded. "My grandmother is having a fit. She loves that dog." He hesitated. "And I like her, too. We want her back."

"You should have thought of that before you helped me steal

those other dogs. I needed one more to make the transport. She was sweet and easy to snatch." He grinned. "That's how it goes."

Ellis's hands clenched into fists, and I watched, wondering if he'd be able to control his impulse to smash the man in the face. I feared if he couldn't control himself, the other man would beat him to a pulp.

"I'm going to get Cupcake back."

"You stay away from those dogs." The bigger man was getting angry now. "I'll make you regret the day you were born."

"You can try." Ellis wasn't going to back down. He had more grit than I'd given him credit for.

"Little man, don't get in my way."

"Or what?" Ellis asked. "You think Rutherford is fond of you? You think he respects you? He thinks you're trash, and you know, he's right."

I felt the weight of the gun in my hand. Ellis was going to get his brains beaten in. I wouldn't shoot the bigger fellow, but I would shoot over his head if I had to. He could easily kill Ellis.

"Little man, you should leave now. While you can."

"I'm going to get Cupcake. You should never have taken my granny's dog. You're a moron, and Rutherford will agree."

I eased onto my knees so I had a stable base if I had to shoot. The pressing need for action was delayed when Zotto walked up to the two men. "What's going on?"

"Nothing," they said in unison. "I'm leaving," Ellis added. He started to back away, but the bigger man grabbed for him.

"You're staying right here. You aren't leaving and causing trouble."

"What's the problem?" Zotto asked. He was calm, but there was an edge in his tone.

"Nothing, Zotto. It's just that Ellis owes me some money. He's trying to skip out on paying me."

"That's a lie," Ellis said. "I'm going to get my granny's dog. Jason is trying to sell her to a lab."

Zotto turned slowly to look at Jason. "You're doing what?"

"It's not your affair."

"I'm making it my business. Where are these dogs?"

"Screw you!" Jason turned on his heel, went inside, and slammed the door.

"Where are the dogs?" Zotto asked Ellis. "Tell me now or I'll beat it out of you."

"They're . . ."

The blow to the back of my head came out of nowhere. I hadn't heard anyone coming up. I fell face-first into the dirt, the gun beneath me. I struggled a moment to pull it out and roll over, but the effort was too great. I slipped into the darkness.

13

When I came to, I knew I'd messed up. I was still on the ground beneath the shrub I'd been hiding in. Ellis, Zotto, and Jason were all gone. Sitting up slowly, I tried to remember what had happened before I lost consciousness. It was clear I'd been hit on the head by someone. Someone with a very hard weapon. Like, maybe a brick. A dull headache throbbed just above my eyes.

I looked around me, but there was nothing on the ground. No sign of my attacker. I heard some people talking outside of another building on the premises, and I got to my feet—a little unsteady—and started toward the voices.

I couldn't make out what they were saying. I went around the big house and to the back patio, where Rutherford Mace was talking with Zotto. Mace had obviously returned from wherever he'd gone.

"Jason is a moron. Fire him and send him packing. He's going to get us all in trouble." When Mace saw me, he stopped talking, signaling Zotto to also shut up. I felt a sense of frustration. I'd lost my best lead and any chance of getting the dogs back. Ellis and Jason were gone.

"Where are the dogs?" I asked.

Mace and Zotto turned to look at me. "Help her into a chair." Mace was all fake concern.

Zotto took my elbow and walked me to a chair on the patio. "Sit down and be quiet," he whispered in my ear.

I wanted to believe he was trying to help me, but I knew better. I'd heard him talking with the two dog thieves. "Where's Ellis? And where are those dogs?"

"We don't know anything about dogs," Mace said. "I told you before to look around. You didn't find any dogs, did you?"

"I did."

"What?" Mace looked perplexed. "What dogs?"

"Just one dog named Avalon. I have her now and she's safe. But where are the other dogs? I heard they were about to be transported somewhere. Like, maybe a research facility."

"I don't know anything about that." Mace came to stand over me. "And I don't like to be accused of things. Especially cruelty to animals."

He sounded sincere. Was it possible he wasn't aware of what was happening on his own property? "There was a dog here. I took her back to Zinnia." I watched his expression closely. He still looked puzzled.

"What dog?" Mace directed the question to Zotto, who shrugged.

"Take it up with Jason," Zotto said. He gave me a piercing look, which I read to mean for me to keep my lips zipped. Because I wanted to see how this played out, I did exactly that.

"Jason Lomus had a dog here?" Mace seemed angry.

"You need to ask him." Zotto wasn't admitting to anything. And since he'd helped me with Avalon, I wasn't about to rat him out.

"Would you mind if I looked around the place? Last time I was here I didn't get a chance."

Mace shrugged. "Knock yourself out. Zotto, go with her and make sure no one bothers her."

That was an ominous statement. But I smiled big. "Thanks."

"Are you okay?" Mace asked. "You looked a little . . . unsteady."

"I'm good." I still had a headache, but I was otherwise unharmed. "I'll just look around and then head out."

"Zotto. Go with her." Mace smiled. "Take good care of her."

He was gracious, but somehow I had the sense that he was sending Zotto to make sure I didn't see anything I shouldn't. The Mace estate was huge. There would be plenty of time for things to be shifted and moved. It might be a game of musical chairs with the dogs. And Zotto could be caught between a rock and a hard place if he was trying to keep his job and also protect dogs like Avalon.

Mace gave a nod of his head and walked away.

Zotto made sure he was gone and then he rounded on me. "You are putting the dogs in danger coming here like this. You need to leave now. And don't come back."

"I'm not going anywhere until I find Jezebel and Cupcake. That Jason seemed to know something about her, and that little rat fink Ellis, too. He's involved in the theft of his own grandmother's dog." He was a terrible human being as far as I could tell.

"Ellis is a joke, Ms. Delaney. He thinks he knows so much and he is truly viewed as a fool here."

"But he and Jason were saying—"

"It doesn't matter. What matters is that you clear out of here and fast. I'm doing what I can."

I had to say it. "I don't trust you, Zotto. I think you're lying to me."

He gave me a long-suffering look. "Think whatever you want, but get out of here now. I mean it. You're going to make things worse for the dogs. I'm trying to help you find them, but you're complicating things for both of us."

"I intend to have a look around."

He waved a hand, indicating I should do my worst. "I'll go with you because Rutherford told me to. So, let's get it done."

I led the way to the first big outbuilding, a bunkhouse situation, only the bunks were all empty and a thick layer of dust coated the flat surfaces. No one had been living there for a while. There was no evidence of dogs.

I went over every building on the property that I could find, but there were plenty of places where kennels could be hidden in the brakes and thick woods. I had no excuse to stay longer, and I worried that Tinkie might have been trying to call me. "I'm going now, Zotto."

"Good. And stay gone. If I see any dogs I'll be in touch."

I wasn't sure if I believed him, but there was no one else I could rely on with access to the Mace property.

I arrived back at Squatty's, hoping to find Tinkie sitting on the front steps waiting for me. I wasn't that lucky. I had to go to the door and knock. When Squatty let me in, I caught sight of Tinkie's face. Thundercloud didn't do it justice. She was upset and I didn't blame her. I'd been gone for several hours and she'd been stranded. Without a word from me. Squatty had probably chewed her ear off.

"Well, where is Cupcake?" Squatty demanded. "You were gone long enough, and you left Mrs. Richmond here. My whole morning is shot."

Graciousness was not a priority for Squatty. "Yes, it was a difficult situation. I hate to be the bearer of bad news"—actually, I didn't—"but Ellis is involved in the abduction of Cupcake. He knows who pulled your fence down and took her."

"That's an outrageous lie!"

"Okay. Kiss your puppy goodbye. Either you can take it up with Ellis and force him to tell us where the dog is, or you can pretend your grandson is a good guy." I knew he was a liar. "But he isn't, and you know it."

Squatty looked from me to Tinkie and back to me. I cast a side glance at Tinkie to discover she was already over her annoyance at being left behind. Tinkie had a hot temper, but it never lasted long. She was one of the most forgiving people I'd ever met.

"Call Ellis," Tinkie told Squatty.

Squatty was reluctant, but she pulled her phone from her pocket and dialed her grandson. "Ellis, I need you at the house, please." There was a pause. "No, now. Right now. It can't wait." She hung up before he could protest more.

I got my phone and called Dawson Reed of the internet pet finders. If Dawson could come over, too, we might get somewhere. My call went to voice mail, and I left Dawson an invitation to Squatty's house. I didn't know if he'd make it or not, but I'd tried.

"When Ellis gets here, what are you going to do?" Squatty asked.

"Force him to tell us where Cupcake is."

"How will you force him?" she asked, wringing her hands. I felt a moment of pity for her. Ellis was a low-down rotten skunk, but he was also her blood. Her inclination would be to protect him, but she had to make a choice. Ellis or her puppy. I wasn't shocked when Cupcake won out.

Tinkie and I went into the kitchen for a cup of coffee and to be out of the main area when Ellis arrived. I wanted Squatty to have a chance to talk to Ellis before I had to twist his arm. If he would tell his granny the truth, it would save us all a lot of heartburn.

Fifteen minutes later, Ellis was walking in the front door, directly into the buzz saw of his grandmother. "Where is Cupcake?" she demanded. "And don't try to pretend you don't know. I have it on good authority you know very well and you know who is responsible. Now, I want my baby back."

"Those detectives!" Ellis was apoplectic. "You believe them over your own grandson?" His indignation sounded real, and I wondered how narcissistic he really was. He'd stolen his grandmother's dog and was now offended that he'd been caught.

I started to go to the foyer where the argument was taking place, but Tinkie caught my arm. "Just wait. See what Squatty can get out of him."

"Where is my baby?" Squatty demanded, and her voice cracked. A pang of sympathy hit me right in the old heart.

"I don't know," Ellis said, his voice much quieter. "I really don't. I had no idea they would take Cupcake. I'm fond of her, too."

"Do you think they would hurt her?" Squatty asked.

Dang! My heart was breaking. No matter how annoying Squatty could be, she loved that puppy. And she was hurting.

"I don't know," Ellis admitted in probably one of the most truthful statements of his life. "I don't know why they took her. I really don't. I do everything they tell me to do. It isn't like I needed to be slapped into line."

That was an interesting way of viewing the set of circumstances. It sounded like Ellis had gotten in over his head with this crew and was doing whatever he could to stay on their good side.

"Those detectives are going to help us find Cupcake. And Jezebel. And any other dogs they've stolen. And you're going to cooperate with them, do you hear?"

"Grandma, you're going to get me hurt." The fear in his voice was real. I looked at Tinkie and we both nodded. If Ellis was afraid, we could ask the police chief or even Coleman to protect him. I wouldn't put any faith in Garwool, but Coleman would keep Ellis safe—unless he was implicated in some crimes.

Finally. Tinkie nodded at me and we both stepped into the foyer. When Ellis saw us, his eyes went big and round. "You tricked me, Granny. You've put my life in danger. They're going to kill me now, for sure."

Squatty sobbed and Tinkie went to her side. "No one is going to kill you, Ellis. Don't be such a drama queen." Tinkie's snappy tone stiffened his spine and he squared his shoulders.

"You don't know how dangerous these men are," he said. "I sure didn't, or I'd never have talked to them." He looked at Squatty. "I'm not involved in the dog stealing. Or the drugs. Or the guns. I was just friendly with the wrong people."

I believed him. Ellis was not a brave man. He was a go-along-to-get-along kind of guy. "Help us find those dogs before they're sold or destroyed."

He nodded. "Okay. I'll do what I can."

"So, who has the dogs?"

"If I tell you, they'll kill me."

"And if you don't tell her right this minute, I'll put you out on the street." Squatty was dishing out some tough love.

Ellis shook his head. "I can't tell. I'll pack my things."

This wasn't the outcome I wanted at all. I couldn't help but feel sorry for Ellis. He was genuinely afraid, and Squatty was absolutely furious with him. "My precious Cupcake is gone because of you and your low-class, thieving friends. I'm sorry, Ellis. I've given you a place to live, food, a vehicle, job and educational opportunities, and my payback is that your friends stole the one creature on the planet I love with all my heart. I fear they will kill her, too. If you won't help us recover her, get your things and get out of my house now."

It was a tough scene to witness, and Tinkie was about to cry. Squatty's eyes were full of tears, but her jaw was set. Ellis looked at both of us and then walked past us to go to the back of the house, presumably to collect his possessions.

"Are you really kicking him out?" Tinkie asked Squatty.

"Of course not. But he doesn't have to know that. I'm hoping he'll lead you two ladies to the place where they're holding the dogs. Get my baby. That's all I ask. Get my baby and I'll pay you twice what Tilly is paying you."

"Our fee isn't a bidding war," I said. I was reluctant to admit we were helping Tilly for free. I didn't want it to get around the county that we were soft touches. "We just want the dogs recovered. That's all."

"That's what I want, too. I'm sorry I was so happy about Tilly suffering. It isn't much fun. I've learned a bitter lesson here. I'll help any way I can to bring all the dogs back home."

"We're going to wait outside and see if Ellis will lead us to the place where the dogs are." I had to get out of the house. It was just too sad.

"Thank you both. Thank you." Squatty pulled us into an embrace before she let us out the front door. I called Coleman on the way to the car.

14

"Budgie ran a background check on that Dawson Reed fellow." Coleman was talking and driving. I had my cell phone on the console set on speaker and Tinkie was in the passenger seat.

"What did Budgie find?" Tinkie asked.

"Dawson Reed has a criminal record."

I wasn't as shocked as I should have been. "For what charge?"

"Assaulting an undercover FBI agent."

Well, that wasn't what I was expecting. "Are you kidding me?"

"Not at all," Coleman said, and I could imagine the big smile on his face. He loved it when he could surprise me. "It's actually an interesting story."

Coleman's definition of interesting and mine weren't always in sync. "Spill it, please. Tinkie and I need to talk to him, and I'd like to be prepared. This may be leverage."

"Well, a criminal record might be a bit of an exaggeration."

Okay, here it came. Coleman had had his fun and now he was going to tell us the truth. "Did he assault an FBI agent?"

"He did. No doubt about it. And he didn't try to pretend he didn't."

Coleman was talking in circles. I had learned to bide my time. Tinkie, though, gave me her frustrated face and made a cutting motion across her throat, telling me she was ready to slit Coleman's gullet.

"Explain, Coleman, or I'm going to bring Tinkie to the sheriff's office to deal with you. She isn't amused."

He laughed. "Bring her to Dahlia House. I'm on my way home. I'll put something on the grill."

"You just redeemed yourself, buddy," Tinkie told him. "Now tell us about Dawson. We need a good lead. We're sitting outside Squatty's place, hoping her grandson heads out to the people holding the dogs."

Coleman's humor was gone. "Now you two don't go off on a tangent. These people aren't to be messed with."

"Coleman, tell us about Dawson. Tell us or I'm hanging up." I was a little agitato by this point.

"Okay, sorry. I just can't resist tormenting you two. Here are the facts. Dawson got into a physical altercation with two men who were transporting dogs to a fight."

I parsed out what he'd said. "And he was arrested for trying to help the dogs?"

"Yes, but he put an FBI agent in the hospital for a week. He clocked him with a tow chain he had in his Jeep. The chain gashed his skull badly and he almost lost an eye."

Those big chains were heavy and unwieldy. It would be difficult to control an attack if Dawson was swinging the chain. Though Dawson was not what I'd call a physically intimidating specimen, the chain would even the score. "But why was an FBI agent involved in dogfighting? And just so you know, I think Dawson was in the right on this one."

"The agent was undercover. Dawson almost blew the whole case, but they managed to arrest five men who are currently serving time in the Mississippi State Penitentiary at Parchman."

That was a relief.

"How is the FBI agent?" Tinkie asked.

"He's okay. Good doctors. And Dawson got off with no jail time and the charge was lowered to simple assault. He didn't know the man was an agent. Dawson really was trying to help the dogs. But you should know he's a loose cannon sometimes. Kind of like you, Sarah Booth."

"Thanks. Last I checked, I haven't assaulted any FBI agents."

"See that you keep it that way," he said. "Now, I'm about to pull into Dahlia House."

"Please make sure Chablis stays with Sweetie Pie and Avalon," Tinkie said. "Tell her I'll be home shortly."

"Will do."

"Gotta go, Coleman. Ellis is getting in his vehicle. We need to follow."

"Be careful, ladies. Call if you need backup."

"You know we will." I hung up and did a U-turn in the road so I could follow Ellis. Wherever he was going, we were going, too.

Tinkie and I stayed a comfortable distance behind Ellis. It wasn't hard. He drove like an old woman. It was clear Ellis wasn't a risk-taker. As we followed behind him, heading out of town on the east side, I wondered if Squatty would ever forgive him about Cupcake. I didn't particularly like Squatty, but she did love her little dog. And Ellis had betrayed her.

Tinkie was lost in thought also, but she was going down a different track all together. "Do you think Dawson is a good person?" she asked.

"He put himself on the line to save a dog." That was in his favor. But he might have used a bit more judgment in the process. Smacking an FBI agent with a heavy chain wasn't the brightest move a person could make.

"Who do you really think is behind the dog thefts?" Tinkie asked.

"You don't think it's a dogfighting ring?"

She hesitated. "I can't say for sure. It just seems . . . peculiar."

I nudged her in the arm and pointed down the street. Ellis was taking a right-hand turn down a driveway nearly concealed in overgrown shrubs and weeds. If I followed him onto private property, I wasn't certain what I might find. Or if I would be able to get away if I needed to.

My cell phone rang. Coleman was calling. He knew I was bird-dogging someone. I didn't answer, and he called right back.

"Something is wrong," Tinkie said. She didn't have the psychic skills of Madame Tomeeka, but she was perceptive.

"What's going on?" I asked when I answered. The phone was again on speaker.

"It's Sweetie Pie and Chablis. Sarah Booth, they're gone."

I felt like I'd been punched in the gut. "What? Are you sure? Maybe they're asleep upstairs." But Coleman didn't make mistakes like this.

"What do you mean 'gone'?" Tinkie asked. She was freaking out, too. "How?"

"The front door was open when I pulled up into the yard. I didn't think much about it until I whistled them up and they didn't come. Only Avalon was here."

"But if Avalon was there . . ." If any of the dogs left, I would have figured it would be her. She was new. She might not understand that she lived at Dahlia House now. Sweetie Pie and Chablis would never just take off. Never. I looked at Tinkie and realized she was thinking the same thing.

"Did someone take them?" I asked.

"I'm afraid that may be the case. Let me check the footage from the front-porch camera I installed."

"I'll wait on the phone." My foot was itching to hit the gas and strike out for home, but if there was an explanation and the dogs were perfectly safe, I didn't want to blow following Ellis.

"I'm pulling it up on my phone now." Coleman's voice went dead. There was only silence.

"What? What is it?" He was making me panic.

"Sarah Booth, the person who took them was driving an old Roadster, like your mama's. The person is small of stature. Face covered by a mask and hoodie. And they disabled the camera. Damn."

"Gertrude." I whispered the name that made my heart contract. Tinkie put her hand on my arm.

"Do you think Gertrude has the dogs?" Tinkie asked, panic lacing her voice.

"Coleman, is it Gertrude Stromm?" Gertrude was my nemesis. She'd developed an irrational hatred of me based on false information and a mind that readily twisted into conspiracy theories. A former bed-and-breakfast owner, Gertrude blamed my mother for the fact that Gertrude had poisoned her own son. "Is it her? Does she have Sweetie Pie and Chablis?"

"I can't be certain, but it looks like her." Coleman kept his voice level. "I'm sending you the footage."

"Where has she been all this time?" Tinkie asked. "I hoped she was dead."

Tinkie wasn't the only one who'd hoped Gertrude was gone from our lives forever. My phone dinged and I checked out the video from the porch camera.

"It's Gertrude." I recognized her. "She was here and she took the dogs. I guess she didn't realize Avalon was my dog, too, or she would have taken her."

"I'll have roadblocks on every rutted pig trail out of the county. We'll catch her and get the dogs back," Coleman assured me. "Don't panic, Sarah Booth. Tinkie, we will find the dogs. I'll see about getting the camera fixed and the others installed. We will find the dogs."

But would we find them alive? That was the question no one could answer. Gertrude was capable of anything.

15

By the time we made it back to Dahlia House, Budgie and DeWayne, Oscar, Harold, Pauline, Maylin, Cece, Millie, and Madame Tomeeka were all waiting for us. Millie had brought food from the café, even though no one was hungry. Avalon ate some treats, but for the most part we were all in a deep depression.

"Does anyone know where Gertrude has been?" Oscar asked. He had his arm around Tinkie, supporting her as she leaned into his chest and cried. Pauline and Maylin tried to comfort her, but she was scared for her pup. Maylin was the love of her life, but Chablis would always be her first baby.

I excused myself and went to check on the horses. I needed a moment alone. I tried not to think of what Gertrude might do to Sweetie Pie and Chablis, and instead I focused on how—and why—Gertrude was somehow involved in the theft of dogs in Sunflower County. It didn't make sense. Yet somehow I had to figure out what had really happened and how I could recover the missing dogs. *All* of the missing dogs.

"Don't give up hope."

The male voice behind me scared me and I sat up, banging my head on a board. "Dammit, Jitty!" I knew it was the Dahlia House haint causing trouble again. I swung around to look at her, taken aback for a moment at the tall man dressed in a three-piece suit from the 1850s. "Who are you?"

He took his top hat off and executed a courtly bow. "Henry Bergh, at your service."

"Who?" I asked.

"Henry Bergh, founder of the American Society for Prevention of Cruelty to Animals."

I took in his dated clothes and did my best to pull up the little bit of knowledge I had on the ASPCA. It was founded in 1866 in New York State—the first of the US states to pass legislation to protect animals. "Do you know where Sweetie Pie is?" I asked. Jitty never helped me with a case, but Sweetie Pie was different. She wasn't just a case; she was family.

"You have no idea how cruel humans can be toward those without a voice," he said.

"Please, don't do this. I can't have those things in my head right now." Jitty was going to break me if she kept going. "I know how awful some people are."

"When I founded the ASPCA, I was mocked and ridiculed. They called me a bleeding heart, a liberal, a man crazed with tender sensibilities."

As worried as I was about the missing dogs, I was equally compelled to listen to the man who was called "the great meddler" because he was not above getting physical with those he found beating horses or abusing dogs, chickens, and cows.

"Why are people so lacking in compassion?"

"I don't know," he said, his voice riddled with sadness. "Compassion for animals is a matter purely of conscience; it has no perplexing side issues."

"Do you know where the dogs are? I'm begging you, Jitty."

As I watched, Henry Bergh morphed and shifted until the tall, top-hatted gentleman was gone and Jitty stood before me. She wore jeans and a sweatshirt—and there were tears in her eyes. "I tried to scare that old biddy away," she said. "I did try, Sarah Booth, but she couldn't see me. She wasn't scared when I slammed the door or rattled the windows. She just snatched up those pups and left."

Jitty was breaking my heart. "Thank you. Thank you, for trying." I felt a storm of tears mounting behind my eyes. "I have to find those dogs, Jitty. I have to."

"What are you going to do?" Jitty asked.

For the first time ever, I realized that Jitty wasn't deviling me. She was genuinely concerned for the dogs. And for me. "I'm going to find the dogs. And Gertrude. And I am going to end her."

"Now, Sarah Booth—" Jitty stepped back into the shadows of a stall when the barn door opened and Tinkie walked in.

"Are you okay, Sarah Booth?" she asked.

"I am, I think." I couldn't explain it, but Jitty's visit had somehow given me strength. "Are you?"

"I don't know. What are we going to do?" she asked.

I had an answer. It came to me like a whisper on the wind, and I wondered if in this one instance, Jitty was offering advice. "We're going to find Ellis and beat the truth out of him if that's what it takes. We can't let Coleman know."

"I'm with you. Let me get Oscar and my crew headed for home. Then we can either get Cece or Millie to leave, too, or maybe they'll help us. But we can't involve Coleman or the deputies. They took an oath to uphold the law, and right this minute, I am very eager to break all the laws I need to break to bring those dogs home."

I held out my hand and we shook. The pact was made.

Somehow we cleared our friends and support group out of my house. I didn't lie to Coleman, but I didn't tell him the truth. Guilt would eat at me for a long time, but saving the doggos was my priority. I would suffer now, and make amends later.

"What's the plan?" Tinkie asked when we were alone in the Delaney Detective Agency office in my home. Here we had access to computers, phones, printers—the basics of doing online checks and writing reports. I looked up Dawson's number and called him. I put the phone on speaker so Tinkie could participate.

"Sarah Booth, what's going on?"

I explained what had happened. "We know who is responsible. We just don't know why she would steal our dogs. It doesn't make sense. I know she hates me, but how is she connected to Cupcake and Jezebel being stolen?"

"Are you sure that she is connected?" Dawson asked the one question that demanded an immediate answer. And I had no clue what that answer might be. How was Gertrude involved? How did she even know about the missing dogs and our new case? We hadn't talked to anyone except Squatty and Tilly and the police chief. "Police chief," I whispered.

Tinkie nodded. "I think you hit the nail on the head. Whether Garwool deliberately or accidentally gave Gertrude the information necessary to hurt you, I think it may have come from him."

I could feel the heat coming off the top of my head and I

recalled the old saying that my hair was about to catch on fire. Garwool didn't seem to want to help us but, by damn, if he was fueling the enemy with information, I was going to hurt him.

"Dawson, can you find out if Garwool did this?" Tinkie asked. She put a supporting hand on my arm.

"Maybe. I have a source in the police department I can ask."

"Would you?"

"Okay. I'll call you back."

"We're driving to Nixville now," I told him. "I have to talk to Tilly, and I need to watch Squatty's house in case Ellis returns. He knows more than he's letting on."

"I'll call when I hear something," Dawson said before he hung up.

"I'm sorry, Tinkie." I was deeply remorseful.

"About what?"

"Gertrude. She has Chablis because of me. She has no fight with you."

"That's not true, Sarah Booth. You forget she's tried to kill me several times. I'm just lucky she didn't succeed, and so are you. Please call Coleman and loop him in on our plans. If we get in trouble with Gertrude, I fear Garwool won't help us. Our only hope will be Coleman. As head law enforcement person in the county, he overrides Garwool, right?"

I didn't know the answer to her question. Not really. The sheriff had jurisdiction all over the county, which included incorporated little towns, but I didn't know if Coleman had more power than Garwool or not. And that was an issue I didn't want to press. Not right now, in case I needed Garwool to step up for the dogs.

Sensing our mood, Pluto didn't even attempt to get in the

car with us. He sat on the front porch of Dahlia House with Poe the raven perched on the back of a rocking chair. The two black figures watched like silhouettes, and seemed to tell me that they'd keep an eye out for the missing dogs. Avalon was in the kitchen sleeping beside the still-warm stove. Coleman would see to her when he got back home; I couldn't leave her free to roam.

Tinkie and I jumped in the car and sped to Nixville.

Our first stop was Tilly's house. She was so excited to see us when she opened the door, but she immediately realized Jezebel wasn't with us. She'd had no ransom requests and few calls on the reward she'd offered. I took the list of names and addresses of those who had called with potential information, and then I showed her a photo of Gertrude I had on my phone. "Do you know this woman?"

Tilly took the phone and examined the photo. "I'm not sure. Why?"

"She's a criminal mastermind and she took our dogs," Tinkie said, her worry and indignation rising to the surface.

"What? She took your dogs?"

"She took Chablis and Sweetie Pie from Sarah Booth's house. She left another dog, Avalon, because she didn't know it belonged to us."

"Why would she do this?" Tilly asked.

"She is a mean and awful human being." Tinkie blinked back tears. "If you know her, tell us. It may help."

Tilly studied the phone again. "She does look familiar. It's that red hair. At her age, it looks fake."

Gertrude's cosmetic routine didn't interest me. I just wanted the dogs back. "Do you recognize her?" I pressed.

"I can't be certain." Tilly focused on the picture again. She used her fingers to enlarge it and studied it more. "I think I have seen her in town, but I don't know her."

"Where did you see her?" Tinkie asked.

Tilly frowned. "Maybe at the grocery store." She nodded. "That was it. She was in the Piggly Wiggly buying steaks. In fact, she asked me what the best cut of meat would be for a dog."

"She asked you that?" I said. That evil woman had bought meat to lure the dogs—and she'd asked a woman whose dog she may have dognapped for advice for cuts of meat.

Tilly closed her eyes. "I didn't put two and two together. I'm sorry. Do you think she took Jezebel as well as your dogs?"

"I don't know," I said honestly. "I really don't know. It doesn't seem possible." I'd known Gertrude was still lurking out there, waiting to hurt me if she could, but I'd never expected her to steal dogs. And we didn't have any proof that she'd been involved in stealing Jezebel and Cupcake. Only Chablis and Sweetie Pie.

"Tilly, do you remember anything this woman said to you?"

She thought a few seconds. "We were at the meat counter and she had some flank steak. I told her that would be easy to cut up for the dogs, but to cook it before she offered it. I know raw meat is supposed to be good for them, but I don't like it." She made a face. "And Jezebel won't eat it raw. She prefers grilled but will take pan seared."

If the circumstances weren't so dire, I would have laughed. Tilly was truly under Jezebel's paw! Just like the rest of us dog lovers. But Gertrude Stromm was far too dangerous to be a laughing matter.

"Did she say anything about the dogs she was buying the meat for?" Tinkie asked.

"Only that she wanted them to have a nice treat before . . ." She faded into silence and then looked away from us.

"Before what?" I tried not to sound aggressive.

"I didn't take it in a negative way when she said it, but now . . ." Tilly put a hand on my arm. "I'm so sorry. I wish I'd paid attention."

"What did she say?" Tinkie was even more upset now.

"Before what, Tilly? Please just tell us. We may be able to stop her if we can find out where she is."

"Before I have to do the responsible thing." She spoke the words softly.

"That doesn't sound so bad," Tinkie said. "Maybe she was taking them to the vet to be checked out."

I only swallowed. Tinkie knew better and so did I. Gertrude wouldn't take an injured human for medical care, and certainly not an animal. She was a horrible person. "Did she indicate where the dogs might be?"

Tilly sighed. "I'm trying to think. She didn't say anything specific, but—" Her eyes opened wide and there was excitement in her face. "She did say that she was going to Zinnia. Does that help?"

"Yes." It didn't really, but Tilly was trying. "Did she say what she was going to Zinnia for?" I asked.

"No. She didn't give any details. But she seemed nice. Are you sure she's involved in this?"

"She has my dog," Tinkie said. "And Sarah Booth's hound. And when we find her, we are going to make her pay."

Tilly looked completely defeated. "Whatever you need, I'll help."

"Tinkie, would you stay here with Tilly and see if she remembers anything else? I'm going to talk to Garwool."

"Sure," Tinkie said. "I can do that. Keep me posted."

Oh, I felt certain if I had to slap the snot out of Garwool, Tinkie and everyone else would hear about it. I'd end up in jail. And I just flatly didn't care. If I could prove Garwool was working with Gertrude—a known criminal and a wanted woman—I intended to run him out of office permanently. After I kicked his butt all over town.

"What about Ellis?" Tinkie whispered to me. "We were going to try to track him down and follow him."

"And we will. Tomorrow." I had a real burn on to get to Garwool. "Can you handle Tilly? Maybe give Squatty a call and see if she's heard anything. You would think her own grandson would work to get *her* dog back, if none of the others."

"I somehow don't think Ellis cares how Squatty feels."

She was likely right about that. But I needed to find the police chief. I couldn't think of anything else until I did. "I'll be back."

"Be careful. Garwool has a mean streak and he can be vindictive." Tinkie held my gaze. "Call if you need me."

"You got it."

16

Tom Terrell was the only person at the police station. It was after hours and Garwool, along with the dispatcher, had gone home. I was disappointed, but I trusted Tom a lot more than I trusted Garwool.

I pulled up Gertrude's photo on my phone and showed it to him. He didn't even have to think it over. "Yeah, she was here. Talked to the chief for over half an hour."

"Do you know about what?" I asked.

"I do not. And when I asked Garwool, he told me to worry about my own business and not his. You look distressed. What's going on?"

"This woman, Gertrude Stromm, stole my dog and Tinkie's dog today. She broke into my home and took them."

He whistled. "Why?"

I shook my head. "I don't know, but I suspect it's for a terrible plan she has to make me suffer."

"She was here right around lunchtime. She holed up with

the chief, and when they both came out of his office, they seemed pretty pleased with themselves."

This was only getting worse and worse. If Gertrude felt like she had the long arm of the law working with her, she would be even more dangerous. "I suppose Garwool isn't aware that there's been a statewide search on for Gertrude for over a year. She's wanted on numerous charges, from one end of the state to the other."

Tom looked down at his desk.

"Was Garwool aware?" I couldn't believe a lawman would behave so recklessly.

Tom finally met my gaze. He motioned me into the tiny kitchenette and poured us both a cup of coffee. "I don't know what Garwool knew exactly. He was just . . . sneaky about talking with her. Which leads me to believe he knew something was wrong."

I didn't want to put Tom on the spot. Garwool was his boss. I would try to finesse my questions. "I'm dating the sheriff of Sunflower County." It was not a great opening, but it got the basic information out there. "Coleman is a good person and a great lawman. How is Garwool to work for?"

"Ever heard the phrase 'discretion is the better part of valor'?"

"I've heard every single adage, wise saying, truism, and cliché in the Southern lexicon. My aunt Loulane lived by those truths."

"Then you won't ask me that again. I want a career in law enforcement. Garwool might not be able to help me a lot, but he damn sure can hurt me. Political interests in the state have split it into two camps. There are those who believe in the rule of law and upholding it, and those who believe the laws only apply to their enemies."

I didn't have to ask him which camp Garwool fell into. It was abundantly clear he had no respect for other law officers. Not even his own men. "If you asked Garwool, would he tell you where Gertrude went?" He sure wouldn't tell me.

"Probably not. If you want anything out of Garwool, you'll have to trick it out of him."

"Any suggestions as to how to do that?"

Tom grinned. "Maybe I have a scheme or two up my sleeve. Where's that blue-eyed partner of yours?"

"She's at Tilly's house. She was also hoping to stop by Squatty's to see if that lout grandson of hers shows back up."

"If Ellis's brain was made of TNT, he wouldn't have enough juice to blow his nose," Tom said. Despite the tension that knotted my shoulders, I had to laugh. Tom had Ellis pegged. Except that while Ellis might be dumb, he was still dangerous.

"Do you know him well?"

"I went to school with Ellis. When he actually made it to class. Ellis always wanted to be a big shot. I think he felt at a real disadvantage because he didn't have a mom or dad, only his grandmother. And you've met Squatty. She's . . ."

"A bitch?" I supplied the term so he didn't have to say it.

"In a word, yes. She is. Squatty tried to give Ellis some advantages. She did. But she also ran her mouth all over town about how she was sacrificing for her grandson. Ellis felt like he was a burden that no one really wanted."

That would be more than hard on a high school kid. "I'm sorry. That must have been painful, but he's a grown man now, and he doesn't appear to be working to build any kind of life for himself. He is mooching off his granny."

Tom nodded. "Yes. That's true. Ellis had a real talent for playing the guitar. I remember him in the tenth grade. He was playing with a little band out of Memphis and they were developing a following. Squatty made him quit."

"Why?" Now, that I didn't grasp at all.

"Drugs. Sex. Girls. Satan. Who knows what some of these people get in their brains. She told him if he continued to play the guitar, he'd have to find his own place to stay. Squatty made sure he'd never feel secure in his own abilities."

The damage that some parents or guardians did to the children in their care haunted the kids the rest of their lives. Some acted unwittingly, and some because they didn't give a damn. I suspected Squatty was the former. For the moment, I was willing to believe she had Ellis's best interests at heart but had not understood what he needed to be happy.

"If Ellis doesn't show up at Squatty's, do you know where he might be?"

"There's a blues club on the outskirts of town. He used to go there." Tom shrugged. "I played the drums in the high school band Ellis was in. He never seemed able to get his feet up under him. Mitchell Rockwell was the chief then, and he enforced the age limits at T-Bone's Juke Joint. Which meant that Ellis and I weren't legal to be in the club."

"Even if you weren't drinking?" I had never really given that aspect of being in a band much thought. But what were high schoolers supposed to do?

"Against the law. Rockwell wasn't a mean guy, but he believed in the law and in enforcing it equally."

I couldn't argue with that. "What happened to him?"

"Oh, he stepped down as chief here and went to work for the MBI, the Mississippi Bureau of Investigation. Last I heard, he was in Jackson."

Then Rockwell would surely know that Gertrude Stromm

was a wanted fugitive. She'd shot a man in the leg—my fiancé at the time, actor Graf Milieu—tried to kill me and Tinkie numerous times, and a number of other horrible deeds.

Things in Nixville had gotten a lot dicier.

"I need to speak with Garwool." I didn't want to. I'd prefer to go home, talk to Coleman, and let him handle the seemingly corrupt police chief. But I was here, and the missing dogs were in danger. Time was crucial. I couldn't walk away.

"He's probably at home. As I was going to suggest, take your partner over to his house. Turn her loose on him."

"You mean ask her to flirt with him?"

Tom grinned. "Garwool has a huge ego. She might be able to shake some information loose if she butters him up." He stood up and gathered the empty coffee cups. "Keep in mind that he doesn't like you. He knows you're dating the sheriff of Sunflower County and he hates that fact. He hates that he's not sheriff. So, leave it up to your partner."

"Tinkie is better at this game than I am anyway."

"I kind of figured that. No offense. She's just got that . . . steel magnolia thing going for her."

"No offense taken. We each have our talents."

"Amen to that. Rattle his tree, Sarah Booth. And good luck. I'm going to patrol the town and if I see Ellis, I'll snatch him up and give you a call."

"Thank you, Tom. Thank you."

We walked out of the police department together and got into our respective vehicles. In a moment I was parking at Tilly's house. Tom had given me Garwool's home address. All I had to do was deliver Tinkie there. She would put the ball in motion.

* * *

I drove Tinkie around Nixville while she worked out her plan of attack. I was glad she was sharing her schemes with me. It also gave me an idea of how long it should take her to accomplish the plot. She was going to flirt with Garwool, make him feel big and strong, and see if he might let something slip about Ellis, Mace, Zotto, or Gertrude. Gertrude, of course, was my priority. It was just a matter of seeing what fell out of the tree when Tinkie gave it a good, hurricane-force shaking.

Tinkie told me that she'd given Squatty a call, but she wasn't helpful with information about Ellis. They had a relationship of benign neglect, which dovetailed with what Tom had told me. While Tinkie was busy with Garwool, I intended to stop by and plumb the depths of Squatty's brain.

When Tinkie was ready for battle, I pulled up in front of Garwool's house, taking in the manicured lawn. This was a man who loved to put chemicals and herbicides on his grass. The house was big, too. At least five thousand square feet, judging from the roofline. I couldn't believe Garwool made that kind of money as police chief of a small Mississippi town. So where was he getting his money? Family inheritance? Maybe. I could do some research on my phone while I waited on Tinkie.

She put her hand on the car door handle. "Give me an hour," she said.

"Not a minute more. Did you let Oscar know we'd be late this evening?"

"I did. He said he'd let Coleman know, too. Let's just get this done and over with. I want to go home to feed Maylin and tuck her into bed."

"You know Oscar has already fed her!" Oscar was no slacker in the daddy-o department.

"Probably, but I can feed her again. It won't hurt her. I just want to snug her tight."

I totally understood. "We'll find the dogs, Tinkie. Don't give up hope."

"See you in an hour." She walked to the front door, squaring her shoulders as she went up the steps. When she rang the bell and Garwool answered, I drove away. Better for him to think she didn't have a ride. He'd have to let her in.

17

Squatty was standing at the sink, washing her dinner dishes when I knocked at her back door. Her face was so hopeful when she recognized me that I felt like a heel.

"I haven't found Cupcake yet. Or Jezebel. Now my dog is missing, and Tinkie's little Chablis is gone, too. We know who stole our dogs, and I believe it's tied to the theft of Cupcake and Jezebel."

"Who is it? Tell me and I'll take care of them."

I deeply appreciated her sentiment, but Squatty had no clue how mean Gertrude Stromm could be. "Tinkie and I are working on it. I can't figure out why this person would take your dog. She hates me and Tinkie, but I can't understand why she'd have a bone to pick with you."

"Who is she?"

What harm would it do to tell her? The chances that her path would ever cross Gertrude's were slim to none. "The woman who took my dog is Gertrude Stromm." I pulled up a photo of her on my phone. "This is her."

Squatty stepped back from me and waved me to a seat at the kitchen table. Her face told me more than I wanted to know.

"Have you seen her?" I asked.

"Yes." Squatty lifted her chin. "I've met her before."

That stopped me in my tracks. "What?"

"I've seen her in the grocery store here."

Which was the same information that Tilly had given me. What in the world was Gertrude doing in Nixville? Other than haunting the grocery aisles.

"Did you talk to her?" I asked.

"She talked to me. She's a friend of Ellis's."

This was not good news. "How long has Gertrude been in town?"

"You'd have to ask Ellis that, if you can find him. He isn't answering my calls."

I actually hated to ask Squatty this question, but I needed to know. "We know Gertrude took our dogs in Zinnia. Just to be clear, why do you believe Ellis is involved in the loss of your little dog?"

To her credit, Squatty paused for a good long time. "Ellis is . . . damaged. I'm partially responsible for this. He has aggression toward me at times. The thing I can't grasp is why he would take it out on Cupcake. That dog adores him. It just doesn't make sense to me."

"And how do you get on with Garwool?"

"Funny you should ask. Two weeks ago, I was at a city aldermen meeting to protest Garwool and the police department."

"Really. What were you protesting?"

"All the stray animals roaming the streets. They are dirty and carry diseases. They—"

I couldn't stop myself. "You realize that Cupcake may be one of those strays now."

Squatty's face went pale. "What?"

"Cupcake might be out there trying to get home. Often stray animals are in a bad position because of the humans who failed them." Squatty's attitude had gotten under my skin.

"You think she's wandering around the streets, hungry, trying to get home?"

I'd struck a nerve, and I hoped it made a difference. "It's possible. Stray animals need help, not condemnation."

"I told Garwool we needed an animal control officer just to get them off the streets, but it could be a good solution. You know the city could write grants, try to build a shelter. Tilly has been saying this for a long time and I mocked her. I've been a fool. And Garwool is worse."

"A humanely run shelter is a good idea." She was seeing the light. "What did Garwool say?"

"That it wasn't his responsibility." She blinked back tears. "It never occurred to me that the strays weren't at fault. I made a mistake. Garwool has no interest in solving the issue."

Attitudes like Garwool's were sadly common. Coleman and his two deputies did double duty when they could, helping move loose livestock, hogs, and sheep off the roads to avoid wrecks, and also picking up strays to take to the vet. Often Coleman paid for that out of his pocket, and we were lucky that Dr. Smith was so generous. He charged the bare minimum. Coleman and his deputies worked with several rescue groups to transport Sunflower County animals to waiting homes. Garwool could—and should—be doing better for the residents of Nixville. Stray animals weren't exactly a crime wave, but they often caused suffering and distress, especially for people who had compassion for them. And since there was no other agency in town to take up the slack, Garwool could have accommodated the public better. Not to mention finding the missing pets, which he'd shown no inclination to even look for.

"Do you think Garwool is an honest man?" I asked Squatty. I was just curious to see how she would respond.

"He doesn't impress me."

It was a hedge, but I could read between the lines. "Where does he get his money? Family inheritance?"

"Because of his big, fine house?"

"Yes."

"No family money that I know of. He was raised in Arkansas, across the river in Helena. His family was poor. But I hear his soon-to-be father-in-law, the mayor, has thrown some lucrative business opportunities his way."

On the face of it, there was nothing illegal about that, but it troubled me. The devil was in the details. To my way of thinking, preachers, law officers, and elected officials could serve only one master and it should be the public. "What kind of business opportunities?" My question was part curiosity and part to be sure Garwool wasn't so compromised that he couldn't perform his police duties.

"I've only heard rumors. He does own a bed-and-breakfast in Pine Bluff, Arkansas, and—"

"Wait. He runs a B and B?"

"I don't know that he actually runs it, but he owns it," Squatty said. "Why are you so shocked?"

I couldn't explain that Gertrude Stromm was also a former B and B owner, and why that alarmed me. I didn't want to scare Squatty any more than I had to. But I couldn't shake the dread that fell over me. Was it possible Gertrude had been hiding out in Pine Bluff, working for Chief Garwool? Oh, I had to get this information to Coleman so he could check it out. And I had to keep a grip on the idea that if Garwool had hired her, he might yet be ignorant of who she really was or what she'd done in the past.

Though I waited the whole hour at Squatty's, Ellis never returned. Squatty made no excuses. "If he comes home, I'll call you," she promised as I went to the door. It was time to pick up Tinkie and get back to Zinnia. It was getting very late.

I texted my partner that I would be waiting outside Garwool's home. I felt a deep weariness as I waited in the car. The night had grown cold. Most often February was the coldest month of the year—but there were days, even weeks, when the promise of spring seemed on the verge of being fulfilled. Then old man winter would make another appearance and freeze our toes nearly off. This was a night when the cold had returned with a vengeance.

Luckily I didn't have long to wait for Tinkie to come out of Garwool's house. I watched her come down the walk as he stood—seeming to glower—in the doorway of his home. Watching her. Watching me. What was his connection to Gertrude, if any?

Tinkie got in the car, and I resisted hurling a hundred questions at her. I waited for her to tell me what had occurred in her own time. It didn't take long. We'd barely cleared the city limits of Nixville when she spoke.

"Garwool is a skunk, Sarah Booth."

That wasn't what I really wanted to hear, though I wasn't shocked. "Why so?"

"His focus is on making his situation better. I don't think

he cares about the people of Nixville, and he certainly doesn't care about the dogs. He told me if he had his way the city would enact a policy where he could shoot any stray animals. That was his solution."

"What did he say about Rutherford Mace and his operation?"

"He was very cagey. He said Mace was a good man and that his wrestling operation—the school and whatever—had been really good for Nixville and the state in general. It is true that it brings in a lot of people from out of town. Mace has a high profile and he's on TV sports shows a lot."

"He had nothing negative to say?"

"Not a word."

"Did you ask him about Gertrude being in town?"

"I did. He denied seeing her."

I told her about the B and B in Pine Bluff, Arkansas.

"He's in bed with her," Tinkie said. "Not literally, but he hasn't been doing his job as police chief if she's running around his town and he's in business with her."

"We have to make sure he's in business with her." I didn't want to tar him with guilt until I had the proof.

"Coleman can find that out," Tinkie said with assurance.

"I hope so. I'm also going to contact Mitchell Rockwell with the MBI. He may have some insight."

"Maybe ask Coleman to do that. You know how lawmen will give more courtesy to another person in a uniform."

"You're right." My partner was smart. "Did you learn anything else?"

"Garwool's fiancée is . . . interesting."

"How so?"

"She's not attractive and she's bossy. She didn't even bother trying to be pleasant to me. She just showed up and took over the conversation. She kept putting him down. And she made sure I knew that her father, the mayor, had helped pay for the house. It was a pre-wedding gift. She's got her hooks in deep and she doesn't mind letting everyone know she rules the money and the roost."

A pre-wedding gift. A big, expensive house. In the past women had sold their independence for such things, but it wasn't all that common for a man to do so, at least in my experience.

"Did Garwool seem to resent her actions?" I was curious.

"No. He just smiled at her and told her he loved her every three minutes. He . . . fawned over her."

"Interesting." And a little unpleasant. But it wasn't my gig to judge. We were halfway back to Zinnia and I followed up on the B and B in Pine Bluff. "Did Garwool or his fiancée say anything about his other business ventures?"

"Not a word," Tinkie said. "Coleman can check on that better than we can, but Harold can also look into the finances."

"What is Garwool's fiancée's name?" I should have asked Squatty, but I hadn't.

"Penelope Fenway. I don't know the family. But Vern Fenway is the mayor. We should be able to dig up some information on him."

"Definitely. And I'll bet Squatty and Tilly both have plenty to say about him. I should have asked them both."

"Tomorrow is another day, Miss Sarah Booth," Tinkie said, quoting one of our favorite heroines. "The problem is that I miss Chablis so much. If it weren't for Maylin, I wouldn't want to go home."

Tinkie hit the nail on the head. I had to remind myself that

Pluto, Poe, Avalon, and the horses were waiting for me. But it wasn't the same without Sweetie Pie. At last, I accepted that I'd have to confront that loss head-on.

"We'll figure this out. We'll find the missing dogs. All of them." I wanted to climb in bed with Coleman and let him warm me up.

"We have to. We don't have another option."

I nodded. Tomorrow was another day, and one that would require a lot of both Tinkie and me. It was time to get some rest.

18

Coleman met me at the barn. He must have been watching for me to come home. I'd tried to be quiet, in case he was sleeping. He worked hard and he needed his rest. But he appeared by Reveler's stall just as I pulled a bale of hay down to give the horses. The night was cold, and a bit of hay would be welcomed by all three of the equines.

Avalon was at Coleman's side, and his hand strayed down to the dog's head. He stroked her as he took in my swollen eyes and stuffy nose. Yes, I'd been crying. Sweetie Pie was my heart. And Chablis, too. I couldn't stop myself from worrying about what had happened to them. Where might they be?

Coleman stepped forward and gathered me in his arms, holding me tight as Avalon licked my hand. Those doggy kisses were my undoing, and I sobbed against Coleman's chest.

He let the storm pass before he lifted my chin. "We will find them."

"I know." I had to be positive. There was no other path.

"I promise you, Sarah Booth. We will find them. Harold is going to bring Roscoe to Dahlia House tomorrow and just let him sniff around. He may be able to pick up a scent." He stroked my back. "I know it's a long shot, but those dogs are psychically connected. You know that. We owe it to Roscoe to give him a chance."

"I agree." It was a long, long shot, but it was one Hail Mary we couldn't pass up without at least trying.

"I have a plate of fried catfish and coleslaw for you. Millie brought it by. She and Cece are very upset. They're digging into some of the back issues of the paper to see what Tilly Lawson stuck her finger in that pissed people off. She mostly turned in articles to the local Nixville weekly, but sometimes she wrote articles for the *Dispatch*. Cece feels the stolen dogs are part of a bigger issue."

That was a terrific angle to work. Tilly's activism might be at the root of all of it, but I had to tell Coleman about Gertrude and the B and B in Arkansas. It could wait until we were in the house and by a fire. The temperatures had dropped, and I was glad to see Coleman had thought to blanket the horses. It was wonderful to have someone who knew, instinctively, what needed to be done.

Avalon led the way back to the house and I sat at the kitchen table while Coleman put the food and a glass of wine in front of me. I wasn't hungry, but I ate because I knew it would only worry him if I didn't. Avalon wasn't averse to having a crispy piece of fish slipped under the table to her. She did look pretty sad. I figured she was missing Sweetie Pie, too.

When enough of the food was gone—a lot of it to Avalon—I stood up and went to Coleman. "I have things to tell you. Let's go to bed."

"I'm at your service," he said, doing a courtly bow that made me smile.

He lit a fire in the bedroom, and when the flames were crackling cheerily, I told him about Gertrude and the B and B. And about the role I suspected that Bill Garwool played. I was holding Coleman's hand, and I felt it curl into a fist. He was very angry.

"I don't have any proof that Garwool knew," I told him. "Maybe he didn't."

"Maybe."

But I could tell Coleman didn't believe that for an instant. And I feared that as soon as Coleman could make it to the Nixville city hall during business hours, Garwool was going to pay a terrible price. One he had likely earned, but I didn't want Coleman jeopardizing his law enforcement career to defend me.

"I've heard other things about Garwool. He's hired by the Nixville mayor and aldermen, so I don't have a say in whether he holds on to his badge or not. But I promise you, if he ignored APBs on Gertrude and hired her anyway, he will be charged and prosecuted. Mitchell Rockwell with the MBI is a good man. I think he'll be straightforward with me."

At least he wasn't talking about beating Garwool to a pulp. No, Coleman was a deliberate and ethical lawman. I was the brawler.

I filled Coleman in on Vern Fenway and his daughter Penelope, Garwool's bride-to-be.

"I know Vern." His tone was completely blank.

"And?" I pressed.

"And he's a piece of work. He's very wealthy. Made a lot of money with a chain of funeral homes along the Gulf Coast."

"He's a mortician?"

"He was a mortician. Now he's a businessman. He hires people to do the actual work. He just rakes in the profits."

"But he's never been accused of illegal business dealings?"

"There have been rumors," Coleman said. "All of them out of my jurisdiction. I can contact the Harrison County sheriff to see what he knows."

"Thank you, Coleman." I didn't want to ask the next question, but I had to. "Are there any leads about the dognappers or dogfighting rings?"

"Nothing solid. But DeWayne, Budgie, and I are on it. You can't think about that if you're going to do your job finding Cupcake and Jezebel."

"You don't think all the dogs are together?"

"Chablis and Sweetie Pie seem a lot more personal. Maybe because it's you and Tinkie. But we believe Gertrude took them. The other two dogs—we just don't know."

He was right. "I had kind of hoped they were all safe together."

He pulled me against his side. "Don't borrow trouble."

Good advice, even if it was impossible to follow. "Tomorrow I'm going to corner Garwool. Tinkie did her best. It's my turn now."

"Let's worry about that in the morning."

Soon, I found myself deep in a forest filled with sunlight, heat, and the calls of birds and other small animals. I knew I was dreaming, but I didn't understand the dream at all. In the distance, I could hear Sweetie Pie's yodel of hound-dog love, accompanied by Chablis's fierce bark. The dogs didn't sound distressed. To the contrary, I would have said they were playing or hot on a trail of something delicious. I felt the need to run to them, to find then. But then, in the way of dreams, something cold and icy cracked in my chest, and I felt the thaw of dread. The dogs were safe. They were okay, though I couldn't see them. But where were we?

I looked down—thinking maybe ruby slippers and a yellow brick road—but all I saw were my barn boots and a dirt path where exotic plants grew so close together it created a tunnel. I had no idea where I was or how I got there.

"Never approach a primate unless you're sure your attentions will be welcomed."

The woman who spoke stood up from behind dense ferns. Her hair was pulled back at the nape of her neck in a neat bun. The air of serenity about her gave me comfort. "Who are you?" I asked.

"Not a big student of anthropology, are you?" she said.

"I was more of a theater student," I told her. "Science and math—never my strong suits." Why was I even telling her this? And who was she? "Where am I?" I tried another question.

"Tanzania."

"How?" I didn't question if it was true, I only wanted to know how I'd gotten there. And where was Coleman? I looked around, but other than a shy chimpanzee now peeking from behind the fern, I didn't see another living creature.

"I'm not qualified to discuss metaphysical events." She smiled. "But I love animals."

That was what I held on to. She was there for Sweetie Pie and Chablis. And for me. She'd transported me to a jungle to help. "What can I do?"

"What you do makes a difference, and you have to decide what kind of difference you want to make."

I recognized the quote. While I wasn't great with science, I did love literature, and that quote was famous. "Jane Good-all." I held out a hand but she didn't shake, she just laughed.

"A pleasure to meet you, Sarah Booth."

"You know me?"

"Enough. I know you care about your dog. All the dogs. I know you understand that animals are every bit as intelligent and sensitive as humans. I know you believe that we must do all in our power to protect animals. They do have a voice, but so many people don't hear it. We must protect them. All of them."

"Yes!" It was such a pleasure to talk with someone who accepted the bond between humans and all other living creatures the way I did. "They are not ours to harm, use, or imprison. They are our partners on the planet. Why can't all people see this?" I asked.

"The fatal flaw of humans is their greed and selfishness. So many animal species share and work together. Not humans. They are out for themselves, for their own family unit, their own tribe."

She was just making me sadder. "What can I do?"

"Exactly what you're doing. Care. Care about all the animals. Speak out for them. They deserve our protection. Remember, until one has loved an animal a part of one's soul remains unawakened."

She was going to leave. I felt it. But I didn't want her to. I looked around me and drank in the verdure of the jungle. I could now detect smaller monkeys and two more chimps. They gathered around Jane and lightly held on to her, like children needing the security of their mother. She also made me feel safe. She'd been a great hero of mine.

"Do you know where Sweetie Pie and Chablis are?" I asked.

She shook her head. "I wish I did."

"I'm sick with worry for them."

"I know."

"Will I find them safe?" My voice cracked.

"I believe you will. But you must believe it, too."

That was the hard part. Believing that something good would come out of something so bad. I wanted to lash out with the indisputable point that I didn't have any freaking ruby slippers on my feet. I found it hard to believe anything good would come of the dogs being stolen. Not even Jane Goodall could restore my faith in Gertrude Stromm.

"Jitty?" I didn't want to play any more games. "Where are Sweetie Pie and Chablis? And the other dogs, too. I have to find them." A tear leaked down my cheek, almost freezing on my face. I realized then that I was no longer in a tropical jungle. The chimps and wildlife were gone. I was in the bedroom in Dahlia House and the fire had gone out. I could turn on the central heat, but I didn't want to leave the warm bed. I reached over for Coleman, and the bed was empty. He was up and gone.

And I had a big suspicion where. I threw back the covers, startling Avalon, who was on the foot of the bed.

"Time to shake a leg," I told her. "Coleman is on the move." I wasn't certain if I wanted to stop him—because I knew what he was going to do—or if I wanted to cheer him on. No matter which, I had to get to Nixville, pronto.

I showered, threw on some warm clothes and boots, and went to get my car keys on the kitchen counter. They were gone. But there was a note: "By the time you find your keys, I will be finished with Garwool. Sorry I had to trick you, but this is better settled between the two of us."

"Aaarrrgh!" I wanted to pummel him with my fists. He'd hidden my car keys so he could sneak out in the predawn and maybe get himself arrested. What a vile prank. But I had a backup plan. I called Tinkie immediately, even though it was the butt-crack of dawn.

"Come get me, please. Coleman hid my keys and he's going to Nixville to thump Garwool into the ground."

"Damn. Be there in fifteen."

19

I loaded Avalon into Tinkie's Caddy and we headed for Nixville. We'd arrive by eight, and city hall was my destination. If Coleman was there, maybe I could head him off.

"Promise me you won't get physically involved." Tinkie was worried that blows would ensue.

"I wish I'd thought to bring my Super Soaker." A good dousing of cold water might break up the fight, if it came to that.

"I wish I'd thought to bring a net." Tinkie referenced an old cartoon meme of bad guys being captured. She wasn't joking.

We whipped to the front of city hall just as the clock struck eight. There was no sign of Coleman's truck. So where was he? I tried to call him, but it went to voice mail.

"Coleman, I'm in Nixville. Where are you? What are you up to?" I wasn't angry any longer. I was worried. Coleman was the most levelheaded man I knew, but even he had a breaking point. If he thought Garwool had anything to do with the abduction of the dogs, he would squeeze him until he told the truth.

"Let's just go inside," Tinkie said.

The heater was on in the car, but it was still cold. February was holding true to form—one extreme or the other. "I heard the weather report this morning. There may be an ice storm tonight." The thought of our dogs, possibly in a cold place instead of safe in our beds, almost made me cry. Tinkie was blinking back tears herself.

"Coleman said Harold was coming by Dahlia House today to see if Roscoe could pick up a scent." I tried to sound positive.

"Gertrude took them in a car." Tinkie was not willing to give in to foolish hopes. "There's not a trail for Roscoe to follow."

"Maybe he can smell their scent, if they're nearby."

"If Gertrude is nearby, I'll stomp a mudhole in her ass and walk it dry."

I didn't try to sooth or placate my partner. Or remind her that as Queen Bee of Delta society, she shouldn't talk that way. I was terrified for the dogs, and so was she. Gertrude might not kill them outright, but she wasn't above letting them freeze to death. And did she have Cupcake and Jezebel? Were the dognappings in Nixville a ploy to work on us? To bring us here so she could steal our beloved pets? It seemed like a very convoluted scheme, but Gertrude was *not* a rational human. A psychiatrist could have a field day plumbing the depths of Gertrude's insanity, but I didn't give a flying . . . hoot. I wanted the dogs back, and I wanted her out of my life. The damage she'd done was irreparable. But that was the past. The future needed only one thing—Gertrude to vanish.

"Look! There's the mayor," Tinkie said as Vern Fenway took out a set of keys to open the door to city hall. It was eight o'clock on the button.

Before I could slow her down, Tinkie was out of the car and flying toward the door of the office complex. She literally pushed Fenway in the door. I was right behind her, but when she had him inside, I heard the door lock. She'd locked me out! Tinkie had locked me out in the cold!

And heaven help Vern Fenway. She was going to hurt him. I knew it in my bones.

I beat on the door, but no one answered. I ran around to a window—even though my hands were freezing—and found a view. In a far corner of a room, Fenway was pressed against a wall with Tinkie on tiptoe and in his face. She was furious.

Using my frozen fists, I pounded on the window but they ignored me. Then I saw Tinkie reach into the waistband of her pants and my heart stopped. Did she have a gun? Was she going to kill the mayor of Nixville? Even if he deserved it, murder wasn't a good idea. "Tinkie! Tinkie! Hold your powder!"

The gun had the desired effect, and Fenway slid down the wall and onto the floor. He was blubbering like a little baby. This was going to be big trouble for Tinkie. A man like Fenway wouldn't take being humiliated lying down—or sitting, for that matter. He would get payback.

I heard another car pull in front of the building and I ran around to find a woman unlocking the door. I brushed past her, though she called out to stop me. Hoofing it like a Thoroughbred, I ran around the corner and down a hallway to the official mayor's office. I locked the door behind me when I got inside. In a matter of seconds, I had the gun from Tinkie and

I offered the mayor a hand and pulled him to his feet. He was a short, balding man with a face as red as a boiled beet. He was very angry. Tinkie, thank goodness, had calmed down.

"Call the police! Call the police!" Fenway screamed.

It was all I could do not to pop him across the mouth with the butt of the gun. But I didn't. Tinkie was likely going to jail, and I had to be able to bail her out. She'd assaulted the mayor. This was going to be ugly.

"Where are the dogs?" Tinkie demanded. She no longer had a gun, but she picked up a letter opener from the mayor's desk. She was in a very bloody frame of mind.

I knocked it from her hand. "Stop it, Tinkie. Stop it."

"Margaret! Call the police!" Fenway wailed.

I picked up the letter opener and pointed it at his throat. "And you shut up, too. I mean it. You're getting on my last nerve. I won't be responsible for what I do next."

The door to the office cracked open, and Margaret peeked in. "Sir?"

"He's fine. Leave before you get caught up in this," I said to her.

"No problem." She quickly closed the door. It would seem that Fenway had earned no respect or protection from the people who worked for him. Margaret had pretty much thrown him to the wolves—which might be the only thing that saved Tinkie's bacon.

"What do you want?" Fenway asked when he realized the cavalry wasn't coming.

"The dogs." Tinkie had no other agenda. "Where are they?"

"Dogs?"

"Don't play dumb with me, or you're going to regret it." Tinkie reached for the gun, but I stepped back.

"I heard someone stole a couple of dogs. Big deal. Go to the pound and get some new ones. I'll even pay the adoption fee."

He was a very, very stupid man.

"Shut up, you mush-brained idiot," Tinkie said.

"Better listen to her," I said. "She's pissed off, and since her daddy owns the local bank and her husband is president of it, I'm pretty sure she could make life difficult for you."

At last, something had penetrated his slick, bald pate. Money. It got them every time.

"You're Mrs. Oscar Richmond?"

"None other," Tinkie said.

"Does your husband know you're here, behaving like a crazy woman?"

"Does your daughter know that you're marrying her off to Garwool to build your empire?" she responded.

It was a zinger, and I had no proof—except for the paleness that touched his face and the sweat that dripped down his cheeks—that her barb had hit the target. Fenway wasn't smart, but like a cockroach, he valued survival.

"What do you want?" He was finally ready to parley.

"The dogs. That's all we want," Tinkie said.

"And a bit of information on one of your Arkansas employees." I wasn't about to let him off the hook for Gertrude.

"What are you talking about? Arkansas employees?"

"At the B and B in Pine Bluff. Don't you co-own that with Garwool?"

I could tell the arrow of truth had struck home. He cleared his throat and went to sit in his chair. I noticed his legs were a little weak. Especially when he looked at Tinkie, who did actually look as if she might rip his throat out with her teeth.

"Garwool is my future son-in-law. We do have some business ventures."

"This woman"—I pulled out my phone and brought up the photo of Gertrude—"stole two dogs from my home in Sunflower County. She is a wanted criminal. The MBI has been looking for her for nearly two years. And you've been supporting her. Garwool should have known she was wanted for crimes. Perhaps he did. Perhaps you did, too."

I let that sink in. Coleman might have to handle Garwool, but roly-poly Fenway was about to pee his pants. We had his number, and I wasn't about to let the pressure off until he squealed.

"We had no idea. We'd never knowingly hire a wanted criminal. I mean she's . . . old. She's an old lady."

"Tell it to the grand jury," I said. Tinkie was wisely holding her water. She could easily be charged with assault, which was something I wanted to avoid. Oscar could thank me later.

"Look at the photo. When was the last time you saw this woman, and where is she now?"

He did look. He was afraid not to. "I'm not certain," he said.

"Tinkie, call Mitchell Rockwell with the Mississippi Bureau of Investigation. He was police chief here before Fenway was elected mayor. I'm sure he'll love to hear what's going on right now in Nixville."

"Wait!" Fenway held up a hand. "I remember now. Yeah, that woman is running the B and B in Arkansas for us. She's in Pine Bluff, as far as I know. She's very efficient and she's done a fine job landscaping the grounds."

Yeah, that was Gertrude's forte. She had a green thumb and a black heart. "Where is she now?"

"How the hell would I know. Arkansas, like I said."

"Think again," Tinkie said. "Think hard."

Fenway looked toward the door, obviously hoping for help. None was coming, and he realized it. "Maybe my daughter did mention that she was in town to discuss a new contract."

"Your daughter is involved in this?" Why in the world would a loving father involve his daughter in a scheme with a wanted criminal?

"Penelope's got a great head for business. Got her MBA from Ole Miss. She's a whiz at this kind of thing."

"How lovely for you," Tinkie said with a sneer. "Where is your daughter?"

"Leave her out of this. Maybe I've been too lenient with Penelope. I haven't really helped her with business plans for the B and B. That's her baby, but I'll get with her and she can fire this woman you seem to hate. How's that?"

"Where are my dogs?" Tinkie asked. "Give us the dogs— all of them—and maybe we won't involve the MBI. It would be bad if your daughter was investigated for criminal behavior because of you."

Fenway looked more angry than disturbed. "My daughter has nothing to do with any of this. Plausible deniability. We hired someone who had great credentials, and she's done a good job for us. That's not a crime."

Technically, he was right. Tinkie and I had lost the advantage. We couldn't bully him any further, and the wise move would be to get out of his office before he decided to charge us with something—like assault with a deadly weapon. Tinkie had some protection with her father and Oscar, but she'd crossed a line. We both knew it.

"Gertrude has been seen in Nixville. Where's she hiding?"

Fenway tucked in his shirt and straightened his tie. "She was staying at the hotel outside of town. I don't know where she is and, just so you know, I'll fire her as soon as I find her."

"Be careful. Gertrude holds a grudge and she won't hesitate to hurt you or your family." Tinkie gave the warning even though it was clear she disliked Fenway. I was proud of her.

"I'm not concerned. Garwool can tell her. She won't mess with an officer of the law."

He was confident, but I knew Gertrude better than that. "She's dangerous. Believe us. You've crawled inside a croaker sack with a rattlesnake. Be careful or you'll be bitten. I'm serious."

Fenway waved his hand at me. "She's old. Really, how much damage could she do?"

I didn't answer, because I knew it wouldn't do any good. His mind was made up. Like I had before him, he dismissed Gertrude because of her age, but she would prove him wrong if he gave her half a chance.

"Where is Chief Garwool?" I asked, remembering that Coleman was at large in Nixville. At least I thought he was in town. And I suspected he was bird-dogging Garwool for a confrontation.

Fenway frowned. "He should be here. We normally have coffee together while we discuss the city."

I caught Tinkie's attention and edged toward the door. "We'll be leaving. If you see Gertrude Stromm, call the sheriff. She's a wanted person. And you'd do yourself a favor if she was behind bars."

"Sure thing." Fenway's focus was on some papers on his desk. At least he wasn't talking about pressing charges against

Tinkie. Oscar had been a "get out of jail free" card for Tinkie on a number of occasions.

I had one more thing to say before we left. "Fenway, if anything happens to my dog, or any of the dogs, I will see to it that you suffer in unimaginable ways. If you know something, you'd better spill it."

"Get out of my office." Fenway wasn't going to play.

20

Tinkie and I made the rounds of Tilly's and Squatty's houses, hoping they had new information for us. Neither woman had heard anything about their lost dogs. Their loss only heightened and exacerbated the feelings that swept over me and, judging from Tinkie's expression, over her, too.

"Do you think we'll find the dogs?" Tinkie asked. She was carefully looking out the window of her Caddy as we drove slowly around the small town, hoping against hope we'd catch a glimpse of one of the missing dogs.

"We will." I said it firmly and with a conviction that I didn't feel. But Tinkie was suffering. Admitting that we might not find our family members was too much. For Tinkie and for me.

A moment later my phone rang and I put it on speaker. "I've been chasing Garwool for the past two hours," Coleman said. "Sorry I hid your keys, but I wanted to confront him alone. You and Tinkie need to be careful. There's a lot going on here."

That was an understatement. "What do the dogs, Garwool, Fenway, Rutherford Mace, and Gertrude have in common?" I asked Coleman.

"I don't have an answer. Yet," Coleman said. "There is a connection. We just have to figure it out and get the pups back."

"Where are you?" He'd failed to tell me.

"Rutherford Mace's place."

"What are you doing there?" Tinkie asked.

"Looking for Ellis Adams."

Coleman was being awfully tight-lipped about what he was up to. "Why Ellis?" I asked.

"What? Are you writing a book?" he responded, making Tinkie giggle.

"I have a score to settle with you already," I told him. "Holding out on me now is only going to make it worse."

Coleman didn't laugh, but I could hear the smile in his voice when he said, "I look forward to . . . paying my debt."

"Cut it out," Tinkie said, trying not to laugh, too. "What are you doing, Coleman?"

"The best I can," Coleman said. "Talk later." And the line went dead.

"You are going to have to stomp his butt," Tinkie said, and she wasn't laughing. "He's deliberately keeping us in the dark."

"Yes, he is. And we're going to find out what he's up to. But first let's find Garwool. That may give us a clue. Coleman was bird-dogging him but dropped back because he went to talk to Mace."

Garwool hadn't been at city hall, and he wasn't with Coleman. So, where was he? We drove back to the office complex and Tinkie went inside to talk to Deputy Tom Terrell. She came back out with a big grin on her face.

"He told you where Garwool is?"

"He did. And I think it gave him pleasure to do so. The chief is getting a haircut at Old Bob's Barbershop. If we go straight there maybe we can catch him."

I'd thought about a private conversation, but maybe an audience would be helpful. Garwool was vain, and he wouldn't want to be played as a fool in front of other men. When we got to the barbershop, we found Garwool under a hot towel, waiting for a shave.

Tinkie signaled the barber to be quiet as she took a seat beside Garwool. I leaned against the wall in a corner. Tinkie was far better at this than I was.

"Hey, Bill," she said in her sexiest voice. "I need some help."

"Give me fifteen minutes and I'll be done." He started to remove the towel from his face, but Tinkie stood and held it in place. "Don't rush. I can sit here and wait for you."

"Now don't keep a pretty lady waiting too long," the barber said, playing right along with us. I gave him a thumbs-up as thanks.

"Who's here?" Garwool asked.

"Just little ol' me," Tinkie said. "I'm one of the people who recently lost a dog. I was hoping you might have some good news, or at least some leads for me."

Garwool started to sit up, but Tinkie stood behind his chair and pressed his shoulders down. "Mr. Barber, I think you need to head down the street for some doughnuts," Tinkie said. "We'll watch the shop for you."

Garwool had grown terribly quiet.

"I'll be back in a jiffy, Chief. I'll get you one of those lemon custards you love so much." And the barber was out the door, the bell jingling merrily. It was just Garwool, Tinkie, and me left in the shop.

Garwool sat up slowly and removed the towel. "I should arrest both of you."

"For what?" I asked. "We haven't done anything."

"She," and he pointed at Tinkie, "put hands on a law officer. That could be considered assault. That's a serious charge."

"Bring it," Tinkie said. "I already don't like you. I'd love nothing better than seeing you mocked and ridiculed in a court of law because you were bested by a woman who is five foot two and weighs a hundred pounds. You will be laughed out of town."

She wasn't wrong about that, so I just grinned.

"I don't have any leads on the missing dogs. I don't care about the missing dogs. And I urge you to leave my town and don't come back."

"Or what?" I asked. It was just my day to poke a snake with a stick.

Garwool rose swiftly from the barber chair. "You two think you're impervious to consequences. You"—pointing at me—"think the sheriff can protect you. And you"—pointing at Tinkie—"think your banker husband can keep you out of trouble. But not here. Not in Nixville. I run the show here, and my word is law."

Oh, if only I'd recorded this little hissy fit. Cece and Millie could have a field day with it at the newspaper and on their podcast. Just in case he pressed his point, I fumbled my phone out of my pocket and discreetly hit record.

"I'm so glad to know that you embody the law, in word and deed," Tinkie said, her tone dripping with sarcasm. "And yet you don't have time to find the missing family members for two women of your town."

"They are dogs. Not family members. You two are fools if you can't tell the difference."

"Did you talk with Coleman this morning?" I asked. I wanted to pop him hard in the mouth, but he would put me in jail and I wouldn't have a leg to stand on. It was best to ignore his obnoxiousness and hope that Coleman would deal with him at a later date. Coleman or the residents of Nixville.

"I heard the sheriff stopped by the PD, but I didn't talk to him. I was busy."

"Have you investigated what's happening at Rutherford Mace's place?" Tinkie asked.

"No need. There's nothing going on there except camps for people who want to wrestle professionally. It's a very good boost to our local economy."

"So we've been told," Tinkie said. "When the word gets out that people's pets aren't safe in Nixville, I suspect that will have a negative influence on the local economy."

"I seriously doubt it." Garwool pulled off the drape the barber had put around him and threw it on the barber's chair. "Now, if you'll excuse me, I have things to do."

My cell phone rang and I checked the caller ID. It was Dawson Reed. Maybe he had an update on the pet finders group. I nodded at Tinkie, who followed Garwool out the door while I took my phone into a corner and whispered.

"What's going on, Dawson?"

"We had a sighting of that big red tic hound of yours. Someone saw it running down Main Street in Nixville this morning. Can you check it out?"

"We're in Nixville right now. We'll go look for Sweetie Pie. Any sightings of the other dogs?"

"Not so far, but that banker friend of yours, Harold Erkwell, is in town and he has his dog with him. Roscoe, I think it is. Someone at the furniture store said that Roscoe had struck a trail. Once you get the big hound dog, maybe she and Roscoe can take you to the others."

"Thank you." If this worked out, it would be one of the best gifts of my lifetime.

21

Dawson Reed was waiting on the corner by the post office and a drugstore. Harold stood beside him with Roscoe on a leash. Roscoe was not happy with the situation. He tugged at the leash, looking south down Main Street and barking like crazy. Though I strained my eyes for a glimpse of Sweetie Pie, I didn't see anything except Tilly coming down the sidewalk toward us. It was clear she'd been crying. My heart dropped.

"What's wrong?" I asked her.

"I got a call on the reward for Jezebel. The man said he was certain he'd seen her. But I went there and . . . nothing. He wasn't there and neither was my dog. Or any dog, for that matter. It was a cruel joke. That's all I can surmise."

Tinkie folded her into an embrace. "I'm so sorry. That is mean. If we find out who did it, I will personally throat punch them for you."

The threat did the trick, and Tilly smiled. "Thank you. Don't do that. You'll go to jail, but I love that you're willing to consider it."

"Tell us exactly what the caller said, please," I said.

"He said that he'd seen Jezebel about two blocks from my house. Not far from Squatty's. I just got my hopes up that maybe both dogs were together and I could find them. I hurried over with my checkbook to pay the reward, but there was nothing. No one on the street. No sign of any dogs. Nothing. And I had the sense that someone was watching me the whole time. Likely watching and laughing at what a fool I was."

"You're not a fool to love an animal," Dawson said. "And you went to try to save your baby. That's what a good parent does."

The bottom line was that it hadn't resulted in anything. "Did you hear anything in the background of the call?" I asked. "Anything that could help us locate where the call came from? Any accents from the caller?"

Tilly pondered my questions. "Yes, I did hear something, now that you mention it."

"What?" we all asked at once.

"I heard men talking in the background. And a sound like a drum or someone beating on a tabletop. And a bell that dinged."

I couldn't be certain, but it sounded like it could be the wrestling program at Rutherford Mace's place. "That's helpful," I said. "Thanks."

"What are you doing here?" Tilly asked. "Standing on a street corner."

It was at that moment that I saw my hound dog come around the side of a little boutique. She spotted me, let out a baleful yodel of a howl, and came at me ninety to nothing. I braced myself and caught her in my arms. Lucky for me, Harold was standing behind me and caught me before I splatted on the sidewalk with a ninety-pound hound dog on top of me.

"Sweetie Pie!" Harold and Tinkie both knelt down to love

on my pup. She was so glad to see us—she licked and howled and talked to us about all of her adventures. Even Dawson Reed looked very pleased at the reunion.

"This is a good first step," Dawson said. "I'm happy for you. But we have to find the others. I'm going home to get on the computer so I can rally the forces. We do have supporters in Nixville canvasing for the dogs. Some volunteers are checking out all the tips on the reward hotline. We had one lead that I thought might get us some results, but so far nothing."

"What lead?" I asked. Dawson should have told us this earlier.

"If it looks promising, I'll let you know. So far, it's been a dud."

I couldn't compel Dawson to share with us, but I could warn him. "I don't know what this lead involves, but be careful. Some of the people I suspect have power and they are up to something."

"Something like what?" Dawson asked.

"Running drugs, dogfighting, criminal activities. And if you threaten them, they will hurt you." I wanted to be crystal clear.

"We have law enforcement backup and some financial incentives to keep safe," Tinkie pointed out. "You could be seriously hurt if you threaten the wrong people."

"I'm a pro at this," Dawson said. "I'll be careful. Now, I have to go. I'll be in touch."

There was nothing else we could say. We watched him walk down the block to his vehicle.

"I hope he's careful," Harold said. "But right now, let's celebrate the return of Sweetie Pie. Roscoe is in bliss."

It was true. The bearded, scruffy little devil dog was as tight against Sweetie as he could get. He loved her just like I did.

"Where have you been?" Tinkie asked Sweetie, a plaintive note in her voice. She looked at me.

"Where is Chablis?" I asked my dog. "Have you been with Chablis? Is she with Jezebel and Cupcake?"

Roscoe licked Sweetie's face and seemed to whisper in her ear. They bounded to their feet, and in a moment, he and Sweetie were headed north down a side street. There was nothing to do but follow.

"Do you think they know where Chablis is?" Tinkie asked as we all hustled down the street. She was breaking my heart, and despite the fact I had no control over the situation, I felt guilty that Sweetie Pie had been returned to me. And I also had a question: Why? If Gertrude had the two dogs, why release mine? She hated me far more than she hated Tinkie. What was that crazy hussy up to? I didn't have time to really think because Sweetie Pie and Roscoe had set a blistering pace. We were all hustling to keep up with them.

The dogs went down the block where Tilly lived, continuing to the area where Squatty lived. What was going on? Tinkie and I had covered these blocks repeatedly when we were looking for Cupcake and Jezebel. We'd turned up nothing. But Sweetie and Roscoe seemed to know something we didn't. I followed them to the area where Squatty's fence had been knocked down.

I hadn't noticed the nearly empty lot next door—it was overgrown with weeds and volunteer trees that no one had bothered to cut back. Tinkie pointed to a small shed. "We never searched there."

We hadn't. It was so close to Squatty's house, I'd assumed she would investigate in case Cupcake got stuck under the old shed.

Sweetie Pie headed straight for the shed. There was nothing for it but to climb the rickety fence and go after her. She and Roscoe were trying to show us something. I just hoped it was something good, and not something awful.

"What are they doing?" Tinkie asked me, and it was clear she was worried.

"Let's find out." I put a hand on her shoulder and held her back as Harold went to the old shed.

"Listen!" He turned back to us. "Do you hear that?"

"What is it?" Tinkie asked.

"It's a whine. A dog is whining inside." He tried the door, and when it wouldn't readily open, he kicked it in. Harold could be a badass when the situation required it. "Stay back," he called out.

My heart dropped to my knees. This couldn't be a tragedy for Tinkie. Or for Squatty or Tilly. The dog inside was alive. And Harold was going to get it.

"Who's in there?" Tinkie asked.

"Stay back." Harold blocked the door until I had my arm around Tinkie and kept her away.

"What is it?" Tinkie pushed away from me and dodged under Harold's arm. She was in the shed before anyone could move to stop her.

"Oh, no! Oh, no!"

I rushed past Harold myself and went to her. She was kneeling on the floor of the shed beside a sun-glitzed bundle of fur. I felt my heart break. Sweetie Pie and Roscoe nudged past me and went to Tinkie. Sweetie Pie gave the saddest howl I'd ever heard.

22

The weak whine that came from the fluff ball made me gasp. The dog was alive. And when Tinkie lifted her into her arms, I knew it was Chablis.

"Let's go!" Harold said, helping Tinkie to her feet. "Sarah Booth, call Dr. Smith and tell him we're on the way."

I was already on the phone.

Harold and Tinkie rushed out of the shed, and I was on their heels with Roscoe, Avalon, and Sweetie following. Harold climbed the fence and took Chablis as Tinkie made her way over. Chablis was breathing and whining, but something was wrong. I couldn't tell if she was hurt, but there was no blood that I could see. I didn't dare ask Tinkie—she was almost catatonic, holding her dog as she slid into the back seat of the car with the other three dogs. Harold jumped into the front seat and in only a few minutes we were in the car headed to the vet.

The minute we went into the clinic, Karl came out to take

Tinkie into an exam room. Harold and I, along with Sweetie Pie, Avalon, and Roscoe, waited in the lobby. I felt like time had stopped. I didn't notice the other clients in the office, and I didn't hear the barking and meowing of the pets. I sat with Sweetie and Avalon on one side of my legs and Roscoe on the other. Harold, too, looked stunned. Sweetie Pie was fine; but what had happened to Tinkie's baby?

"Did you see any injuries on Chablis?" I asked. It was a silly question. Harold didn't know anything more than I did.

"I couldn't tell. She wasn't bleeding."

"Do you think she was poisoned?" I had a long list of things I didn't want to ask.

"I don't know. Let's just wait, Sarah Booth. We can make ourselves sick with worry. The question you need to be asking is how did Chablis get from Zinnia into a shed in Nixville."

"Gertrude."

"Yes, Gertrude. But how and why? I mean Gertrude had disappeared. The heat was off, for a while, at least. Now she's in the gunsights of every law officer in the state."

I texted Coleman to let him know Sweetie Pie was fine and Chablis was at the vet.

"Need me to come?" he asked.

He'd already been to Nixville that morning. And there was nothing he could do but hold me while we waited. I wanted him beside me, but that wasn't a fair request. He had his own job to do. "No. I'll let you know when we hear something."

"The very minute you hear."

"I swear." I hung up with a great sense of loss.

Harold pulled out his phone. "I'll let Oscar know. Tinkie may need him."

I got up and went outside with Sweetie and Avalon to pace.

The day was cold but sunny, and we walked the parking lot back and forth. I couldn't sit still, and I didn't want to disturb the other pets and clients who were waiting to be seen.

At last, the front door opened and Harold and Roscoe came out. Sweetie rushed Roscoe and they licked each other, as if they were offering comfort. "Did you hear anything?" I asked.

"Chablis is going to be okay." Harold looked wrung out. "It was a very close call, but Karl said she would be all right as long as they keep pumping fluids and she responds."

I felt the tears accumulate and fall down my face. "What's wrong with her?"

"Tinkie said Chablis was dehydrated and exhausted. They're giving her fluids in an IV and will keep her overnight. But she should be fine."

"And Tinkie?"

Harold put his arm around me. "She is going to be fine, too. I promise."

Maybe. Maybe not. Someone had struck a devastating blow at Tinkie's heart—and at her ability to keep those she loved safe. That was the fallout from an attack like this. Our sense of security had been horribly violated. Tinkie and I had dealt with some mean characters in our career. My dad, a lawyer and a judge, had often talked to me about human nature and how dangerous a person without morality or ethics could be. We'd suffered that firsthand when Gertrude took Sweetie and Chablis, two innocent animals who had nothing to do with the bad blood between us and Gertrude. It would take a while before we felt secure leaving the animals anywhere unattended.

Tinkie came out to the parking lot and signaled us inside. "Would you let Sweetie Pie stay the night with Chablis?" she asked me. "I don't want to leave her alone, and Karl said they could stay together in side-by-side kennels. It will give Chablis a lot of comfort."

I wasn't hot to leave Sweetie, especially since I'd just gotten her back and wanted to wallow in the bed and love on her. But Chablis was her best friend. And Tinkie was mine. "Sure. That would be a good idea."

"Thank you." Tinkie raised on tiptoes to kiss my cheek. "You're the best friend ever. Come back and see my little girl. She looks about eighty percent better than she did when I brought her in."

Tinkie spoke the truth. Chablis's head lifted when she heard Sweetie's yodel, and her little ears perked forward. She let out a whimper that instantly drew Sweetie and Roscoe to her side. Avalon watched from the doorway until Sweetie Pie gave a short bark—obviously an invitation to enter. Avalon hurried over to the patient. Sweetie tenderly licked her friend, finally settling on a soft bed by the kennel door.

"I do think she wants to stay," I said.

"I agree." Harold knelt down to pet them all. Roscoe gave an evil little snort-bark and then beat it out of the kennel area and into the waiting room, where all hell broke loose. He took off after a big tabby tomcat who jumped on the counter and knocked a stack of business cards, heartworm meds, and a lit candle to the floor. Harold was right behind him, stomping out the candle and catching Roscoe by the collar. Roscoe was a demon. A demon that I loved.

While Harold sorted the mayhem in the front office, I put my arm around my friend as she knelt beside her dog.

"You're going to be fine," Tinkie told Chablis. A vet tech came in to check her IV and to set Sweetie Pie up in a kennel.

They couldn't allow Sweetie free range with no one in the building. There were too many things for her to get into that could harm her. But I would be there first thing in the morning to get both of the dogs.

Tinkie was crying when we left, and I put an arm around her. We drove Harold back to his truck in downtown Nixville, and then we headed back to Zinnia. Whatever we'd hoped to accomplish, it could wait until we'd both recovered from the shock and joy of finding our dogs. But the fact remained that Jezebel and Cupcake were still missing. If Chablis's condition was an indicator, we had a right to be worried about the two missing pups. Maybe Gertrude didn't have them. But if not her, then who? And were they being cared for? The nights were bitter cold. At least for tonight, Sweetie Pie and Chablis would be in the vet clinic with an on-duty tech looking out for them. And tomorrow, Chablis would go home!

Oscar was waiting for Tinkie at Hilltop when I dropped her off. Harold had followed me there, just to be sure we were both okay. We were—and Tinkie wasn't alone. She had Maylin, Pauline, and her husband. Oscar had left the bank to be with her, and Harold and I watched as she ran into his arms and he held her.

When I'd first met Oscar, I'd had little use for him. He seemed to be a dandy, an entitled, privileged asshat. But in the time I'd been back in Mississippi, I'd come to view him in a different light. The one thing I knew without reservation was that he would do everything in his power to protect Tinkie and Maylin and keep them happy and safe.

"Do you want to go inside?" Harold asked me.

"No. I think Tinkie needs the comfort of her husband, and you need to go back to the bank and finish your work. Especially if Oscar is going to stay home with his family."

"What are you going to do?" Harold asked. I detected a hint of excitement in his voice.

"I'm going back to Nixville. I believe Cupcake and Jezebel are near that shed. I have to look more thoroughly. What if they're right there, desperate for water?"

"We do need to find them. Have there been any sightings?" Harold asked.

"No." That was the bitter truth. "It's just a gut feeling I have." Coleman would call it a hunch. He never trusted a hunch he couldn't verify, but he loved it when he had a good one. And I did, too.

"I'll go with you," Harold said. "Since Sweetie Pie is playing nursemaid, Roscoe may prove to be an asset."

"Yes, Roscoe is a great asset. As are you." Harold was a good PI, though it wasn't a vocation he wanted to pursue. He had a logical brain that often led him to conclusions based only on facts. I was more emotional and intuitive. Tinkie fell in between the extremes of us.

I stopped by Dahlia House, contemplating the possibility of leaving Roscoe and Avalon. We could use their help, but I had to factor in the reality that it was too cold to leave them in the car if Harold and I hit a good lead. I was about to put them in Dahlia House when I stopped. Harold only looked over at me.

"I can't leave them. Not with what had happened to Chablis and Sweetie Pie."

So, the four of us headed to Nixville. With any luck at all,

I'd be home by five o'clock to cook supper and give Coleman the attention he deserved. And also to bleed his brain for any leads he might be withholding. I had a sneaky suspicion that he knew more than he'd let on about how Sweetie and Chablis had ended up in that shed in Nixville.

Our first stop was the vet clinic, to check on Chablis and Sweetie Pie. They were snugged up, side by side, in their kennels. Chablis had improved remarkably, and I knew she'd be going home the next day. What a relief. I snapped a photo of the doggie lovefest and sent it to Tinkie to let her know Chablis was well on the way to recovery.

"What next?" Harold asked when we were back in the car. Avalon and Roscoe were in the back seat.

I, frankly, wasn't certain what to do next. Harold brought a skill set to the day that I didn't always have at my disposal. Along with the fact that he was a financial brain, he was also pretty handy with technology.

"Let's find Dawson Reed. His internet pet finders group may have some information. Dawson might be an interesting person for you to know."

"Bring it on," Harold said. He rubbed his hands in anticipation. "I love a good scavenger hunt on the internet. Or in person, for that matter. Let's get after it."

We hopped in the car with the dogs and I texted Dawson while Harold drove. We were at Dawson's place in fifteen minutes.

Dawson's house was a modest brick ranch-style house on the outskirts of Zinnia. The yard was maintained, but not immaculate. Plenty of pollinator plants had been left to grow in jumbles around the building. Dawson came out with a blue heeler following closely by his leg.

"This is Ziggy," Dawson said. "He wants to help, too."

Ziggy darted from his side and jumped up on the car door so that he could nose and sniff with Avalon and Roscoe. They were excited to meet. I got out and opened the door to let them romp a bit. It was a joy to see them so happy to play, and I couldn't wait until Chablis and Sweetie were able to be there with them. The three dogs tore around Dawson's yard and then disappeared around the corner of his house. The games were on!

"Any leads on the missing dogs?" Harold asked. He was taking Dawson's measure.

"In fact, I just got a message," Dawson said. His face lit up in eagerness. "Someone thinks they saw Jezebel. I mean, it's impossible to tell because those fuzzy white dogs look a lot alike. But . . ." He tapped on his phone and then showed it to us. "That looks like Jezebel."

He was correct. The dog did look exactly like Tilly's pet. Was it possible we'd finally caught a break?

I studied the photo of the charming white dog facing the camera. She was on a sidewalk by a well-maintained grassy verge planted with daffodils. The flowers told me the photo was recent, and that the dog was in a community that had public plantings. In the background were several parked cars, but, search as I might, there was nothing that I could identify as a location. The disappointment was bitter.

"Where was this taken?" I asked.

"We haven't pinpointed the exact location. It came in anonymously," Dawson admitted. "My IT guy is trying to find out where it was sent from."

"Can you message the person who sent it?" Harold asked. "Maybe they would volunteer more information."

"Already have," Dawson said. "The thing in our favor is they asked about the reward. That two grand really got folks paying attention. So, I need to notify Tilly and make sure if she talks to them that we're included in the conversation. I don't want anyone to take advantage of her and I don't want to miss an opportunity to get more data if we can."

"And we need to recover the dog—alive and safe." That was my priority. "The one good thing is if that is Jezebel, she seems healthy and fine."

"She won't be for long if she's running around loose," Harold pointed out. "She could get hit by a car or another dog could attack her. Or someone with a black heart could pick her up."

Harold was right. I didn't like hearing it, but the days of dogs—even country dogs—running loose were over. People were mean.

"May I see the photo?" Harold asked.

"Sure." Dawson passed him the phone, and Harold studied it. "I may know where this is," he said, to the surprise of both Dawson and myself.

"Where?" we said.

"Look at the pavement. Old brick. There's nothing like that in Nixville, but there is in Zinnia. I think that dog is here."

23

It wasn't a great lead, but it was one we could follow. Especially since Harold had a location in mind. "Let's go!"

Harold and I got back in the car; Dawson followed in his vehicle with his cattle dog, Ziggy, riding shotgun. All of the dogs might come in handy. Roscoe was a pretty good tracker—though not as good as Sweetie Pie, with her hound-dog sensibilities—and his determination was legendary. And Ziggy might also catch Jezebel's scent. Dogs were so much smarter than most people gave them credit for being.

We ended up on Second Street in Zinnia. The road was paved with bricks, as were many of the old streets in the Delta towns that had sprung up around the cotton industry. Harold was driving slowly so we could look for the location.

"There!" He pointed to an area on a residential street. In a moment he'd maneuvered the car so that I could compare the view out my window with the photo of the white dog loose on a street.

"This may be it." Excitement crept into my voice. "Let's get out and look around."

Avalon and Roscoe were barking in the back seat, eager to hit the bricks. When I opened the door, they bounded onto the sidewalk, sniffing and coursing back and forth. Avalon had enough hound in her that when she caught a scent, she was ready to give chase.

Dawson arrived with Ziggy on a leash, and I admired his intelligence. I wished I'd thought to bring one. Roscoe would mind us—sort of—but Avalon was a dog I didn't know well. I was worried she might bolt and get hurt. I didn't have much time to think about potential disaster. The dogs packed up, barking like banshees, and Roscoe began to howl like a demon was chewing his tail.

"They're on to something," Dawson said as Ziggy dragged him forward to join in with Avalon and Roscoe.

"But what do they sense?" I asked. "It's nuts that they would catch the scent of Jezebel just because we're looking for her. We don't even know when that photo was taken. It could have been two days ago. If that's Jezebel at all." I wanted it to be true, but I'd given up on fairy tales when I was twelve.

"Never underestimate a dog," Harold said. "Humans will disappoint you again and again. A dog, never!"

The words were barely out of his mouth when Ziggy bolted forward. She snatched the leash out of Dawson's hand and was down the block before I could even get behind the steering wheel of the car to give chase. Harold and Dawson pounded down the sidewalk on foot, with Avalon and Roscoe in hot pursuit. Where in the world was Ziggy heading? There was nothing to do but chase after her, since I couldn't manage to head her off at the pass.

Ziggy raced down Second Street and I pulled over to let Harold and Dawson hustle into the car. Then I put the gas pedal to the floor as I went after the dogs. They were staying on the sidewalk but galloping like their tails were on fire. Luckily, there was no traffic on the narrow side road and we could easily follow them. My concern was that the canine posse was heading out of town. We were hot on their heels, but just outside of the Zinnia city limits, the land opened up to vast stretches of fallow fields. If the dogs decided to chase into the wooded areas, we wouldn't be able to drive after them and we didn't stand a chance at keeping up on foot.

I gave Harold my phone and asked him to call Coleman to let him know our location and plan, just in case we ran into Gertrude or some other dognapper. I had a gun in the back of the car in the spare wheel well, but Coleman would be upset if I had to use it to plug an older woman. Even if that woman was Gertrude.

"You're heading out of town on Second Street?" Coleman asked. "I'm in a situation, but I'll put out a call for Budgie and DeWayne. They're heading back to town from that general direction. If we have to block the dogs, the deputies might come in handy."

We'd gone two miles and the dogs were unflagging in their pursuit of whatever in the world they'd caught the scent of. The residential homes on narrow patches of grass had given way to rural homes on acreage. We were leaving residential Zinnia behind, and I couldn't believe the dogs could continue to run so fast.

"Step on the gas, Sarah Booth," Harold said. "They're pulling away from us!"

Indeed they were. My tires squealed around a corner, hot

on their tracks. That's when I saw an old Mercedes Roadster
that looked like the one my mama used to drive. Only my
car was in the barn at Dahlia House. Or at least it had been
this morning when I fed the horses. I loved that car for many
reasons, but I'd retired it when I bought a newer vehicle. The
Roadster, because of its antique status and beauty, drew too
much attention. I'd opted for a dark gray hybrid crossover. It
looked like a million other cars on the road.

"Is that your car?" Harold asked.

"I don't know. It sure looks like it." Chinese red, with a
dove gray interior. I felt a cold cramp in my stomach. If that
was my mother's Roadster, it could mean only one thing—
Gertrude had gotten into my barn and hot-wired the car. Gertrude had a thing for antique Roadsters, too.

I pulled up beside the car and asked Harold to get out and
check. A half mile down the road, two patrol cruisers were
headed our way. Budgie and DeWayne whipped around to
block the road as they got out and pursued the dogs on foot. It
took them only a moment to catch Ziggy's leash, and Avalon
and Roscoe fell into line, rushing DeWayne for snuggles. Everyone was contained, but we still needed to figure out what the
dogs were chasing so . . . doggedly.

"Hey, it *is* your car, Sarah Booth," Harold said. "The ignition has been popped. Go get the pups and I'll stay here. I
want to thoroughly examine the car." The dogs were a good
three hundred yards away, and I wasn't one to argue with free
help.

It was a good plan. I pulled down the road and the deputies
loaded the dogs into the back seat of the car. "Where were
they going in such a hurry?" DeWayne asked.

"I wish I knew," I told him.

"Then let's find out. Let's give the dogs a chance to show us what they were pursuing." He got a leash from his patrol car—he carried one at all times in case he needed to help a stray. He clipped it onto Avalon's collar before he let the dogs out of the back seat. We set off down the road on foot, though at a more reasonable pace this time.

Ziggy was still dragging Dawson, but Avalon and Roscoe had settled into a nice, brisk walk. The day was sunny and chill. It felt good to stretch my legs, all the while I was looking for any sign of a fuzzy white dog. Jezebel had to be somewhere around this area.

I turned to Dawson. "Did you set up any kind of meeting with the person who sent you the photo of the white dog?"

"I need to do that. I did inform Tilly, and she is supposed to speak with the tipster. She's the one who has to pay out the reward. We pet finders don't get involved in the money aspect in any way. I can say with one hundred percent certainty that ninety-nine percent of the people who help us locate missing pets are honorable and dependable. But there is always that one person that makes life difficult; therefore, we don't handle any money at all. But you guys could do that for Tilly and maybe Squatty, right?"

"We'd be happy to do that." Tinkie and I had handled one or two scenarios where a monetary reward was offered. We'd never had a problem, but I could see where Dawson wouldn't want to engage his online group in it. If someone was unethical and only trying to snap up a reward, it could really backfire on him. Tinkie and I had only ourselves to worry about, and I knew my partner was rock solid. She had more money than she could ever spend, but aside from that she had ethics. She had the same confidence in me.

I turned to Dawson. "Can you call Tilly and see if the tipster got in touch? I wonder if it was a ruse." We'd been searching for nearly half an hour and there'd been no sign of Jezebel or any other loose dog. I hadn't anticipated driving down the street and seeing Jezebel just waiting for a ride home. But I couldn't help the fact that I felt our lead with Jezebel was slipping away.

We'd covered a lot of ground and we hadn't seen a sign of a dog. Any dog. The tip Tilly had received was beginning to look more and more like a cruel prank. It was exactly something that Gertrude would do, and the Roadster was evidence she'd been in this area. Had she dumped Jezebel somewhere on the edge of town? The dog was too far from her home in Nixville to easily make it back to Tilly.

While we were walking, I called Tinkie to fill her in. She didn't answer, so I left a message and then hurried to catch up with Dawson and Harold. They were making tracks. De-Wayne and Budgie had received a call they had to answer, but they promised to rush back out if we found anything. I didn't relish the idea of meeting Gertrude in a rural setting, but I couldn't expect the deputies to hold my hand. We were on our own, following the dogs as they sniffed the air and kept moving. If they were discouraged, they didn't show it. Perhaps we just needed to take a little guidance from our pooches.

We were still headed out of town, and I glanced back. The Roadster was long out of sight. "Should I retrieve my car?" I asked Harold. "I could hurry back to pick y'all up."

"Or I could run and get my vehicle," Dawson offered. "You could take Ziggy's leash."

"Either way works for me." I could hustle back to where we'd left our vehicles, or I could keep walking forward. Six of one, half a dozen of the other. The one thing I wanted to do was talk to Coleman about the Roadster. Unless Gertrude showed up to steal it again, the car was safely parked on a Zinnia street. And DeWayne had indicated that he'd make sure Coleman sent a wrecker to pick it up. That was all well and good, but I was eager to get the car back to the barn so I could fully examine it. Harold was also chomping at the bit to see if he could find any clues. Gertrude was smart and careful, but there was always a chance she'd left evidence or a hint of her plans in the car. I knew that if Coleman had time, he'd examine the car before it was even moved. He had a big job to do, and he was on standby to testify in a trial.

"Hey!"

Dawson's sharp retort drew my attention. He was pointing to a clump of trees that seemed to front a little creek. "What is that?" he asked as he left the side of the paved road and began cutting across a weed-choked field.

I saw movement. Something white was shifting through the underbrush. It looked like . . . a dog! "Jezebel!" I cried out, and the animal turned to look at me. She hesitated only a moment and then she ran toward me full-tilt boogie.

"Jezebel!" Harold dropped to one knee and opened his arms wide for the white fur ball that hurtled toward us. It was indeed the missing dog.

The minute Harold had his hands on Jezebel, I heaved a sigh of relief. Tilly's dog squirmed and licked. I had no doubt it was Jezebel. We'd successfully recovered three of the missing dogs. Only Cupcake remained unaccounted for. And I hoped that Jezebel might lead us to her.

When Jezebel was in his arms, Harold stood up, holding her. She looked a lot heavier than she was because of all the fur. He lifted her as if she weighed only a few ounces. And I felt my heart swell with joy. I texted Tinkie immediately to let her know we had Jezebel. When she didn't respond, I almost called, but I didn't. Like Coleman, Tinkie also had a very full plate with our work and her family. Maybe she was having a little me time with Maylin. She deserved that without me calling to make her feel guilty.

"Jezebel is safe!" I typed. "We have her and we're going to look for Cupcake a little longer. I'm nearly positive Gertrude stole my mother's Roadster out of the barn, but it's okay. She abandoned it on the side of Second Street on the outskirts of town. Coleman is sending a wrecker to take it home for me. I'll pick you up as soon as I finish here so we can take Jezebel home to Tilly in Nixville. Oh, and the horses are fine. De-Wayne said he checked them just before he came to help us."

24

Harold, Dawson, and I spent the next two hours giving the dogs every opportunity to pick up Cupcake's scent. There were several times I thought the hounds had hit a trail, but they never went far, and came hurrying back to us as if they sought consolation. I had no doubt they were aware how dangerous it was for Cupcake to be out on her own. She was a delicate little indoor dog. If she was out in the fields and we didn't find her before nightfall, she might not make it. The temperatures were supposed to drop into the low teens. It was another log added to the bonfire of my worries.

"I hate to admit defeat, but I don't think Cupcake is here," Dawson finally said. Even though the day was cold, he wiped sweat from his brow. We'd been moving fast for a long time. I was tired, and even Harold looked like he could use a sit-down.

"I agree." It hurt me to give up, but it seemed pointless.

My phone buzzed and I answered to hear Budgie's voice.

"Coleman had your car towed to Bailey Automotive. He's asked a friend of his who works for the crime lab in Jackson to go over it."

"Thanks." They could do a better job than either Harold or I could.

"He's pretty sure Gertrude took it," Budgie continued. "He's going to get the ignition fixed for you while Bailey has it there."

Coleman was a tender and thoughtful man. He understood that knowing the car was damaged would prey on my mind. "Tell him thank you."

"He tore out of here like a cat after a catnip mouse."

This was news to me. "Where did he go?"

Budgie hesitated. "Well, he didn't say."

That wasn't like Coleman. He was big on everyone keeping tabs on everyone else in case there was trouble. "What exactly did he say?"

"Only that he had to take care of something and would be back by afternoon."

I checked my watch, which was unnecessary since my stomach was growling like a famished lion. It was well beyond lunchtime. "Was he headed somewhere dangerous?" I had to ask.

"He didn't say, Sarah Booth. He really didn't. But I got a sense that he was going after someone he considered . . . unsavory, if not dangerous."

"Gertrude." Her name popped out of my mouth.

"That would be my guess," Budgie said. "But it's only a guess. You have no idea how much he hates her for the pain she's caused you."

I didn't quite buy that Budgie didn't know Coleman's whereabouts, but I dropped it. I had another plan. "We're going to call off the search for Cupcake. I'm going to talk to Tinkie, then pick her up and head over to Nixville. Please leave a note for Coleman, telling him I must talk to Squatty and return Jezebel to Tilly. She is going to be over the moon with joy."

"I'll tell him." Budgie cleared his throat. "Do you know a lawyer named Julian Dickerson?"

"Not personally, but I'm familiar. He's a native of Nixville. Big lawyer in Jackson now."

"Yeah, so I understand."

"Has Coleman gone to talk to him?" It would account for the large chunk of time Coleman planned to be gone.

"I don't know. But he'd written the name on the blotter on his desk. Don't tell him I told you. I'm just worried. Coleman was hot under the collar about your car. I think he found some link between Dickerson and Gertrude Stromm."

Oh, that would light Coleman's fuse—no doubt about it.

"Thanks, Budgie. This is very helpful."

"Promise me you'll play it safe. He's going to be furious if I told you something that got you hurt."

"No worries. I will use all care, and I'm taking Tinkie with me."

I dropped Harold and Roscoe at his vehicle. He was going to the bank to work but said he'd keep his phone active so we could call if we needed him. When I stopped to get Tinkie, I filled her in.

Tinkie was as excited to see Jezebel as I'd been, but she brought up a great point. Winter days were short and severe thunderstorm warnings were up. A large thunderstorm with lightning, hail, and ice would move into Sunflower County within the next two hours.

"We can take Jezebel home first thing in the morning and

pick up Sweetie Pie and Chablis," Tinkie said. "I'll call Tilly and tell her we have the dog safe. But let's wait until morning to take her. I'll keep Jezebel here with me. It will help me with missing Chablis."

Even though I knew she was right, I wanted to argue. I was ready to deliver Jezebel to her owner, to see the relief and joy on Tilly's face. But that was selfish. The smart thing to do was to be safe on the roads and safe with my partner and the dogs. Coleman would agree with Tinkie. And ultimately I did, too.

I got back in the car with Avalon. How I missed Sweetie Pie, but she was performing her nursemaid duties with Chablis. And she was safe. Whatever Gertrude had meant to do to them, Sweetie Pie and Chablis had escaped her clutches. I couldn't help but think of Dorothy and Toto. Which made Gertrude the Wicked Witch. But we had thwarted her, for the moment, at least. How had Sweetie gotten away? And why had the dogs been put in that shed? What was Gertrude or her evil henchmen up to? Questions better answered in the daylight than on a dark and stormy night.

As I turned my car around to head home, I could feel the electricity in the air. Lightning forked to the north, creating an eerie illumination of a completely black vista. There were no stars, no streetlights—just the velvet darkness of February in the Mississippi Delta.

25

Snugged against Coleman's back, I finally drifted off to sleep. The storm raged outside Dahlia House, and sometime in the early morning I woke up worried about Tilly missing her pup. And Cupcake was still out there somewhere, waiting for us to rescue her. I had a lot on my mind.

Coleman had spoken with Mitchell Rockwell, the former police chief of Nixville who now worked for the MBI. Rockwell had nothing good to say about Garwool or the mayor. But he didn't have any proof that could be used to bring charges, either. He'd told Coleman that he wouldn't be averse to a sting operation if Coleman was up to helping. Such an endeavor would take planning and strategy. It wouldn't help me find Cupcake or punish those responsible for stealing the dogs. But it was a great future plan.

Avalon had eased up onto the foot of the bed, which made me miss Sweetie Pie more than ever. Luckily, Pluto had taken to the gray hound, and even Poe seemed to accept our newest family member. Coleman had teased me, saying in another year I'd have twenty dogs and cats and an uncountable number of other "dependents."

If I had my way, I'd have every stray animal in the world living at Dahlia House. But even I knew that was silly. One person could only do so much. Each animal deserved time and attention and love. I couldn't expand time so that I had more of it. With the horses, dogs, cat, and Poe, I was stretched thin.

And worried about Cupcake.

Avalon sighed in her sleep and I smiled. Sweetie Pie was a soft moaner when she was on the bed. I found the nocturnal noises of the animals so comforting. Even Coleman's tiny snorts and grumbles made me feel safe and loved. I slipped out from beneath the covers and went to the fireplace. The embers had burned low, but Coleman had brought in more wood. We had central air and heat, but I loved the fireplaces. I stoked the fire, put on more logs, and hurried to the kitchen to make coffee. It wasn't even five, but there was no going back to sleep. I was eager to take Jezebel back to Tilly, and we had to find Cupcake. Sweetie Pie would help us once we sprang her and Chablis from the vet clinic. Yes, returning Jezebel and getting Sweetie and Chablis back—those were things to look forward to. And I did.

I took a cup of freshly brewed coffee to my office. The heat was on in there and it was cozy. As I sat and worked at the computer, I could hear pings of hail against the window. It was going to be a very cold and slick morning when the sun finally arrived. This storm wasn't as bad as some of the winter storms that hit so hard and cold, with freezing rain. The ice accumulation pulled entire sections of the power lines down. Weather predictions were for a warming trend as soon as the sun came up. That was good news.

My search for any information on Gertrude Stromm was frustrating. I found where a woman with a name I didn't recognize—obviously an alias for Gertrude—had been running a B and B in Pine Bluff, Arkansas. There were photos of the B and B and I saw Gertrude's green thumb at work in the beautiful flower beds. At the end of the article, there was a photo of the proprietress. It was Gertrude. I didn't doubt it for a minute. And now, believe it or not, the B and B had suddenly closed. Apparently, Garwool and the mayor, Vern Fenway, had second thoughts about a business that was operated by a woman who was wanted by all the law enforcement agencies in the state of Mississippi. Whatever the reasons, it was a smart move on their part to shut down the place and send Gertrude packing. But where had she gone? That was something I intended to find out.

Dawn broke over the eastern horizon, and I was ready to rock and roll. I'd had a shower, made breakfast for Coleman, and talked with Nixville police deputy Tom Terrell. Avalon and Pluto were frisking in the front yard, and I sipped another hot cup of coffee and watched them as the horses frolicked in the pasture.

Tinkie's Cadillac came down the drive, and just behind her was Harold. I couldn't believe he was taking another day off work at the bank, but it was possible he was only obeying Oscar's orders. When Tinkie's health was involved, Oscar didn't mind sending his employees to keep her out of trouble.

Jezebel jumped out of Tinkie's Caddy and greeted us with boisterous barks. I waved my friends in for some caffeine before we left to track down Cupcake. I was curious about what

Harold was planning on doing. He satisfied my curiosity right off the bat.

"I'm meeting with Vern Fenway at eight thirty this morning," Harold said. "He's been trying to get some of his businesses refinanced. Oscar wanted me to give his requests a . . . personal touch."

Lord-a-mercy, Oscar was putting the squeeze on Fenway like some mafia don. I wanted to watch Harold work this situation, but I had my own chores to attend to. And I knew that Harold would be more effective without me and Tinkie playing lookie-loos.

We made a plan to meet at Millie's for lunch unless one of us ran up on a good lead about Cupcake. Harold and Roscoe, who was of course riding shotgun, took off while Tinkie put Jezebel and Avalon in the back seat of my car. I couldn't wait to see Tilly's face. But I sure didn't want to run into Squatty until we had her dog recovered, too.

We drove straight to Tilly's, and we were in luck. She was in her front yard, pulling a few weeds. At the sound of the car, she turned around. I saw the emotions move across her face—from hopeful expectation to dread, and then the moment she saw Jezebel in the back seat of the car: joy!

"My baby!" She dropped her tools and gloves and came straight to the car. I opened the back door and Jezebel flew out of the back seat and into her arms. Tinkie's eyes teared up at the happy reunion. Mine, too, but I turned away. I didn't need a reputation as a soft touch.

"What about Cupcake?" she asked after she'd held and snuggled Jezebel, kissing her face and crying her joy.

"Not yet," I said. "Have you talked to Squatty?"

"Yesterday. She's in a bad way. I never realized how much

she loves her little dog. And that grandson, Ellis. I think she wants to kill him, but is afraid of going to jail."

"She shouldn't hurt him." Tinkie was all over that. "She would go to jail and it would be awful."

I had a hunch to play. "Tilly, do you know a lawyer named Julian Dickerson?"

"Oh, Julian. Yes, I know him. His mother and I were in the garden club together. She had her hands full with him."

This was interesting. "How so?"

"Julian is extremely smart. Maybe the smartest person I've ever met. Smart people, without proper direction, can end up in dark places. Julian's friends were sometimes questionable. But he outgrew those impulses, it seems."

I was getting a different picture of Julian than the one I'd had in my head. Smart, successful, and with a history of walking on the dark side. "Were any charges ever brought against Julian?"

"Not that I know of," Tilly said, "but we all know Julian has the juice to get such things taken care of. I'm sure you catch my drift."

Oh, I did. Julian was special—protected by the powers that be. This was also interesting. "Do you know if Julian was involved with Rutherford Mace?"

Tilly stepped back. "You're asking a lot of questions that could get you in big trouble with Fenway and Garwool."

"I don't really give two figs about those two men," I said. "I want to find Cupcake and then get my hands on the people responsible for taking the dogs in the first place. We've recovered three of the four—none of them were turned in for rewards. The dogs have been found wandering around all over the place. They were left out along roads in a place they weren't familiar with, and could have been injured or killed. Now I'm just hoping we can find Cupcake and get her home."

Tilly touched my arm. "I don't want Squatty to know I have Jezebel back. It will break her heart. And it could push her into committing a violent act against Ellis. In the last day or so she has really grown to hate him. She blames him."

It would be hard not to blame the little fink. He'd known what was happening and done nothing to protect his grandmother's beloved pet. He was a skunk of the highest order.

"What's Ellis's connection to Rutherford Mace?" I asked.

Tilly shook her head. "When he was younger he ran around town wearing a wrestling outfit and pretending to be with the WWE. He thought he would seem glamorous, but the girls only laughed at him. So many young men can't seem to grasp that a young woman wants a partner who is kind and compassionate, not a cartoon character."

"You sound like you know Ellis," Tinkie observed.

"Only a little. He cut my grass one summer and we talked a little. He was a likeable young man, but he reeked of desperation. He only wanted to make friends. The boy didn't have a clue how to go about doing that."

"But Squatty is so social," Tinkie pointed out.

"Squatty isn't an eighteen-year-old boy. Cool for a tea party isn't cool for a high school boy. Everything Squatty tried— and she did try—backfired. I knew it was a trainwreck headed straight for Ellis, but no one could stop it. Never tell her I said this, but Squatty cares about her grandson. If you prove he took Cupcake, it will damage her. Keep that in mind."

Another sticky wicket thrust in our faces. I didn't like Ellis, and I disliked even more the impact he could have on his granny's emotional health. "Do you think Ellis would harm Cupcake?" I asked.

"I honestly don't know. Not the Ellis I knew when he was fourteen and cutting my lawn. He was a tender kid. He loved animals and was careful of wildlife when he cut the backyard. We'd have rabbits or such come up to nest sometimes. And he was completely trustworthy. He had a key to the toolshed and used the equipment. He always cleaned it up nicely and there was never even a question of his honesty. So, I don't know who Ellis is today. But in the past, he was a good person."

This was a view of Ellis I'd never really heard. "Thanks, Tilly. And I'm so glad Jezebel is home. Just keep her inside until this passes over."

"If she goes outside she'll be on a leash. I swear to you. And don't count me out of the investigation. Jezebel is home, but what about the other dogs missing? We know about Cupcake, but surely there are many others. Probably hundreds."

"That's likely true." I still didn't have a handle on why Cupcake and Jezebel had been taken in the first place. And we hadn't connected their abduction to Gertrude stealing Sweetie Pie and Chablis. The only link was that Gertrude worked for the mayor and police chief of Nixville, and the minute Tinkie and I went to investigate the dog thefts, Gertrude stole our babies. But I couldn't put my finger on how all of these events were related.

"Do you think Gertrude is working with a dog-theft ring?" Tinkie asked. She made a face that let me know she found this highly unlikely. But I had other thoughts.

Gertrude was an arch criminal with nefarious skills. She'd eluded law enforcement for many months now. But dog theft? Unless it was an organized ring that sold the dogs for medical experimentation or for bait dogs in dogfighting, I didn't see the motive. As Garwool had pointed out, the lack of spay-and-neuter laws in the Southern states, along with a complete lack of enforcement of cruelty laws, had created an atmosphere where thousands of stray dogs were destroyed each year. And even more cats. No one in authority seemed to care at all.

"I'm not seeing the profit motive," I admitted. "But Gertrude sometimes does things just to be mean."

"She's an evil person," Tinkie agreed. "But I contend there has to be a bigger picture. Bigger stakes. She's aging, and she's essentially homeless now that you routed her from Pine Bluff, Arkansas." Tinkie bit her bottom lip. "She's going to be meaner than a sack full of cottonmouths, Sarah Booth."

"I may have unleashed the Kraken." I tried to make a joke, but Tinkie was worried, and so was I. "Coleman is fixing the camera on the porch, and as soon as possible he's also putting up game cameras around the farm. They'll alert us on our phones of any activity in the barn, the pastures, or the house." Material things could be replaced, but the animals were irreplaceable, and they were the things that worried me whenever Gertrude's name came up.

"Let's go get Sweetie Pie and Chablis," Tinkie said. Our babies were waiting at the vet clinic. "Once I have my fluff ball back, I'll be able to think more clearly."

"Me, too!"

"Tilly, call us if you get any more info on the dog situation. Someone may call the tip line. We're still trying to figure out who sent the tip on Jezebel. No one has stepped forward to claim the reward you offered, but keep reposting the reward information on social media. Dawson is helping to spread the word with his group." I sighed. "If we knew where Jezebel had been, we might find Cupcake."

"Good plan," Tilly said. "I'll do everything I can to help. And here." She held out a check for our fee, plus a bit extra.

Tinkie and I exchanged looks. "We can't take that," Tinkie said. "We're glad Jezebel is back. And we need to get to the bottom of this. Maybe donate that to Dawson and the pet finders."

I nodded my agreement.

"Okay," Tilly agreed. "Now, go get your babies."

26

The minute we walked into Karl's vet clinic and Tinkie opened her mouth, I heard Chablis's excited squeals. Sweetie Pie chimed in with loud, yodeling cries of joy. Two vet assistants brought them out from the back, and before they could stop them, the dogs hurled themselves at us. Sweetie clocked in at about ninety pounds, and when she jumped into my arms, she knocked me backward into a chair. It was hysterical and delicious and filled with love.

"Chablis is ready to go home," Karl told us. "She's perfectly fine now. She just got dehydrated in that shed." He gave me a long look. "Be careful. All of you. Anyone who would leave a dog to die like that is capable of anything."

He wasn't wrong about that. "Did you find anything on Chablis that might indicate who had her or where she's been?" I asked.

Karl shook his head. "Nothing I could pinpoint specifically. She was in that shed for at least twelve hours. Maybe longer.

The dirt from the last rain we had was crusted in her fur, but there was no indication of how she got there. I mean, Chablis came from Zinnia to Nixville. That's not such a terribly long distance, maybe ten or fifteen miles. But it's a long, long way for such a tiny little pup."

"She didn't walk it on her own. And even if she had been intent on walking, she would never have run away from Tinkie or me. What we need to know is why Gertrude took her, and why she left her in that shed." The more I fretted about this, the angrier I grew.

"I checked her paws and pads, and she wasn't walking a long distance on rough terrain," Karl said. "My educated guess is that she was driven from Zinnia to here. You need to determine if Gertrude had an accomplice. Someone who kept the dogs detained."

Karl shook his head and continued talking. "I'm afraid I don't have an answer. I did talk to Chief Garwool about running some forensic tests on the soil I recovered from her feet, but he refused."

"No big shock there." I said it with bitterness.

"I know," Karl said. "It's disheartening. But I'm going to pay a call on Rutherford and Zotto today. I have some questions for them, which I hope will yield some answers."

"Thanks." I gave the veterinarian a hug. "And be careful. Coleman hasn't turned up anything illegal involving Mace or the wrestlers, but he's still looking. Sunflower County can't afford for you to be hurt."

He only laughed. "I'm more like a tick than a spider. Once I'm dug in I'm hard to shake."

"Just be careful."

Tinkie paid her bill and we made ready to leave. We had

to find Cupcake before the day was out. The problem was we didn't know where to start looking for her. We'd check all the places we knew to look, but I had a feeling Cupcake was in a house somewhere—someplace where she couldn't get out to go home. I feared she was with Gertrude's confederate, as I had come to believe someone was working with Gertrude.

When we'd cleared the clinic and put the dogs in the car, I looked at my partner. "Any idea what to do next?"

"My gut always tells me to follow the money. When something is wrong, money is almost always at the bottom of it."

"Who or what is the money we should follow?" There was Fenway and his development company, for one. But Tinkie surprised me.

"Julian Dickerson. That's who we're going to investigate this morning." She pulled out her phone. "In fact, we're going to engage a rock star of an investigator."

"Cece Dee Falcon, right?"

"Cece has all the resources of a news organization. She can find more info in data banks than we can by asking and hoping people tell the truth."

Tinkie was right. And I hadn't really asked Coleman to dig for anything specific for us—other than looking into Garwool's past. Maybe a trip to the local library and a call to Cece were the next steps. The library first. We were in Nixville, and now was the time to pursue the leads we could find here.

Tilly, who had some pull with the head librarian, called ahead for us and so we were allowed to take Chablis, Sweetie Pie, and Avalon into the office. Our dogs were well-behaved and settled down on a rug like little sardines in a can. In under two minutes they were all fast asleep. Tinkie and I were left to our own devices to dig up what we could.

Frasier Bland was the head librarian, and he brought me a stack of genealogy books when I asked about the Dickerson family. But even better, he took some time to talk to me while Tinkie researched Rutherford Mace and the wrestling mecca he'd built.

Before long, I was deep in the tangled web of family ties and connections as I tried to figure out if Julian Dickerson played a role in the missing dogs. Family history might not be the best avenue to stroll down, but I had asked Budgie to check on criminal records, etc. Nothing. Dickerson was a highly regarded criminal lawyer who had a big practice in Jackson. He did some pro bono work in Sunflower County for a couple of charities—foster kids and cancer research. I wondered what the story there might be. I found it interesting to search out what charities—and why—touched the hearts of some people.

I learned that Julian had never married. He had no siblings, and he'd inherited money and land in Nixville from his parents. His adopted parents. They had taken him in as a three-year-old when his biological parents disappeared from the scene. The adoption was closed, and there was no indication of who his birth parents had been. He'd suddenly become the ward—and then the adopted son—of Boice and Janey Dickerson. The adoption had been so private, it seemed that few people in Nixville were even aware he was adopted.

I heard an exclamation of surprise from Frasier, and I looked up and realized I'd lost an hour going down the rabbit hole of what looked like a fairy-tale adoption. I'd learned nothing of significance, but I'd wasted an hour.

"Where did this dog come from?" Frasier asked—and he was directing the question to me.

I stood up and went into his office. For a moment I thought

my eyes were wonky. There were four dogs sleeping on the rug. The extra dog was a little reddish-blond-and-buff-colored scruffy dog with legs a mile long. She was snoring, pressed close against Sweetie Pie's stomach.

"Where did she come from?" Frasier repeated.

"I don't know." And I really didn't. She hadn't come in with us. Or any other client that Frasier could remember. "Look, there's something taped to her collar." I bent down and removed the note that had been attached.

"My name is Pumpkin. I'm heartworm negative, have had all my shots, and I am a very naughty dog. My mama can't keep me because everyone wants to kill me. Please let me live with you."

"Where did this dog come from?" I was panicking. I had acquired a second dog only a few days ago. I sure didn't need a third one, and I didn't need a naughty puppy, either.

"Let me take a look," Frasier said. When he leaned down to pick Pumpkin up, she snapped and growled, then burrowed deeper into Sweetie Pie's comforting belly.

"You need to do something with that dog before she bites a library patron," Frasier said.

Suddenly the extra dog was my problem. "She isn't mine. I don't know where she came from." I was too loud, and Tinkie heard me and came over.

"What's going on?" she asked.

I pointed to the dog. "This is Pumpkin. She just showed up like an apport. Now Frasier says she's mine."

"I let you bring your dogs in here and now you've got a ringer to deal with." Frasier looked too jovial to be angry. No, he was having fun with my predicament.

"She's really cute!" Tinkie knelt down to pet her, and Pumpkin wiggled with delight.

"She tried to bite me," Frasier told her.

"I wonder why." Tinkie was droll and funny. We all laughed, but it didn't resolve the issue of the dog.

"I don't need three dogs," I whispered to Tinkie.

"No worries! I have a plan."

"What kind of plan?"

"Look at that Pumpkin dog. She would make the perfect bride."

"Bride? What in the Sam Hill are you talking about?" Tinkie was the logical partner, but sometimes I couldn't follow her line of thinking.

"One word. Roscoe. It's like Frankenstein and his bride! A match made in heaven. Roscoe and Pumpkin, sitting in a tree, k-i-s-s-i-n-g!" Tinkie sang the ditty from our childhoods.

And I didn't argue, because she was a hundred percent right. All we had to do was get Harold to agree.

27

I accepted we wouldn't leave the library without Pumpkin, but the dogs were asleep again, and Tinkie and I had to finish our research. She was pouring over the history of wrestling in Nixville and the number of celebrity wrestlers who'd been trained at the place Rutherford Mace owned. I was buried in the tortured history of the Dickersons.

The Dickerson family had deep roots in Mississippi. Joshua Dickerson had served as one of the first appointed federal judges in the state. The family had always had a close connection with the law. It was no shock that Julian had pursued a legal career. But had he taken his sharp mind and legal training one step beyond the law? That's what I needed to find out.

In the strange way of library research, I found myself going through an old Nixville High School annual. I was a sucker for the past, and the memories any yearbook kicked up in me. There were photos of the Nixville band with drum majorettes and flag twirlers. I smiled at the photos of Most Popular, Most Likely to Succeed, Most Athletic of Julian's senior class. He was crowned Mr. Nixville High School with his pretty female contemporary, Carrie Wells. They did make an attractive couple.

Technically, I was waiting for Tinkie to finish up. I'd gone down the genealogy rabbit hole and found nothing worthwhile, but Tinkie was still poring over a computer screen and some books. She seemed to be finding something. I almost went over, but I decided not to interrupt. I flipped another page of the annual and stopped. There was a Beta Club photo of Julian Dickerson and a handsome young man with a cocky smile. It took me a minute to realize it was Rutherford Mace.

Mace wasn't named in the photo of the group taken for the Beta Club, but I knew it was him. And he was chummy with Julian. Very chummy. That brought up some important questions for me.

When I looked up, Tinkie was putting away her research materials. She gave me a thumbs-up to indicate she'd found something of interest.

I photocopied some pages from the annual and some other interesting data I found, returning all the materials to the place where I'd gotten them. I held on to the yearbook. I had some things to discuss with my partner.

The friendship between Dickerson and Mace was perfectly legal, but why hadn't Julian mentioned it when I'd talked to him? Was he hiding this, or was it just an oversight? In the annual photo, they looked like close friends, but high school was far in the past for all of us. Things changed, especially friendships. Still, it was worth checking out. And I lucked upon another familiar face in the Beta Club photo. Tom Terrell, the police officer. He was standing beside Julian and a pretty young woman who wasn't identified.

When Tinkie finished putting away her research material, I signaled her over to look at the annual. She instantly saw the same thing—Dickerson and Mace, yukking it up.

"Good find, Sarah Booth. That's a link we need to pursue." She nodded with a grin. "And I found out some stuff about Mace, too."

"What's that?" I asked.

"Mace and Dickerson are best friends. Or they were. And that friendship involved some trouble with the law."

That piqued my interest. "What kind of trouble?"

"Kid stuff, mostly. Egging a teacher's house, stealing toilet paper from the public schools and courthouse to roll yards. Nothing terrible that I could find, but in every instance, Mace stepped up and took the blame."

She was right. When I took a look at her research, it seemed Mace and Dickerson were hellions in high school. Boys with a penchant for what I termed pranks, but activities that could have resulted in an arrest. A record, even as a juvenile, could have gravely impacted Dickerson's future. And each time they'd pulled a stunt, Mace had taken the blame. What did it mean? And did it really even matter to the case of the missing dogs?

"Mace and Dickerson seemed to go to great pains to smother this information," Tinkie said.

"Why would this be a secret?" I asked.

"No clue. But that's the very reason we should look into it," she said. "Where there's smoke, there's almost always fire."

"I wonder who would be the more forthcoming with facts," I said, "Mace or Julian Dickerson?"

"Good question. Mace is local, though, so that's the place to start."

"Better idea—let's start with the deputy, Tom Terrell. He's a classmate. Maybe he knows the scoop."

"I'd trust him a lot more than Mace or Dickerson," Tinkie said, expressing my exact thought. "Let's head over there."

"Let's call first. I don't want to run into Garwool or the mayor. I'm pretty sure they both hate our guts by now."

"Should we ask Coleman or even Harold to do it?" Tinkie asked.

"No, let's do it ourselves. If we don't get any satisfaction, we can call in reinforcements."

I dialed the police department, and when Tom answered, I asked if he could meet us for coffee. He was more than glad to get out of the office for a little while. "Maybelline's is a great place for coffee and pie," he suggested.

It was a five-minute drive, and I parked around behind the café just to keep the Nosey Parkers from gossiping. I'd come to view Nixville as a small town where eyes were everywhere. Nixville didn't need the controversial CCTV cameras. The residents were constantly watching. To that end, I was glad to keep as low a profile as I could manage.

We'd just sat down at a table when Tom arrived. He slid into a chair and held up one finger, then two. He made a motion circling the table and then held up three fingers.

"Code?" Tinkie asked.

"One for coffee, and two for apple pie. It's the best pie you'll ever eat. Three, indicating how many servings. I hope you don't mind that I ordered for you."

I didn't mind—apple pie sounded fortifying. It might give me the energy to keep after this case. Tinkie had other ideas, though.

"I don't know that this could be the best pie. We have Millie's Café in Zinnia," Tinkie said, stoutly defensive of our friend, who ran it. "Millie's pies are the best I've ever eaten."

"Not taking a thing away from Ms. Roberts," Tom said, "but the apple pie here is really the best. Hands down."

Tom didn't lie. On a scale of best pies, Millie made a coconut cream pie and a lemon meringue pie that no one could beat. But the apple pie in Maybelline's was to die for.

I'd been tempted to "borrow" the high school annual from the library, but I hadn't done it. I was afraid my mama would rise from the grave to scold me. Libraries were sacred to her. Even a temporary theft of reference material was unforgivable. I'd have to rely on the copies I made and the photos I took with my phone.

We'd almost finished our delicious pie—it was really so good no one wanted to talk—before I broached the subject of Mace and Dickerson. Tom was sipping his coffee, waiting for me to begin. I brought out the photocopied page of the school annual and handed it to him. "What do you know about Rutherford Mace and Julian Dickerson?"

"We all went to high school together. Mace became a successful television wrestler who now has a thriving business training other wrestlers. Dickerson went to law school and has a high-end criminal-law practice in Jackson." He shrugged. "They were good friends in high school, but we've drifted apart."

"Are they related?" I asked.

He looked at me for a long moment. "I've heard rumors, but I think it was only because they were two peas in a pod. If you said 'Rutherford,' look behind him and Dickerson was right there."

It was strange. In a small town, this kind of gossip would be well-known. "Just rumors?"

He wiped his mouth with a paper napkin. "Everyone in town loved Boise and Janey Dickerson. When they said they'd adopted a baby boy, folks were overjoyed for them, and from what I can tell, Julian has delivered for them. He was a standout academically and athletically, and he's now a big-time lawyer. They would be very proud."

I noticed the past tense. "What happened to them?"

"Car accident," he said. "It was a real tragedy. Julian was in law school at Ole Miss and, as I understand it, they were driving up to Oxford to meet him for a tailgate at the homecoming football game. It was terrible."

I swallowed the familiar emotion that rose in my throat. Loss was never easy, and I felt for Julian. But I still had questions to ask.

"Would you say Julian is a good guy?"

"Why do you ask?" Tom countered.

"I don't know." It was the truth. "There's something going on with these dogs. And if there is a connection between the two men, it might help explain some of this."

"I don't understand how." Tom wasn't dense, but he didn't see how the connection would work. I wasn't sure I did, either.

When we'd first taken the case, it had seemed that Rutherford Mace might be involved in a dog-theft ring and also dogfighting. Was it possible someone was attempting to set Mace up for trouble? Someone who might want revenge for some unknown act? I was stretching. A long stretch. But who had taken Jezebel? How had she been returned to Zinnia? And where was Cupcake? The latter question was the most important.

"You never answered her question," Tinkie said. "Do you view Julian as a good guy?"

Tom sighed. "He's a criminal defense lawyer. I'm a police officer. We take different approaches to crime. He's smart, and he uses every advantage to his favor. I don't care for some of his tactics, but isn't that what he's paid to do? In that regard, he's a very good guy."

Yet again, I was impressed with Tom Terrell and his balanced outlook. He embodied many of the qualities I valued in Coleman. He probably detested Julian Dickerson for his legal work, but Tom was able to step back and understand that advocacy for a client made the system work. The justice system was built on the principle that every person charged deserved a competent legal defense. The rich ones could afford competency and so much more.

"And what about Garwool? Is there a connection to him?" I was just covering all my bases.

"None that I know of, but his fiancée, Penelope Fenway, dated Julian and Mace at different times. It was something of a town scandal until Garwool put an engagement ring on her finger. The talk died down, and to be fair, Penelope dated Julian when he was going to Ole Miss and she was still in high school. It wasn't serious."

"What about Mace? Did they date long?"

"I don't believe that was serious, either." He tapped a finger on his chin. "But it seems she also dated Zotto. Now I don't know this for certain, but I've heard talk. You can check it out."

"Seems like Penelope gets around in the dating world." I didn't say that she was lucky her daddy's money offered her some protection, since she appeared to dabble with criminals and kingpins. But it was a possible lead that I needed to check.

"Penelope doesn't have a mean bone in her body," Tom said. "Folks take advantage of her. Her family has money and she's an easy mark."

One of the oldest stories in the world. And it was possible the woman was merely a pawn in a game played by the men around her. Garwool had certainly feathered his nest by asking her to marry him.

28

It was time for us to take action.

"I think we should talk to Penelope," Tinkie said softly.

I was in total agreement. "Does Penelope work?" I asked Tom.

He snorted with laugher. "That girl has never worked a day in her life. She's probably at home or maybe at the gym. She works out a lot."

"Does she have any dogs?" I asked.

Tom shook his head. "She's not really a dog person. She's a little on the . . . froufrou side."

"Thanks, Tom."

"Good luck. I hope you get some information."

We stepped out into the sun and Tinkie gave me a thumbs-up. "There's only one gym in Nixville, so she shouldn't be hard to find."

"I'm going to drop you off at the gym. Keep her busy. I'm going to her place to see if I can hear a dog." My intention went a little further than that. I would hear the dog, see it, then grab it. It was the biggest reason I didn't want Tinkie with me. She had a position in society. I didn't. If I got caught stealing the dog, it wouldn't impact my social life.

"You think she has Cupcake?" Tinkie was excited at the thought.

"Maybe. It doesn't hurt to check."

I pulled up to the gym and saw a red-haired woman on an elliptical machine in the front window. She was very fit and pounding away, and I suspected that might be Penelope. I watched as Tinkie went in, talked to the receptionist at the desk, and then walked to the elliptical machine. The woman stopped, got down, and motioned Tinkie away from the window. Tinkie gave me a subtle thumbs-up and I was out of there. I had to make my time count.

I called city hall to be sure the mayor was in his office, and then I went to his home. I parked down the street and slipped through the hedges until I made it into the backyard. There was no sign of a dog—no food or water dishes. No poop. I was about to accept defeat when I saw someone coming toward the back door. Damn! The mayor had come home, and I was trespassing in his yard.

I ducked down behind a thick holly bush and held my breath. The back door opened—I couldn't see who opened it—and a fluff of fur came running out into the yard. The little dog sniffed around and peed. The person had closed the back door, and I crept closer. It looked like it could be Cupcake. I pulled up the photo of the dog on my phone and tried to compare. But this little dog had been recently shaved and was wearing a pink tutu. Was it the same one? I couldn't be certain. And I sure didn't want to accuse the mayor of being a dog thief unless I was one hundred percent certain.

The pup turned away from me to do her business—the

little tutu shimmering in the breeze. I crept closer, looking for a way to really identify the dog. Cupcake was a cute little mutt with unruly fur and an underbite. I whistled softly.

The dog whipped around and came after me, barking to beat the band. I wasn't afraid of being bitten—poor little thing had such a savage underbite—but I was concerned that the dog would rouse the mayor, who would come out and catch me red-handed. But I had to get a photo of the dog, so I could compare. If Tinkie said it was Cupcake, I'd come back and get the dog.

Someone had put little pink bows above the dog's ears, which would be an insult to every canine I'd ever known. But this was a prissy dog. She came up to me, growling and having a fit. I snapped the picture showing her underbite. When I had the shot, I backed to the fence, scaled over it, and hid in the thick bushes until I was sure I could get back to the car without alerting the mayor. First I'd show Tinkie and then Squatty. If they agreed it was Cupcake, our work on this case would be done.

Or would it?

Would I be able to ignore the fact that a dogfighting ring might be working in Sunflower County? No. I could not. And neither would Tinkie. Or Harold. Or Coleman. Just because these pups we cared about were safe didn't mean we could walk away from the torture or maiming of other living creatures. Even if taking on the people who did such things was dangerous.

The little dog barked hysterically, and I heard the back door open. I peered through a knot hole in the privacy fence and watched as Fenway came out the back door.

"Shut up, you little piece of crap." He yelled at the dog. "Shut up!"

I thought for a minute he might rush into the yard and hurt the puppy, but he didn't. And it was a good thing he didn't, because I could scale the fence lickety-split and I would teach him a hard lesson about hurting defenseless creatures. I didn't much like him, anyway. I was about to leave my post at the fence when the back door of the house opened and Ellis Adams came out. He glanced at the dog, but otherwise ignored it.

The mayor picked up the dog and took her back inside, moving Ellis inside with them. The door closed and there was nothing left to see. It was cold out, and I was relieved they were keeping the dog inside. Cupcake wasn't a tough hound—she was eight pounds of fuzz and dazzle.

I slowly made my way back to the road and to my car. Tinkie would be waiting for me.

When I got back to the gym, I found that Penelope was gone. Tinkie eyed a rowing machine that looked like a torture device. I showed her the photos. She took her time and really studied them.

"That looks like Cupcake, doesn't it?" I was impatient.

"It does. What are we going to do?"

"Ellis was at the mayor's house when the dog came outside. Ellis saw the dog, so I can only conclude he is involved in snatching Cupcake and working with Fenway on his devious plots. If that dog is his grandmother's pet, you would think he'd say something." I really was ready to knock a knot on Ellis's pinhead. He actions made no sense to me.

"If this is Cupcake and Ellis knew where the dog was, will you tell Squatty?"

"Absolutely." I didn't hesitate. "She deserves to know who her kin values. He's mooching off her, and if he stole her dog . . . I'd completely disinherit him."

"Then let's talk to her."

"I'm going to drop you off at Squatty's with the photos so you can get a positive ID on the dog. I need to go back to the mayor's house. If Squatty says it's Cupcake, text me."

"What are you planning?" Tinkie knew me too well. She took my phone and sent the photos I'd taken of the dog to her phone so she had them.

"I need to see if I can find out what Ellis and Fenway are up to."

"And how are you going to do that?" Tinkie was the practical one.

I didn't have a lot of tricks up my sleeve, but I figured reconnaissance was one option. I could sneak back into the yard and try spying through some windows. Or I could knock on the door and barge in, hoping to find something useful. Snooping was probably the better option.

"I'll just see what I can find. If Zotto or Rutherford Mace shows up there, too, we'll have some answers."

"You'll be able to draw some conclusions, but unless they talk to us, we don't have any proof."

She was right. "Maybe I can change that. Maybe I'll see or hear something that we can take to Coleman." There was no point in trying to talk to Garwool. He was never going to go against Fenway.

"Okay. Drop me off." Tinkie checked her watch. "But if you aren't back in an hour, I'm calling Coleman."

"I'll keep that in mind." I pulled up at Squatty's and let her out. When she was safely in the house, I headed back to Fenway's and a hiding spot in the bushes in the backyard. Maybe I'd learn something worthwhile. The one thing I could do was make sure no one from the Fenway house left with that little dog. I hadn't spoken my concern out loud to Tinkie, but the possibility that Cupcake—if that was indeed Cupcake— would disappear again was a knot of worry in my gut. How I might stop that from happening wasn't clear in my mind. Calling the police wouldn't do any good, but I would cross that bridge when I came to it.

I shifted into the backyard, moving from clump of shrubbery to bush or tree, taking care that no one in the house was looking outside to discover me. At last, I found a great hiding place in a clump of bottlebrush trees where I had an excellent view through the patio doors and into the house. The little blond dog pranced around the den, ignored by the humans who walked back and forth in front of the window. I recognized Fenway and Penelope. Ellis had disappeared.

I checked my watch—I didn't want to frighten Tinkie by running late to pick her up, but it looked like I was going to have to wait. I settled into a comfortable position and watched. Would I get a lucky break and see something that gave me answers?

I felt a gentle tap on my shoulder. It scared me so bad I whipped around to find myself staring into the baby blues of Betty White. Her hair, as always, was perfect and she smiled.

"I used to loooove washing dishes! In Minnesota, the whole family'd get together and wash dishes. Even Uncle Gustav, after the giant Swiss Army Knife accident, learned to dry dishes with his feet. We used to laugh and carry on and have such a happy time."

I recognized the quote from one of my favorite episodes of *The Golden Girls.* "Jitty, stop it! You're no Rose Nylund."

"I beg to differ. I'm just as sweet and innocent and naïve as Rose."

I rolled my eyes. "Can't you see I'm trying to concentrate on watching this house?"

"I can see that you're sitting on your butt under a bush on a very cold day. How smart is that? Even Blanche is smarter than you."

"I don't have time for your foolishness now. Why are you here?" She wouldn't tell me, but I asked anyway. Then I had a hunch. "Betty White was a huge animal lover. She left over three hundred thousand dollars to animal charities when she died. Are you here to help me get that dog?" Maybe Jitty would create a distraction. That would be superb.

My phone dinged and I grabbed it. Sure enough, it was Tinkie with the news I was waiting to hear. "Squatty says that *is* Cupcake," Tinkie texted. "She'll bring me to help you grab the dog."

That wasn't what I wanted to happen. "Stay there," I texted back. "I've got this under control."

"It's rude to play on your phone when someone is trying to talk to you," Jitty/Betty/Rose blurted out.

I waved her to go away, to no avail. She was on me like beggar's lice on cotton socks. "Not now."

"Who are you talking to?" Tinkie asked in her next text. She'd obviously overheard my side of the conversation with Jitty/Rose.

"Oh, no one. Just a demon who is deviling me," I answered her, glaring at Jitty, who patted her blond hair and twinkled her blue eyes at me. She did look and act just like Betty White.

"Are you losing it, Sarah Booth?" Tinkie asked in a text with too many exclamation points.

"No. I'm just watching Cupcake through the patio doors. She's in the den in a wretched pink tutu. Who would put a dog in a pink tutu?" My goal was to distract Tinkie with details.

"Sarah Booth, you sound . . . insane." She added a stupid smiley face.

Tinkie wasn't lying. I did sound nuts. But I snapped another photo and sent it to her so she could see the ridiculous getup they'd put the dog in.

"Oh, that is a crime," Tinkie wrote. "I stand corrected. But Squatty wants to come over there and confront the mayor about having her dog."

"Talk her out of it—and you stay clear of here, too. I have a plan. I'll get Cupcake and meet you at Squatty's. Wait there for me. Promise."

"I'm not certain I can convince Squatty not to storm the mayor's house." The texts were flying fast and furious.

"Try. I'll stand a better chance of getting the dog if I'm working alone. If I get in trouble, you and Squatty can rescue me. Now I have to go." Jitty was giving me a death stare, and someone in the den opened the back door to let Cupcake out into the yard. Now was my chance. I gathered myself.

"Wait!" Betty White held up a hand. "Don't do that. It's a crime."

"I know it's a crime. Now, be quiet. I'm going to nab that dog and take her back to Squatty."

"We'll be arrested!"

"No, you won't." Lord, Jitty was a trial today.

"I've never been in jail. I won't make it. They always prey on the weak and innocent. The others will taunt me for trying to excel at my work in the laundry. I'll fall in with a bad crowd whose leader looks like Ethel Merman. And I'll be forced to engineer a daring prison break using my laundry cart. From that time on, I won't know a moment's peace. I'll scar my fingerprints with battery acid and run from town to town, taking jobs that people who got bad grades in school have. And then one day, they'll find me, holed up in a little shack in the Louisiana bayou. And a sheriff named Bull will call my name out over a megaphone, and when I make a run for it, he'll riddle my body with bullets! Oh, please don't let them take me downtown! I want to live! I want to live!"

I stood up in the crowded confines of the bushes. "Shut up, Rose." I had to stop the gush of confusion Jitty was spewing. I had to grab Cupcake and beat it the hell out of Dodge.

The little dog came prancing toward my hiding place. No one was in the back window. The coast seemed clear. I darted out of the bushes, ignoring Jitty's wails, and scooped Cupcake into my arms. Without even slowing down I used a trumpet vine for a toehold to vault over the back fence. Five minutes later I was in my car headed for Squatty's house and the reunion of pupster and owner.

I was about to heave a sigh of relief when I realized that Rose Nylund was in the passenger seat of my car. Jitty had followed me. She was impossible to shake, because she was a ghost and could just appear. She didn't walk, she glided most of the time. And teleported. She had all the good tricks!

"You have to leave," I told her. "Tinkie already thinks I'm losing my mind. If she sees me talking to you, she is going to have me committed. Then I can never, ever get pregnant and you will never have an heir to haunt."

"Coleman can do his business in an asylum as easily as he can at Dahlia House." Jitty, still portraying Rose, smirked at me. "That man has plenty of stamina and sex appeal. It's a good thing Blanche isn't here. She'd show him a really good time."

"No one gets to show Coleman anything." Jitty was getting under my skin. She was good at that, if nothing else.

"You have a jealous boner for that man, don't you?" Rose smiled so sweetly at me.

I didn't want to get into the terminology of *boner* with Rose—or Jitty. It was a self-defeating argument that she would pretend to misunderstand. Just so she could drive me crazy. Rose might be naïve, but Jitty was a devil.

"You have to get out of the car," I said to her.

"It's moving." Rose gave me a look like I was feeble-minded. "I can't jump out of a moving car."

I whipped to the side of the road and stopped. Little Cupcake almost lost her balance on the seat, but she recovered. "Get out, Jitty."

"If I have to call Dorothy, you'll be sorry."

She was right. Bea Arthur could put the fear of god in me. "Out. Bring on Dorothy, Blanche, and Sophia. Do your worst. Just get out and let me take Cupcake to her owner. You love dogs. Help me out."

"I do love dogs. And for that reason, I'm out of here."

Jitty snapped her fingers and five little dog treats appeared in the air and fell onto the seat with Cupcake. Whatever they were, she scarfed them up. And then Jitty was gone. I put the car in gear and drove to Squatty's.

29

I'd just pulled up to Squatty's when my cell phone buzzed. It was Tom Terrell. "What's up?" I asked as I put the car in park but left it running so the heater was working.

"Did you steal a dog from Fenway's backyard?"

The direct question left me flustered for a split second. "Of course not. I'm trying to find stolen dogs. Why would I steal one?"

"Don't apply logic to this situation. Just tell me the truth. I want to help you."

For some reason, I believed he wanted to help. "Fenway had Cupcake. I did snatch her and I'm taking her home to Squatty right now."

"Don't!"

He was so emphatic he stopped me in my tracks. "Why not?"

"Garwool is on his way over to Squatty's to see if she has the dog. Scram! Right now. Take that dog and drive away. Tell Squatty to act like she doesn't know where Cupcake is."

"What is going on?" I didn't understand how Fenway or Garwool would have the nerve to try to intimidate Squatty when they were the ones who'd been in possession of a stolen canine.

"Don't ask questions. Just clear out of town right now."

I leaned on the horn and watched for Squatty's front door to open. She and Tinkie came boiling out of the house. "Lock the front door!" I ordered them and then waved them into the car. Squatty had hurled herself at Cupcake. She pulled the little dog to her and let out a wail of joy. "My baby!"

"Close the door," I told her. We didn't have time for a re-union. Not now. She'd barely gotten her foot in the car when I took off. And just in time. I could see the patrol cruiser headed for Squatty's house. I turned my attention to my phone and spoke to the police officer.

"Tom, we made our escape. I'm taking Squatty and Cup-cake to Zinnia to hide out."

"Do me a favor and pick up Tilly and Jezebel, too. Just take both ladies and their dogs and hide them for a while. Until I can figure out what Garwool and Fenway are up to."

It was good to know we had an officer of the law helping us out. "Do you have any idea what Garwool and Fenway hope to accomplish by terrorizing two older women and stealing their pets?"

"I do."

"Do tell! I'm putting you on speaker."

"Get Tilly and do it fast," Tom said. "She called the *Com-mercial Appeal* in Memphis and has given an interview accus-ing Fenway and Garwool of some pretty evil deeds. They are furious."

I had to glory in Tilly's spunk. She had her dog back, but

she wasn't backing down. The world needed more people like her. She was a-okay in my book!

"She accused Fenway and Garwool of misappropriation of funds. I heard them yelling at each other in the mayor's office. Fenway blames Garwool, and vice versa."

"Did they say anything about dogfighting rings?" I asked.

"No, but Tilly did. She had some printed information about how some members of the Nixville aldermen and also members of the state legislature are involved in dogfighting."

Oh, lord. Tilly was going to get herself killed. I whipped the car around a corner and stopped in front of Tilly's house.

"I'll get her," Tinkie volunteered.

"Be fast," I urged her as I kept an eye on the rearview mirror. Any minute now Garwool might pull up behind us. I didn't trust him not to plug us in the back—especially if he thought Tilly was in the vehicle. I could see where she'd earned the police chief's spleen.

Tinkie—who'd chosen the cutest little witchy boots ever instead of her normal four-inch stilettos—ran up the sidewalk and to the front door. When she pounded, it was loud enough to wake the dead. Tilly came to the door, Jezebel at her knee. When she saw Tinkie, she threw the door open. "Come in!"

Tinkie put a hand on her elbow. "Come with me. Right now. I'll explain in the car. Bring Jezebel."

Tilly must have sensed the panic just beneath Tinkie's words, because she didn't resist. She stepped onto the porch, locked the door, and hustled with Tinkie back to the car. As soon as they were in the back seat, I stepped on the gas. And just in the nick of time. I saw the cruiser coming toward us.

"Duck! Everyone in the back seat duck now!"

We passed the cruiser and kept going at a steady pace, careful not to speed. When I turned the corner, though, and the cruiser was out of sight, I pressed the gas pedal hard. In a matter of moments, we were passing the city limits of Nixville.

"Where are we going?" Tilly asked.

I didn't have an answer. The safest place was probably Dahlia House. Especially once Coleman got there. There were plenty of guest rooms, and the dogs were always welcome. "Why don't we go to my house? You can stay there until we figure out what's going on with Garwool and Fenway."

"Those two stole my dog," Squatty said. "They need to pay."

Nixville was in the rearview mirror and we were out in the open land of the barren cotton fields. It was too early in the year for the fields to be planted. And it occurred to me that the vista I saw might soon be fading from existence. Climate change was taking a toll on farmers all over the world, and the Mississippi Delta was no exception. But it wasn't climate I needed to talk about. "I hate to have to tell you this, Squatty, but Ellis was at the Fenway house. He knew Cupcake was there."

Squatty's face settled into a mask of fury. "Are you sure?" she asked.

"I saw him. I have photos." I wasn't going to sugarcoat the truth. Something was wrong with Ellis. He'd betrayed his grandmother and a little dog who clearly cared for him. In my opinion, he deserved what he was going to get.

"He is dead to me. I need to go home so I can throw all of his belongings out into the street. I put him out of the house several days ago, but some of his things are still there. And I'm telling him that he's disinherited. I'll leave everything to a dog charity."

I didn't blame her, but now wasn't the time for revenge. "Let's make sure the dogs are safe and then we can fight over what to do to Ellis."

"We need toiletries and some clean clothes," Tilly said. "If we're going to spend the night with you, we need some things."

"Whatever you need that I don't have at Dahlia House, I promise to pick up at the store for you. We just can't go back to Nixville right now. Not when Garwool and Fenway are looking for both of you, and you especially, Tilly. You grabbed 'em by the short hairs with that interview and they want to hurt you now."

"I didn't do anything wrong. I alerted a newspaper to what I suspected Fenway and Garwool are up to. That's all."

"What did you tell the newspaper?" Tinkie asked. We were halfway to Zinnia.

"I told them that Garwool and Fenway were running a dogfighting ring."

I kept my dismay to myself. "Can you prove that allegation?"

"I can," Tilly said. "I have photos and receipts."

As soon as we got to Dahlia House, I'd make sure she told me about her evidence. If there was enough, Coleman could charge Fenway and Garwool with something. Probably lots of somethings. If they were involved in a dogfighting ring, I would do my level best to put them "under the jail," as Aunt Loulane used to say.

At last, I turned down the long driveway lined with sycamore trees that led to my home. My mind had turned to what I might make for dinner, since we had guests that I hadn't anticipated. Of course, we could always go to Millie's Café, which sounded like the perfect solution.

But as I drew closer to the old plantation, my heart thudded to my feet. The front door was open and I could see flames licking inside the doorway. Someone had set fire to Dahlia House.

"Sarah Booth!" Tinkie pointed. "Where are Sweetie Pie, Chablis, and Avalon?"

"Harold has them." I said it with such relief.

Tinkie whipped out her phone and called the fire department and Oscar. "Call Coleman and tell him to come home," she whispered to her husband.

I parked back from the house and got out. The flames were licking at the doorframe, but they hadn't caught the carpet or coatrack in the foyer. I knew what I had to do. I rushed to the side of the house and got the hose. In a matter of minutes, I had the flames doused, and a lot to think about. Mostly, I was thinking about Gertrude.

30

There was little damage to Dahlia House—a burned place on the doorframe where the flames had licked up the wood, and some scarring on the oak floor. Nothing that couldn't be repaired and covered up. Except covering it up wouldn't change the fact that it had happened. I would not forget. Someone had set fire to my family home. And I think I knew who.

I fought back nausea while pretending hard not to be upset. Going to pieces wouldn't help anything right now. Later, when Coleman was on the scene to hold me, I would weep at the damage to my home. And then I would plot my revenge. I would make Gertrude pay. All of the mean stuff she'd done to me and the people I loved—that bill was coming due. And sooner rather than later.

Tinkie made some coffee and helped Tilly and Squatty settle into guest rooms. She called Harold, who brought the pups home and took a look at the fire damage.

"It could be worse, Sarah Booth. I know that's no consolation, but this can all be repaired and no one will ever know."

"No one except me."

He put his arm around me. "I know what you're saying. It's a violation. I get it. You'll find Gertrude—or whoever did this—and Coleman will put them in jail. Then you'll feel better."

Harold was right. His calm way of evaluating the situation did made me feel better. And the important thing was that none of the animals were hurt. Pluto finally came up from the shrubs in front of the house. He lounged on the front porch by the rocker, where Poe had settled. He'd clearly been through a trauma, but he was physically fine.

Avalon, Roscoe, Cupcake, Pumpkin, and Jezebel were having the time of their lives with Sweetie Pie and Chablis. They raced through the barn, around the yard, in the back door, and out the front. It seemed to me Roscoe had developed a bit of a crush on Pumpkin. I watched him prance up to the gangly fuzz-faced pup, drop into that playful pose where his butt was in the air, and then nudge her with his snout. She took off running and he was after her. The others joined in, with Pluto and Poe bringing up the rear. It soothed my heart to see the critters playing, unconcerned.

And the horses were safe in the pasture. My world was okay, but I no longer felt completely safe. Gertrude—or whoever had done this—had taken that away from me. But these feelings were temporary. I would feel safe again. I would not let that crazy woman take away my joy.

We'd settled on the front porch to sip our coffee when Coleman arrived. His brow was knotted in anger as he looked at the damage to the house. While he was friendly to my guests, he had safety precautions on his mind. He excused himself to get to work and reinstall the porch camera.

Coleman was pissed off—but he didn't show it. I could read the signs: the silence, the tense jaw, the way he hammered with precise power. He was furious. And it made me feel good that he cared so much. Tinkie and I could—and had—taken care of many things ourselves. But it was lovely to have Coleman, and also Oscar and Harold, care so much.

The ladies and I walked with Coleman and Harold to the barn to put cameras up there. Coleman had bought seven of them, to give coverage from all angles. My home was going to be a fortress. The cameras were controlled by our phones, and with the phones we could check on Dahlia House and the animals in real time. Hammering up the cameras did give me some peace and solace, but I'd feel a lot better when Gertrude was found. I was pretty certain she'd done the terrible deed, and it was well past time for her to be in jail and charged with a laundry list of crimes.

Yet I also knew that if she'd wanted to burn Dahlia House down, she could have set the fire in the parlor or the kitchen or even one of the bedrooms upstairs. She must have somehow had a key made to the house, and she'd had plenty of time to slip inside and do real damage if she'd chosen to do that. She hadn't wanted to burn the place down, she'd only wanted to terrify me. In that, she'd partially succeeded.

Once the cameras were up, Coleman pulled me aside. "Are you okay?"

I stepped into him, hugging him close. "I am now."

"I'm going to find Gertrude. I promise you."

I nodded against his chest. His tenderness was almost my undoing. "I know you will." Coleman, the Mississippi Bureau of Investigation, the state highway patrol, and numerous jurisdictions in Mississippi had been trying to snare Gertrude for nearly two years. All without success.

Coleman pulled me in so he could whisper in my ear. "When I find her, don't ask any questions about what happened to her."

If any other man said such a thing, I'd be worried. Coleman was furious, but he wasn't a fool. Coleman wouldn't break the law. Not even for me. And I loved him more for that. "What do you think Gertrude is really up to?"

"I wish I could be certain," he said. He and I had walked away from the house so we could speak privately. He was watching Tilly, Squatty, and Tinkie on the front porch as we talked. Tinkie had made drinks and was serving them. Harold walked up and was telling a story. The dogs were frisking about, and even Pluto, who was curled in one of the front porch rockers, seemed to be listening.

"We're going to Millie's Café for supper," I told Coleman. "But I want to talk to Tilly alone. She wrote an article for the newspaper and accused Garwool and Fenway of participating in dogfighting. I'm worried they might really hurt her."

"Does she have a death—"

"She says she has the proof." I couldn't help but wonder if she really did. What would the proof be?

"I don't know what Fenway is up to. Something nefarious, if I had to guess. I believe Garwool is assisting him. But at what?"

"Dogfighting?" I asked.

"I just don't see it," Coleman said. "Fenway is a businessman. He wants to make money. No doubt about that. Dogfighting isn't that lucrative."

"Gambling is lucrative," I said.

"Yes, you're right. Gambling is very lucrative, and with the internet, it opens up the world to would-be betters. But to bet on the life of a dog . . ." Even talking about it made Coleman mad. His blue eyes sparked flames. "They'll pay, Sarah Booth. I promise."

"I know they will. And Gertrude, too."

"What do Fenway, Garwool, and Gertrude hope to gain by this?" he asked, speaking as much to himself as to me.

"Money. Maybe a bigger slice of the gaming pie in the Delta." I was thinking of the Mississippi Gulf Coast, where gambling casinos were big business. Back in the day, when my folks had been growing up, the Dixie Mafia had run the gambling and prostitution businesses on the Gulf Coast. There had been local bars and dives where card games took place in the backroom and prostitutes could be hired by talking to the bartender.

When gambling was legalized in the state—even though at first it was only on floating casino barges docked offshore—it became clear that people had an appetite for games of chance. Money poured into the state. Coleman knew the history far better than I did. We had a casino near us in Tunica on the Mississippi River. But it was nothing compared to the coast, where the casinos had moved up on the land and were meccas of gaming, chance, and other vices.

Coleman stroked my hair and looked into my eyes. "Card games, betting on sports, those things don't bother me. Dog-and horse racing, cockfighting, dogfighting—the people who promote those activities need to be punished for cruelty."

How I loved this man. "I agree. I know some of the towns have benefitted from the casinos on the rivers and lakes in the interior, but unregulated gambling brings an element to the state that we don't really need."

Coleman wasn't the fun police, but wherever gambling arrived, there was always big money, drugs, and prostitution right behind. My uncle Crabtree had been a compulsive gambler. When he'd been caught, after losing the grocery money and the land payment, his wife and other family members had staged an intervention.

Uncle Crabtree had sworn off big bets, but he could never completely stop gambling. He told me one day when I was sitting on the front porch with him that a gambling man would always find something to bet on. "See those crows on the telephone line?" he asked.

When I nodded, he continued. "The one on the right. I'll bet you your allowance that it flies away before the other one leaves. If you win, I'll double your allowance."

It was more money than I could pass up, so I took the bet. He was right! And I lost my allowance that day, which was a grand lesson. I never developed the itch to lose good money on games of chance.

"Farmers have always been gamblers," Coleman said, practically reading my mind. "The weather is the biggest gamble of all time."

"Let's head to Millie's," I told him.

"Harold has volunteered to stay here with all the doggos," Coleman said. "We have the cameras up, but I think it would be a good plan to have a living, breathing human here just in case Gertrude comes back."

"But she could hurt Harold." I didn't trust Gertrude as far as I could throw her.

"DeWayne has agreed to come and stay with him. Oscar is going to meet us at Millie's."

Coleman had planned it all out, putting the safety of my beloved pets first. "DeWayne is a good friend. He loves the dogs, horses, and even the cat."

"But Poe gets on his nerves."

I had to laugh, because Poe did devil him. I'd seen the raven flying around DeWayne's head, trying to snatch clumps of hair. "Poe is a good lookout, though. He'll let DeWayne and Harold know if someone is on the property." He would, too. Poe was clever, and he loved me and Dahlia House.

"Let's go," Coleman said. "I'm eager to get to town, get some grub, and get back here to sleep. I need to make some phone calls tomorrow. I'm not going to give Fenway and Garwool a pass on this. I intend to find out what they're up to, and if it is illegal, as I suspect it is, they are going to pay a hefty price."

"I love it when you talk all badass lawman."

"Now, I hear some fried dill pickles calling my name! Put in an order for me, please. And hamburger steak smothered in onions."

"I can do that." I kissed his cheek and went to the front of Dahlia House to herd the women into my car so we could get some supper. Tomorrow, I could go to the grocery and get provisions for my guests.

31

Squatty and Tilly fell in love with Millie and Cece, who also showed up at the café, along with Tammy, who Tilly knew as Madame Tomeeka. Tilly and Tammy instantly fell into deep conversation, and they were thick as thieves at one corner of the table. Though I strove to hear their conversation, I couldn't make it out. Drat! I'd check later with Tammy to get the scoop.

I had a glimmer of hope that maybe Tammy would have an idea where Gertrude could be holed up. But while Tammy had strange and unusual talents, she couldn't always marshal them to a specific chore.

Even though we were under stress, we laughed and ate. When we were all members of the Clean Plate Club, we settled the tab and prepared to load up for the ride home. Millie had kindly made cardboard take-out cartons for all the dogs, and also for DeWayne and Harold.

Oscar had joined us, and he gently led Tinkie to his car

when we were done at the café. He left before us and took Tinkie to Dahlia House to retrieve Chablis while Coleman would drive Tilly, Squatty, and me. Tinkie was eager to get her pup and get back to Hilltop to see her beautiful little baby girl.

I took a moment and pulled Tammy aside. "Do you know anything about who is stealing dogs and why? Or where Gertrude is?"

"I need to scry for Gertrude," Tammy said. "I tried earlier, but it was inconclusive." She checked her watch, obviously eager to be somewhere else.

"Can you tell me anything?" I asked.

Tammy said she would get with me later on. She was strangely evasive, which only whetted my appetite for our chat. She would talk when she was good and ready—and not before.

At last Coleman handed me into the front seat and Squatty and Tilly into the back. "You have great friends," Squatty said to me as we drove through the falling dusk.

"I do. I'm very lucky."

"Sarah Booth is a good friend to others," Coleman said. "That's why she attracts people who know the value of friendship."

"Cupcake is my best friend," Squatty said.

"And Jezebel is mine," Tilly said.

Squatty sighed heavily. "I always thought that Ellis would be the fallback position for me, the family member who looked in on me periodically to make sure I was doing okay. He's my only grandchild. And as you know, the only family I have. But in good conscience, I can't trust him any longer. Even if he offered to be my advocate, I can't do it." She blinked rapidly and turned to look out the truck window. "It is difficult to get to the end of life and realize that nothing anchors you to the present, and certainly nothing to the future."

Though I kept my gaze out the front windshield, I felt a moment of sorrow for Squatty. Her closest living relative had betrayed her. That was a hard pill to swallow. Squatty had, ultimately, Cupcake as her family. If Ellis ended up in jail, the dog would be her sole companion. And Tilly was in much the same boat.

Dahlia House was our destination—we were only about four miles away. Silence had fallen over the car. Tilly and Squatty were in the back seat with the boxes of food. I was in the front seat with Coleman. Poe had been following us, but at the moment I didn't see him winging along beside the truck.

I heard a cawing in the sky, and I rolled down the window and leaned out, trying to find the raven in the gathering night. What was that rascal Poe up to? He was a smart bird with strong opinions.

I was looking west when a large black thing flew in the truck window—straight in the window and into the cab of the truck. It startled me to the point that I yelled and ducked down. Coleman grasped the wheel and turned sharply to the left, putting the car in a near spin—and just in time! The front windshield exploded, showering us all with glass. Poe flew out through the blasted front window, a black arrow headed down the highway.

"What the hell?" I said, struggling to sit up. Before I could look out, Coleman put his hand on my head and pushed me down again. "Tilly, Squatty, drop to the floorboard!" he ordered.

I could hear them scrabbling in the back seat as the rear

window shattered from another gunshot. Someone was shooting at us, and they weren't playing. They meant to harm us.

Coleman braked and turned the vehicle around. "Stay down!"

It was killing me not to look, but I did as he said because I didn't want to put anyone else at risk. And I wanted Coleman free to focus on his driving.

"Did you see who is shooting at us?" Tilly asked from the back seat.

"Stay down." Coleman's voice cracked like a whip. He'd cut the lights on the car, and in the gathering dark, we had a tiny bit of cover. But we had to find the shooter. Was it Gertrude or someone else?

Coleman had put the truck in motion, but hugging the floorboard like I was doing, I couldn't tell where we were headed. At last, I felt his hand on my shoulder. "Sit up," he whispered. "I need your help."

I eased into the seat with DeWayne's dinner still in my arms. Tilly and Squatty were traumatized, but they followed Coleman's instructions and stayed hunkered down on the floorboard. They were terrified, and rightly so.

"Who is doing this?" Tilly asked. Panic threaded her voice. "Why do they want to kill us?"

If only I had the answer, but I didn't. "The question is, which one of us are they really trying to kill?" I asked. "Is it one of you, me, or is Coleman the target?"

I had a sudden inspiration. "Ladies, is it possible all of this has nothing to do with dogs and everything to do with an inheritance, political power, family ties, or something else?"

"Not me," Tilly said instantly. "Nothing in my life has changed."

"Other than that scoundrel Ellis and whatever crazy ideas he may have come up with, I can't think of anything."

"No sudden income? No change in fortune?"

"No." They spoke in unison.

There was no point pressing the issue. I let it go. But in my black little heart, I knew that someone had a big debt to settle and I would be delighted to make them pay their tab. The goal right now, though, was to get home without getting shot or freezing to death.

We weren't far from Dahlia House, but Coleman made a U-turn in the middle of the highway and headed back on a farm-to-market road that cut across the county. As soon as he could pull over, he called DeWayne at Dahlia House and filled him in on what had happened.

Coleman was kind enough to put the call on speaker, and I was relieved to hear DeWayne say that everything at the farm had been quiet. The horses were fed and blanketed, and he and his girlfriend said they'd wait there until we came home.

I knew without asking that DeWayne and his girl were sitting on the front porch, bundled up in quilts and holding pump shotguns. Nobody had better show up to threaten the animals, or they would regret it deeply. "Thank you both," I said.

"By the way, thank you, Sarah Booth, for the cookies you left on the counter for us. I'm afraid we got into them. You may have to make some more," he said.

"Eat them," I replied. "Eat them all. Thank you for being there." I would have baked DeWayne a passel of cookies. And the truth was, I'd forgotten all about the tins of Valentine's Day cookies I'd worked so hard on before Jezebel had been stolen and Gertrude had returned to Sunflower County. Since that turn of events, I hadn't even thought of the cookies. It was just as well for DeWayne and his girlfriend to eat them while they were still crisp. I had six more days until Valentine's Day. I could bake plenty more, but I couldn't replace a single one of my critters.

Coleman coordinated his plans with DeWayne, who was going to catch Budgie, the other deputy, up on the plan. Once Coleman figured out a roundabout way back to Dahlia House, the lawmen were going to gather and prepare a trap. It wouldn't be the first trap that had been set—unsuccessfully in the past—to catch Gertrude. Somehow she'd evaded several well-planned attempts to bring her to justice.

"You should let Tinkie know about the shots," Coleman told me.

He was absolutely right. I decided to text her instead of calling. The cold coming in through the blown-out window was making my teeth chatter. That would only upset my partner. I texted her an upbeat message about the attack, making it clear we weren't harmed. I was aggravated about the truck windows, though. At least Coleman could park it in the barn until the windows were replaced.

Tinkie and Oscar offered to come help, but I gently dissuaded them. Maylin needed them. If Coleman and the deputies were going hunting tonight, I wanted Tinkie to be safely at home. What she didn't know wouldn't hurt her—but she might be mad at me for a good long while for leaving her out of the loop. It didn't matter. I'd take the heat because I loved her too much to put her in danger.

"Where are we going?" Tilly asked. She was still hunkered down, but she'd eased up by the front console.

"Back to my house. Just in a roundabout way."

"Who is this Gertrude woman and why does she hate you so much?" she asked.

"I wish I knew. The truth is, she's out of her mind."

"My ex-husband used to tell me that crazy people were dangerous, but they were a lot of fun in bed," Squatty said. "That's why we're divorced. He had a weird idea of fun."

For the first time since we'd been shot at, I laughed out loud. "I don't blame you, Squatty."

"I'm not trying to scare you, ladies. But I need to say this. Gertrude is a dangerous woman," Coleman told them. "I know you met her in Nixville. I know she seemed like a harmless older woman. We all wish we knew why she decided to hate Sarah Booth so much. Regardless, she will hurt you, especially if she thinks it will impact Sarah Booth."

"Do you think she was the one who took Jezebel and Cupcake?" Squatty asked.

"I do." I wanted them to grasp the seriousness of the situation. "Gertrude has hurt a lot of innocent people. She is very dangerous."

"And you think she's involved in the dog thefts?" Squatty asked.

"I do," Coleman said. "Though, why stealing your dogs would impact Sarah Booth doesn't make any sense."

"Because it put me in the right place to hire Sarah Booth," Tilly said. "Remember, I went to see Madame Tomeeka about Jezebel. And that's when Madame recommended Delaney Detective Agency. If you step back and look at it, you can clearly see how these parts fit together. Add to that the fact that I was in the Piggly Wiggly talking about how wonderful Jezebel is only a few hours before my dog went missing. Gertrude was in the store. She heard me talking. She even asked me what meat I used for Jezebel, and like a fool I told her. I'm pretty sure that's how she managed to trick her into getting a leash on her collar."

She was right. The theft of Jezebel led straight to the hiring of Tinkie and me. So that much at least made sense. Gertrude could have stolen the dog so Tilly would engage us. Then she stole Cupcake to add to the nightmare. But how was she involved with Mace, Dickerson, Zotto, Garwool, or Fenway? Yes, she'd worked for the mayor and the police chief at a B and B in Arkansas, but was there a deeper connection? That's what I had to find out—and quickly. We had the dogs back, but were more dogs in danger? Was Gertrude involved in gambling and also the drugs that went hand in glove with dogfighting? I had to find the answers, and fast!

32

"How are we going to get back to Dahlia House?" I whispered to Coleman. There were roads that cut through the cotton fields—fallow now until the sun warmed the soil a bit—but the person who'd shot at us was between us and home.

"We can cut in back of my neighbor Luther's cornfield and angle around until we're on the south side of the house."

He knew the roads and he also knew the conditions of the fields. At times the perimeter roads around the fields were as good as paved. But in rainy weather, they were like a tar pit. The rich Delta soil turned to a gumbo mixture that could suck the shoes off a person's feet and grab hold of car tires and hold a vehicle in place. But I trusted Coleman to know which roads were safe to travel and which were death traps. I sure didn't want to get stuck in a field with someone shooting at us.

A gibbous moon climbed the sky, and the night grew even colder, if possible. I knew Squatty and Tilly were freezing, but to their credit, they didn't complain. They'd gotten back in their seats, but they were swiveling from side to side, looking for a possible attack. Coleman was still driving without headlights, and I figured that was smart. It made it difficult to assess the road, though. If we hit a patch of gumbo, he had the skills to plough us through it. I was glad he was driving.

When he took a turn down a road that led to Luther's fields, I knew where we were at last. He was angling back to Dahlia House from the back. We'd end up coming across the horse pasture. I sat up, ready to hop out and open the gate to the pasture.

As we came to the fence, I heard the pounding of hooves. My horses! They were coming to greet us. I felt sweet relief. I knew they were fine. DeWayne had said so, but seeing them crest a tiny rise and come at me, eyes flashing in the moonlight, I knew for the first time in a long time that everything was going to be okay. We would catch Gertrude, find any other poor stolen dogs, put some dogfighters and drug dealers behind bars, and close out this case so I could bake more cookies. This domestic yen I was suffering from would shock my friends, no doubt.

The lights of Dahlia House and the barn came up as Coleman drove slowly across the pasture. The horses followed behind the car, snorting and bucking in the cold night. How I loved watching them. When at last we pulled up by the barn, I got out again and opened the big door wide so Coleman could drive in. No rain was in the forecast, but it would be silly to leave the truck out in the weather with the front and back windows gone.

Coleman pulled in, killed the ignition, and the ladies got out, helping me carry the food from Millie's inside. DeWayne, his girlfriend, Budgie, and the dogs gathered in the kitchen. The dogs whined and Avalon stood up and begged. She was the cutest thing. Coleman and I had not discussed keeping her on the farm, but I knew I wanted to. I was pretty certain I could convince Coleman that he wanted to keep Avalon, too. Not to be outdone, Pumpkin danced around the other dogs like a little princess. She should have had the dang tutu. I would need Tinkie's help to convince Harold—and Roscoe—to take her on.

When the feeding frenzy was over and my guests had warmed in the kitchen, I was more than ready for bed. Tilly and Squatty took their dogs to their respective rooms, and Coleman and I trudged upstairs with my critters. We needed to talk. Coleman had chosen not to pursue the shooter—his first priority was keeping me and the ladies safe. The second issue that prevented pursuit was that in the dark, he could too easily run into another ambush.

He built up the fire in the bedroom and I delighted in watching the muscles ripple beneath his thermal shirt. He was a handsome man in his prime. Thank heavens he didn't seem to know that—he was humble and modest. Traits I truly enjoyed. I sighed and wriggled my way beneath the quilts.

When the flames were licking the dry oak logs, he slipped beneath the covers. I snuggled against his side, resting my head on his shoulder. My hand was on his heart and the steady thrum beneath my palm gave me solace and comfort. I wore his engagement ring, a beautiful yellow diamond, though in the past few months we hadn't talked permanent plans. I just wasn't ready yet, and he respected that.

After he snapped off the light, I inhaled. "Coleman, do you think it was Gertrude shooting at us?"

"Yes. I would say it's likely her. But tomorrow I'll look for evidence."

He was hedging—just a little. He didn't want me scared or

worried. And I loved him for the kindness. "Who else could it be?" I asked.

"Look, you don't know who or what Squatty or Tilly may have pissed off. It could be revenge against them and have nothing to do with you."

"But you don't believe that." He didn't. I could tell by his tone.

"No, I don't. But I also don't believe in jumping to conclusions. Let's see what the deputies and I can find tomorrow."

"I'll be happy to help look."

"I want you to take Squatty and Tilly and their dogs over to Memphis. Take Pumpkin, too. She'll be safer with them. Find a hotel that accepts pets and put them there until we can figure this out. I mean it. If that was Gertrude last night, she doesn't care who she hurts or kills. Let's get them out of the way so we can do our jobs."

While I didn't want to be the Uber service for Squatty and Tilly, I agreed that getting them out of the state might be a wise move. I could take them to Memphis and get back within six hours. If I was lucky, Madame Tomeeka or maybe Cece would offer to drive them. It would be a great opportunity for Cece to interview them about the dog thefts and what was happening in Nixville. But that was worry for tomorrow.

I felt my eyelids growing heavy. Coleman was like a two-hundred-pound sleep pillow. Curved against his side, listening to his heartbeat and regular breathing, I felt myself relax. I hadn't realized how tense I'd been. I drifted into sweet blackness.

I woke up in the middle of the night. The fire was out, and Coleman was breathing deeply beside me. I pulled the covers up to my chin and edged closer to him with the goal of going back to sleep. Sweetie Pie, Pumpkin, and Avalon had gotten up on the bed. Avalon, who was still underweight and recovering from the abuse she'd endured, was snoring gently.

I burrowed deeper into Coleman's side and sighed. At the top of my head, Pluto stood up on the pillow. His hiss was soft and sibilant—a sound that was gentle, and yet terrifying.

I froze, listening. Avalon continued to snore, and even Sweetie Pie was sound asleep. They'd both had exhausting days. Pluto was on red alert. He'd heard something and he was letting me know. He patted my cheek with a gentle paw, making sure his claws were sheathed. I let out a long breath so he would know I was awake.

Someone was walking in the hallway outside the bedroom. The person had a light tread, but I could hear them on the hardwood floor. I listened carefully. They stopped outside my bedroom door. The pause had me slowly sitting up. Were they going to burst into my room, maybe with a gun?

I put a hand out to wake Coleman, but stopped. The person outside my door walked away. He or she went on down the hall. Panic choked me as I thought of Squatty and Tilly, both probably sound asleep and unaware that danger was stalking them. Should I scream? Or would that provoke the intruder to do something dastardly?

Pluto jumped to the foot of the bed, stomping all over Sweetie Pie as he went. "Shush," I murmured to the dogs. I didn't want them barking or raising hell for the same reason I didn't scream. But I had to do something.

Coleman always left his firearm and holster in the gun safe in the closet, and I slipped out of bed, opened the closet door, and worked the lock on the safe. When I had his weapon in my hand, I eased to the door, listening to the sounds in the hallway. Who the hell was in my house?

Sweetie Pie oozed onto the floor without making a sound.

She didn't even disturb Pumpkin. She was at my side instantly. Avalon watched us, with Pluto sitting beside her. I signaled them to remain and be quiet.

I didn't hear anything in the hallway, so I eased the door open. The long corridor was pitch-black. I couldn't see anything, but Sweetie Pie could.

She rushed out the door. Her yodeling cry was loud and eerie enough to draw a scream from the intruder. Sweetie Pie rushed the figure dressed all in black and I followed behind her.

"Stop!" The voice that cried out was female, but it was too late to stop Sweetie Pie, who charged into the intruder and struck with such force that the person rocked backward, lost their balance, and tumbled down the stairs.

I flipped on the hall light and rushed down, gun at the ready. To my shock, Penelope Fenway was crumpled in a heap at the bottom of the stairs. Blood leaked from a head wound.

"Coleman! Come quick!" I called out.

Coleman came running down the stairs barefoot and panicked without his gun. "What's wrong?"

Squatty and Tilly were right behind him, followed by the dogs, the cat, and, lastly, Poe. The raven had been roosting on the curtain rod in my bedroom and was late to the circus. He made up for it by flying in circles around Penelope, cawing at her in his raspy voice. It sounded like he was hexing her.

"Who is that?" Coleman asked. He turned a flashlight on and the high beam caught Penelope in the eyes. She groaned and shielded her face.

"The mayor's daughter," Tilly said. "What is she doing here?"

"Good question," I said.

33

Penelope made no move to get to her feet. She was smarter than she looked. "I came for the dog," she said haltingly. "It's my dog. I know you took her, Sarah Booth. I know you did. She's my dog."

Her lie only irritated Cupcake. She came to the bottom step and growled at Penelope.

"That dog hates you," Tilly said. "Jesus, you steal a dog and it hates you. What a piece of tapeworm you are!"

"How dare you—" Penelope started to her feet, but Squatty stepped forward and pushed her with her foot.

"Stay down if you know what's good for you," Squatty said, and even I wouldn't have challenged her. She was mad as a hornet. The glint in her eye told me she wanted to take her heel and crush it into Penelope's face.

"You stole Squatty's dog," I said. "Who do you think you are?"

"Daddy said I could have her."

That was even more than I could take in. "Your father told you it was okay to steal a pet?"

"I wanted her." Penelope remained prone on the floor, but it was clear she wanted to put her hands on her hips and demand the dog. Fat lot of good that would do her. Squatty would kick her in the face, given half a chance.

"You think it's okay to steal someone else's pet?" Coleman asked her. His tone was level, but I knew he was angry, too.

"Ellis gave her to me. He said Squatty ignored her and didn't want her."

Oh, no. That was exactly the wrong thing for Penelope to say. Squatty was going to tear her limb from limb and then go after her worthless, thieving grandson. I wanted a front-row seat.

"If you wanted a pet, why didn't you go to the shelter and adopt one?" Coleman asked her.

"A stray?" Penelope curled her lip. "I need a purebred dog. I don't want some cur."

Oh, lord, it was going to be a toss-up whether the ladies, Coleman, or I killed the silly little witch. Before any of us could react, Coleman leaned down and pulled her to her feet. I don't know where he had the handcuffs secreted, but he whipped them out and put them on her. "Call Budgie," he said to me. "Tell him we're bringing a prisoner in."

"You can't arrest me," Penelope said. She was indignant. "I haven't done anything wrong. Who do you think you are? My daddy is mayor and he will put a stop to this."

"He's the mayor of Nixville, not Zinnia. Breaking and entering is a felony. Does that ring a bell?" Squatty said. She pretended to slip on the step and stumbled into Penelope, kicking her hard in the shin.

"You hurt me." Penelope was incredulous. "You hurt me! Who do you think you are? My daddy is going to make you pay."

It was still the dead of night and the house was cold. We were all freezing, teeth chattering, but in the distance I heard the sirens. DeWayne and Budgie weren't waiting for us to show up at the jail. They were coming to take custody of the prisoner. I was going to really enjoy this. But before Penelope went, I had a few questions.

"How do you know Gertrude Stromm?" I asked her.

"The woman who runs the B and B in Pine Bluff. She's a total sweetheart."

This woman/child had the judgment of a cat in heat. "Where did you meet Gertrude?" I asked.

"She was at one of Daddy's aldermen meetings. She has a lot of good ideas for Nixville and Sunflower County. She's a lot smarter than you people are."

"What kind of ideas?" I asked.

"Gambling. Ms. Stromm has a plan to legalize gambling in Sunflower County. On land. Not just the boats on the river. It's going to be a gold mine for Daddy and his friends. Just watch and see. Now, give me a phone so I can call my daddy."

For a split second, Gertrude's vision of gambling hell stretched out in front of me. I could see the neon, the flashing lights, hear the whir and clanking of the one-armed bandits . . . I viewed it as hell, but Gertrude would see only money.

"Penelope Fenway, you're under arrest for breaking and entering and assault." Coleman read her her rights as he waited for DeWayne and Budgie to come in the front door.

"What about dog theft?" Squatty asked. "She stole my dog and she meant to keep her."

Cupcake took that moment to let her feelings for Penelope be known. She came down the hallway and went halfway down the stairs before she stopped, looked at Penelope, and growled.

"That's my girl," Squatty said. "She picked up the little dog and went down to the bottom of the steps where Coleman held Penelope's arm. He had cuffed her hands behind her.

"I should punch you in the nose," Squatty said. "In fact, I think I will." She drew back her fist, but before she could strike, Coleman stepped between her and Penelope.

"Don't do anything you could get arrested for doing," Coleman warned her. "If you attack her, I'll have to charge you, too."

"Oh, boo-hoo!" Penelope said. "Haul me off to jail. I get one phone call and I'll get Mr. Dickerson here to handle this ridiculous charge. I'm going to sue you for false arrest." She looked around Dalia House. "I'm going to own this place."

"I highly doubt that," Tilly said as she went down the stairs to stand beside Squatty. "You're going to look mighty good in orange, though. I'll call that reporter Cece Dee Falcon and get her to do a Sunday feature on you and prison fashion."

"You wouldn't dare!" Penelope looked a lot more worried about a society newspaper story than a criminal charge. That was just her mentality, though. She really thought her dad could get her out of her legal peccadillos. She was about to learn a very hard lesson. I intended to prosecute her to the fullest extent of the law. I didn't believe she'd stolen Cupcake—I believed it was that ne'er-do-well Ellis who'd originally snatched the puppy. But Penelope had broken into my home and was trying to steal Cupcake back. So, she was going to pay.

Squatty whipped out her phone and dialed the *Zinnia Dis-*

patch, the local newspaper where Cece worked. "Yes, I have a big scoop for Ms. Cece Dee Falcon. Ask her to return my call." She left her cell phone number.

When she'd slid her phone into the pocket of her pajamas, she smiled at Penelope. "I'll send Ms. Falcon over to the jail to interview you. Should be a blast."

Penelope finally took Squatty seriously, and she was angry. "That grandson of yours, just wait until I tell everyone what he's up to. I'm going to ruin him and you."

"Well, aren't you just a little primped-up huckster," Squatty said.

No one else had a chance to respond. I heard the sirens stop out in the front of Dahlia House and in a moment DeWayne and Budgie came in. They took in the scene and then tried to hide their smiles. Coleman was at the foot of the stairs, holding Penelope by the arm, while Squatty and Tilly, in the pink Barbie pajamas Tinkie had found for them and had delivered, were facing off with her. I had picked up Pluto and taken a seat on the top step. It was like a high school drama production. All I needed was popcorn.

"Take Penelope Fenway to the courthouse and put her in a cell," Coleman told the deputies.

"You'd better not," Penelope said. She glared at the deputies. "You'd better not touch me."

Coleman grasped her upper arm and frog-marched her to the front door, down the steps, and into the back of a patrol car. "Take her now, before I do something I'll regret," he said.

The show was over, so I stood. The sun was coming up and soon it would be time to take Squatty and Tilly to Memphis. I walked out to the front porch to watch as the deputies took Penelope away. It was going to be a tough day for Coleman once Fenway found out his daughter had been charged and locked in a cell.

But I was willing to bet it was going to be an even worse day for Ellis Adams, once Squatty got ahold of him. I couldn't wait!

34

Coleman and I took steaming mugs of coffee to the front porch to wave goodbye as Cece drove away with Tilly, Squatty, and their two dogs. Tinkie said she would talk to Harold and convince him to keep Pumpkin as company for Roscoe. The truth was, a doggy friend might help keep Roscoe home and out of so much mischief.

Cece had eagerly agreed to drive the women to Memphis, where Coleman had booked rooms in a pet-friendly motel. He'd used fake names, of course.

The two Nixville women had tried to resist Coleman's plan, but he'd persisted and won. I had to admit to a real sense of relief, too. I was worried about Gertrude's potential destruction of anyone and anything that stood in her way. How Squatty and Tilly and the dogs were in the way wasn't clear to me. And it was far past time to figure it out.

When the car had cleared the driveway and was on the county road to Memphis, I went to Coleman. He put his arm around my shoulders and held me close.

His cell phone rang and I was pretty sure it was Budgie. He listened a moment, mumbled something, and closed the phone. "Mayor Fenway and Chief Garwool are at my office. They urgently want to speak with me."

"Good luck with that," I mumbled. I had a real burn on for Fenway and Garwool and everything they stood for.

"I'm going into the office," Coleman said. "And you?"

I didn't have a plan—just a sense that I needed to take action. But I had too many puzzle pieces and no clear picture of what any of them meant. I decided to approach the problem from another angle. His name was Dawson Reed. The Hound Dog Patrol group that worked to find and help dogs and cats seemed to be the best option for me to explore. Since Gertrude's arrival on the scene, I'd lost sight of my original purpose—to find two missing dogs. The dogs had been recovered and were perfectly fine, but I still had no explanation for why they'd been taken.

Sure, Penelope wanted Cupcake, but that didn't make sense, either. Why steal, when she could adopt a dog just like Cupcake? And Squatty had made it clear that Cupcake wasn't a purebred. Not to mention that plenty of purebred dogs were being killed in Southern animal shelters every single day.

Before Coleman could get away, I grabbed his hand and pulled him back for a real kiss. I put a lip-lock on him that made his forehead break out in a sweat even though it was freezing. "I'll see you tonight," I told him. "We have a date with destiny."

"I think I should run," he quipped. "Before you render me a helpless babe."

Then, it was time to go inside, get dressed, and head out to work. I wanted to find all the dogfighting rings and put the participants in prison. It was a worthy goal for a brisk February day.

My hand was on the front doorknob when I heard someone singing "Yesterday." It sounded just like Paul McCartney. But Sir Paul was in England, not Zinnia. Had someone turned the record player on? I'd already dealt with a crazed intruder in my home, and I was determined to find this sing-along culprit and put them out in the yard, too. My last nerve was shot.

Then I realized I was alone. Coleman had gone to work. The ladies were on the way to Memphis. Even Sweetie Pie, Avalon, and Pluto were nowhere to be found. Only Poe remained. The raven perched on the back of a rocking chair and watched me, turning his head this way and that as if he were keeping time with the music.

"'All my troubles seemed so far away,'" the vocalist sang. Dang. It sounded just like McCartney and the Beatles. Had I slipped into a time warp?

I opened the door and followed the singing to the music room. The melody flowed all around me. A solitary figure, back turned to me, stood by the piano. When he turned around, my heart almost stopped. Paul McCartney—the young Paul of my mother's fierce crush—was singing to me. I thought I might swoon. Then I realized it made no sense that one of the Beatles was in Dahlia House. No matter how much I loved the crooning, I had to accept that it was only Jitty, giving me a hard time.

"What do you want?" I asked her. Paul, with those twinkling hazel eyes, smiled. Even knowing it was Jitty and an illusion, I couldn't help myself. My heart fluttered.

"I've been vegan since I was twenty." Paul lounged against the piano. "We need to help others see the benefits of a vegan life. Sarah Booth, you need to give up meat and dairy. You'll be so much healthier, and so will the planet."

I believed him. "I'll work harder at giving up animal products," I said. My family had never been huge carnivores, but a serving of meat was part of a balanced plate. Or so I had been raised. My folks grew up at a time when the USDA food pyramid was sacrosanct, even though it had been proven inaccurate. Sir Paul was one hundred percent right. Change was difficult but necessary to help the planet. And I didn't want to eat my animal friends.

"We can all do better," Paul said. "And we are going to find the dogfighters. We are. And Coleman will bring them to justice. Things are going to change for animals in Sunflower County."

Jitty had a lot of faith in Coleman. And so did I. I wanted to believe that good people could bring about good change.

Paul went on. "I wrote 'Yesterday' because I think we all find the past to be easier. Folks romanticize the past. Because we've survived it, the past seems less dangerous. But yesterday is gone. Today is all we have."

He gave that boyish grin that worked like magic on me. He could have sold me hot coffee in hell and I would have paid a premium price for it. "Thank you, Sir Paul. You've helped me rethink my food choices, but what about these dogs? Do you know where the dogfighters are? Will you tell me?" Jitty never helped me with anything regarding a case, but Paul might make her see the light of reason.

"There are people who crave brutality." Paul was beginning to fade a little.

"Is that a clue?" I asked.

"Use it if you can. Now it's time for me to move along."

Before I could ask another question, Jitty twirled in a circle and snapped her fingers. Little black treble notes filled the air around her and then poof, she was gone.

It was time for me to get to work.

I whistled up the dogs and got them loaded in my car. On the way to Hilltop, I called Tinkie. I would have been happy to leave her in Zinnia to be with Maylin, but she was having none of that. Technically, we'd resolved the case of the stolen dogs and both had been returned to their happy owners, so we could say the case was closed. But this was bigger than a dognapping of two pets. Beneath the surface, there was big money and many more missing pets. I wasn't about to give up.

Tinkie was waiting for me on the front porch of Hilltop. I called Avalon and Sweetie Pie out of my car. I intended to leave them with Oscar and Pauline, but they had other plans. I got them out of the car, but they ran around the vehicle and jumped in from the passenger side when Tinkie opened the door. All of my dogs were in total rebellion.

I tried to call them out again, but the dogs ignored me. They sat in the back seat, looking out the window and completely ignoring me. My cell phone rang and I looked at it. An unknown number. I hesitated, but I finally took the call.

"Sarah Booth," the male voice said, "mind your own business or suffer the consequences."

The voice was dead—no emotion at all. "Who is this?"

"Someone who means what he says. Stay away from Nixville. Mind your own affairs. Don't come back, or you'll regret it."

The line went dead.

To my knowledge, I hadn't done anything in Nixville to warrant a threat. Now in Zinnia, I'd had Penelope arrested and charged with breaking and entering as well as dog theft. That was probably sufficient to earn me the ire of Mayor Fenway and Chief Garwool, but neither of them had been the threatening caller. I would be able to identify their voices.

I was thinking about Jitty's appearance as Paul McCartney when I finally got Tinkie in the front seat and the doggos in the back. I'd given up trying to leave them at Hilltop. They were determined to come along. It just wasn't worth a big battle to leave them behind.

Once we were headed to Nixville, I called Dawson Reed. He'd been strangely silent for a man who was supposed to be working a dog-theft case. The call went to voice mail, and I asked him to give me a call back. A little niggle of concern flashed through my brain, but I pushed it aside. Dawson was a busy man. He had a lot of irons in the fire. But he had been checking on some things for me, and now he was radio silent.

"I'm worried, too," Tinkie said. She could read me too easily. "Dawson should have been in touch by now. The good news, though, is that Harold is smitten with Pumpkin. I think Harold will keep her."

That was delightful news, and it did ease my anxiety. Instead of going to Nixville, we decided to detour to Dawson's place. He lived on the outskirts of Nixville. Tinkie was a pro at directions, and she guided me there. We got out and knocked on the door. The dogs were pawing at the car windows for their freedom. When the door of Dawson's home swung open at our touch, I went to the car and let the pups out. Chablis had stayed home with Maylin and Pauline, and I was glad. She was fierce, but she also weighed less than eight pounds and could easily be hurt. I loved Sweetie Pie and Avalon, but they were bigger and tougher. Chablis also had an underbite that lessened the ferocity of her attack mode. Sweetie Pie and Avalon—those two could tear a hunk of flesh right off the bone.

We stood at the open door and peered into the house, which seemed to be empty.

"Dawson!" Tinkie called out. "Dawson, are you here?"

Silence was the only answer.

"I'm going to the back." I eased across the small porch and went around the house to the back. Along the way I peeked in the windows, but I didn't see anyone in the house. My worry escalated. It only grew when I saw the back of the house.

The back door was standing wide open when I got there. With the dogs at my side, I slipped into a mudroom that led to a big kitchen. When I looked into the bedroom, I saw Dawson's computer equipment. Someone had smashed it to bits and thrown it all over the room. My heart raced. "Don't come in here," I called out to Tinkie, but it was too late. She came down the hallway and stopped at the bedroom.

"Holy crap. Any sign of Dawson?"

"Not so far," I answered. Taking great care to be alert to anyone hiding on the premises, we walked around the bedroom. Dawson's equipment was completely vandalized. Like someone had taken a baseball bat to it.

The scene was concerning, but it was the message written on the living room wall that stopped us in our tracks: "Meddlers will die."

It appeared to be written in blood.

35

The logical person to call would be Garwool, but I was having none of that. I didn't trust that man, and I felt I had good reason for my assessment. Instead, I called an honorable lawman—Coleman.

"Don't touch anything." Coleman gave the standard warning not to mess up his crime scene. Tinkie and I knew the drill, but it never hurt to be reminded.

"We'll wait outside for you, once I make sure Dawson isn't here." If he was injured, I needed to find him and get help. Something about the scene—the way everything was brutally destroyed—made me worried that Dawson had also been hurt. It was strange how his home was wide open and there wasn't a trace of him.

"I'm going to check the building out back," Tinkie said. "If someone dangerous broke in, he might have escaped and gone to the shed. He may be hiding there."

"Wait and I'll go with you." Something about the situation

had me on edge. I didn't want Tinkie pushing into a storage area without backup.

"I can manage." Tinkie was already at the back door.

My partner was a little testy—and doubly independent. She resented when I tried to protect her, and I didn't blame her a bit. I didn't like it when Coleman did the same to me.

"I'll check the rest of the house and join you." There was no point arguing with her. I needed to clear the house and then go and join her at the shed.

I turned my attention to the closed door down the hallway. I didn't have my gun, but I approached the door with caution and cracked it open. Before I could react, a scraggly buff-colored dog rushed out into the hall, jumped up on me, and almost knocked me over. The dog jumped in the air, twirling and barking with excitement. She was like some demented and crazed creature hopped up on speed. Pumpkin! How in the hell had she gotten from Harold's house to Dawson's home so quickly? It was only a few miles, but still. She was such a little escape artist. She'd shown up at the library and now she was here.

I rushed to the back door to be sure it was closed. I sure didn't want Pumpkin to get away.

I found a leash and captured the whirling dervish and headed out to join Tinkie at the back shed. When I got there, the door was open but there was no sign of Tinkie. And the dog, all thirty-five pounds of scraggly hair and long legs, tugged at the leash. She was determined to get in the shed. I followed the dog inside the shed.

"Tinkie?" I didn't see my partner anywhere. The shed was as dark as a cave. I reached along the wall for a light switch, but I couldn't find one. I pulled out my phone to use the light on it. The illumination was weak, but it gave me a view of a storage shed that was chock-full of kitchen supplies, old mattresses, chairs, and lord knew what else. There was no sign of Tinkie or Dawson. No sign of anyone alive in the backyard storage shanty.

The little demon dog pulled hard at the leash and almost caused me to fall. I managed to get her under control and we searched the whole shed. Tinkie was gone. She'd vanished. A cold chill gripped my heart. I dialed Coleman.

"Tinkie has disappeared."

He must have heard the panic in my voice. He didn't ask any questions. "I'm on the way. Send the address and wait there for me. Budgie and DeWayne will come, too, to process the house. Be careful, Sarah Booth. Someone could be hiding on the property."

He wasn't wrong about that. And I was beginning to believe the message written on the wall in Dawson's home was not just meant for him—but also for me and Tinkie. "Meddlers will die."

I wrangled the wild demon dog around to the front of the house, where I let Sweetie Pie and Avalon free. They took off for the shed like torpedoes. The little buff-colored terrorist and I followed. Holding on to the dog's leash was like trying to hold on to a whirlwind.

I'd finished a search of the shed, again, with the help of the dogs. Sweetie Pie and Avalon returned to the house on their own—sniffing all about—while Pumpkin and I followed. I kept her on the leash to be safe. We went through every room. There wasn't a sign of the two missing people. Where had Tinkie gone? She'd been there and then five minutes later, she'd vanished. I tried not to think about the dire things that could have happened. It didn't make sense that she'd been abducted in that short space of time and without leaving any evidence. But it also didn't make sense that she'd left under her own power. She wouldn't do that knowing how much I'd worry.

I was sitting on the steps with the dogs when DeWayne and Budgie arrived. They brought their evidence-collection kits and set about processing the house. I paced the front yard, working with Pumpkin to try to teach her manners on a leash. Anything to keep my mind from going to a dark place. I started twice to call Oscar, but I stopped myself. Why get Oscar all worked up before Coleman and the deputies had even had a chance to search? It would be cruel.

When Coleman pulled up and got out of his truck, I ran to him and buried myself against his chest. "Pumpkin is here, but Tinkie is missing. She went to search the shed and she's just gone. I've looked everywhere. Dawson is gone, too, and his house is trashed."

"Send Sweetie Pie to find Tinkie," he said. "I'm here to follow up with you."

"What about Pumpkin?" I asked. "I don't trust her to come if I call her. She's kind of a little doggie terrorist."

"Let her go, too. She may find Dawson."

I unhooked the leash and looked at the dogs. "Find Tinkie and Dawson," I told them. "Find them now."

The dogs, with Avalon bringing up the rear, set off toward the backyard. I wasn't sure what talent Pumpkin or Avalon had as trackers, but Sweetie Pie had one of the finest noses in the South. Pumpkin, as adorable as she looked, had a nose for trouble and not much else.

Coleman left the deputies to process Dawson's house. He told me he'd have to call Garwool eventually, but right now he was happy to let his exceedingly professional deputies do the work they excelled at. He would involve the Nixville police chief at the last minute. Garwool brought nothing to the table that would help us find Dawson or Tinkie. Unless, of course, he was the one who'd spirited them away. I wouldn't put it past Mayor Fenway to do something awful like kidnapping as a payback for Coleman arresting Penelope, who remained behind bars in Zinnia.

The dogs found a hole in Dawson's backyard fence, and they'd crawled through. Coleman gave me a boost over the fence and he cleared it himself as I gave chase to the dogs. I found myself in a tangle of weeds and vines, low shrubs, and volunteer trees. The terrain sloped, and I suspected that at the bottom of the incline, I'd find a small creek.

Coleman grabbed my arm to help me make a better speed. The dogs were on a trail. Sweetie Pie snuffled and crashed through the underbrush until she gave her signature howl. To my pleased shock, Avalon started baying, too, and even little Pumpkin tried to get in on the act. For a dog who had run away from Harold's house and traveled several miles, she was actually minding fairly well.

Coleman's cell phone rang, and he answered it while still keeping a brisk pace through the underbrush. "Got it," he said. "Thanks. I'll relay the info."

When he hung up, he didn't slow down. Instead, he notched up his speed. "DeWayne said Dawson has been spotted driving out to Rutherford Mace's place."

"What?"

"A friend of DeWayne's saw him and called. DeWayne is going out there while Budgie finishes up at Dawson's house."

"And Tinkie?" I wanted to talk to Dawson, but I *needed* to find my partner.

We trudged deeper into the woods. The dogs were going slower because of the thick undergrowth. Sweetie Pie could run through it like the track star she was, but Avalon was still out of shape. No telling how long she'd been tied up, unable to really move around and exercise. And Pumpkin seemed oblivious to the other dogs and to me and Coleman. She ran through the woods, jumping fallen trees, snapping at branches with leaves on them, twirling, barking, and in general gallivanting hither and yon. I'd never had a DNA test done on a dog before, but Pumpkin tempted me to do so. She looked to be Parsons Jack Russell terrier mixed with Beelzebub. She was in her own little world, but she was fascinating to watch. She moved with such grace and total abandon, I would have named her Isadora Duncan.

"Sarah Booth, come on!" Coleman was calling me. Somehow I'd dropped behind him and he was out of sight.

"Coming!"

The word had barely left my mouth when I stumbled over something solid on the forest floor. I went down and knocked the breath out of myself. It took a few moments of heaving to get my wind back, but when I finally sat up and looked at what had tripped me, I cried out. "Coleman! Help!"

It was Tinkie. She was face down in a pile of leaves, unmoving.

36

Coleman was on his radio in a flash. I knelt on the ground, holding my partner's head in my lap. She was breathing raggedly, and her face was pale. So very pale. I touched her forehead and it was cool. I didn't know if that was a good sign or a bad one.

"The road is just about a hundred yards to the west," Coleman said. He scooped Tinkie into his arms and carried her.

I followed, whistling for the dogs. Surely Sweetie Pie would obey. To my everlasting shock, all three of the dogs fell in behind me as I followed Coleman. I ran up to him. "I can go get my car. We can drive her to the hospital."

A soft moan let me know Tinkie was coming to. When we got to the verge beside County Road 534, Coleman gently put Tinkie on the ground. Her baby blues fluttered open, and she looked first at Coleman, then at me. Pumpkin ran up and planted a French kiss right on her mouth.

"Gag! Ack! Ugh!" Tinkie struggled to sit up. "Where did that raggedy-ass dog come from?"

My relief was so profound, I burst into tears.

"What's wrong with her?" Tinkie, pointing at me, asked Coleman.

He grinned wide. "I think I know, and if you aren't careful, she's going to knock you out again and I wouldn't blame her."

Tinkie reached up and rubbed her head. "Who hit me?"

"That was the question we hoped you could answer," Coleman said. "You didn't see your attacker?"

She thought a minute, and then her face changed. "It was Dawson! I remember now. He was hiding in the shed and when I shined the flashlight in his face, he ran away. I chased after him. He hit me with something really hard."

I started to say that Dawson had been spotted driving out of town, but Coleman signaled me to keep quiet. So, I asked, "Why would Dawson attack you?" I was perplexed. Dawson had volunteered to help us. Why would he hurt Tinkie? Did he have something to hide? Dawson's role in this whole business was problematic. He and Ellis Adams seemed to have conflicting interests. To be honest, a lot of the people in Nixville seemed to be serving two masters.

"Do you know where Dawson went?" Coleman asked Tinkie.

"He didn't say." She rubbed her head. "I feel like I'm forgetting something important, though." She frowned in concentration. "Wait, it's something about a website. Dawson was in the shed when I went down to check. He was talking on his phone. He said something about the pet finders website."

I pulled out my phone and looked it up. I gave a low whistle. "It's Pumpkin the dog," I said softly. "There's a five-thousand-dollar reward for her. Jody Holm is desperate to get her back." If Jody was the real owner, my hopes for a happy family with Harold were dashed.

"I don't know who she is, but let's return her dog," Tinkie said, "before she kisses me on the mouth again. I thought she was going to stick her tongue down my throat to my diaphragm."

Pumpkin rushed up to Tinkie, jumped high in the air, and planted another kiss on her lips.

When Coleman tried to carry Tinkie, she squawked and bellowed until he put her down to walk by herself. "Take her to the hospital," he told me.

"Okay." The thunderhead on Tinkie's brow said otherwise, though. "I'll do my best," I told him. "Where are you going?"

"To find Dawson and Garwool. Penelope made her call to her father, so I'm sure he's got a lawyer on the way to her now."

"Like Julian Dickerson," I said.

"The criminal lawyer from Jackson?" Coleman knew of him.

"That's the one. He's in tight with Fenway and Garwool."

"There's something dirty going on here," Coleman said. "The stolen dogs, the dogfighting rings, the proliferation of drugs in Nixville. Budgie did some research on near overdoses, and Nixville has a real problem. I have my suspicions about who is involved, but we need proof."

"I'll take Tinkie to be checked out, and then find Jody Holm and return Pumpkin. If there is a reward, Dawson should probably get it. I mean, Pumpkin did come here when she left Harold's house."

"Not on your life," Tinkie said. "I'll take the reward and do something really good with it. If Jody really wants that naughty little dog back, she should have her." Tinkie held her hand up to cover her mouth. Pumpkin was quick and deadly accurate with the tongue kisses. Tinkie wasn't a germaphobe, but dog throat swabs were a bit more than she wanted to indulge in.

"I'll get my car," I told Coleman, and then left him with Tinkie and the dogs while I cut back through the woods. Fifteen minutes later, I was on the street, waiting in my car with the heater going wide open. The dogs were loaded in the back seat, with Pumpkin leading the way. She was a bossy little thing who took it upon herself to make the other dogs behave. If Jody Holm didn't want her back, she'd be perfect for Roscoe. The two of them could tear Sunflower County apart. But right now, Tinkie and I had another agenda.

Doc Sawyer met us in the emergency room, and though Tinkie protested profusely, he gave her a once-over and a clean bill of health. "Your head is so hard no damage was done," he teased her. "You might not be so lucky again. Sarah Booth, keep her out of trouble."

"I'm not a miracle worker," I told him, but I gave Tinkie a wink so she knew I was messing with her. It was good to see Doc, though. With his nimbus of white hair and his ultimate kindness, he never changed.

"Doc, have you noticed any unusual activity with drugs in Sunflower County?" I hadn't really thought about posing this question until that very moment.

"Now that you mention it," he said. "We had three kids come in with overdoses just since Monday."

"Overdoses of what?" Tinkie asked. She was combing her hair.

"There's a lot of pot laced with fentanyl in the area," Doc said. "We have at least one overdose a day. Sometimes more. I don't know where the drugs are coming from." He frowned.

"The truth is, if they legalized marijuana for recreational use, it would cut down on a lot of the harder drug overdoses. I personally believe people are making so much money on these illegal drugs they don't want to fix the problem."

"Doc, do you know Dawson Reed?"

"The pet finder. Sure. He's a good kid."

He wasn't a kid, but to Doc he was a whippersnapper.

"Dawson is the person who hit Tinkie." I still didn't know how Dawson could be in two places at once, but I'd see Doc's reaction. Disbelief, then confusion washed over Doc's face.

"Why would he do that?"

"I was hoping you might know."

Doc shook his head. "A lot of the drug overdoses seem to come from the rural area around Nixville. I've heard there are dogfighting rings there. Drugs and abuse of animals go hand in hand."

That was the link I had to prove. And time was a-wasting. How I planned to make that connection, I wasn't certain. But it was time to go back out to Rutherford Mace's place, and this time I wasn't leaving until I had the proof I needed.

37

Tinkie refused to get in my car unless I promised her I wouldn't take her back to Zinnia. She also demanded that I not call Oscar and tell him what was going on. Weighing what I owed my partner and what I owed Oscar, I felt like I was being pulled apart by two different loyalties. Ultimately, I sided with Tinkie. I agreed not to tell her husband about the attack. I also promised to talk to Coleman about holding off on talking to Oscar until Tinkie had had a chance to break the news of the most recent attack to him.

Aunt Loulane had often cautioned me that knowing right from wrong wasn't the hard part—what was difficult was figuring out the most ethical choice when right and wrong were so tangled together. This was one of those instances.

I drove to Dr. Smith's clinic with Pumpkin in tow. She rushed around the back of the car and into the clinic, ran and leaped at all the dogs waiting in kennels, twirled on her hind legs, and licked the wallpaper border that contained butterflies. The vet tech and other clients were either amused or aghast.

I didn't know how or where Pumpkin came from, but she deserved all the care we could give her. Life on the lam was dicey for any dog, but one as naughty as Pumpkin—well, a lot of people might want to do her in. I hated to leave her at the clinic, but I had a bad feeling that danger would be walking hand in hand with us. I wanted Pumpkin to be safe. I texted Harold to let him know where she was in case anything happened to me. He responded back and agreed to reach out to Jody. One way or the other, Pumpkin would have a great home.

When I got back in the car, Tinkie looked unhappy. "I feel I should have brought Chablis. I never should have left her home. She hates being left out. So does Pumpkin."

I frowned. "But Pumpkin is safe here." I knew that would make Tinkie feel better. She always put the safety of her loved ones first. "And Chablis is safe at Hilltop, too. It's the best place."

"She is, I know. But she could probably find the dogs when we go out to Mace's place to search for the dogfighters."

Chablis was very clever. I couldn't deny it. But Tinkie was acting as if we were going to raid Rutherford Mace's wrestling facility and property. I didn't think that was a wise plan—and Tinkie was normally the pragmatic person. My plan was to sneak in, surveil, make photos to document our case, and get the hell out of there without being hurt. I couldn't trust Pumpkin to be quiet and well-behaved.

"Tinkie, we have to be very careful. And I need to talk to you about who hit you. Are you sure it was Dawson?" The car was running for the heat, but I made no effort to pull away from the curb.

Tinkie turned in her seat. She petted Avalon and Sweetie Pie in the back seat. "Why are you questioning me?"

"At the time you were attacked, Dawson was seen driving out to Mace's place. He couldn't be in two locations at once."

"Who saw him?"

This was the rub. "I don't know. Someone told Budgie."

"But I *heard* his voice. He came up behind me. I turned around—I remember his shoes."

"Did you see his face?" I hated to grill her, but these were questions that needed an answer.

She thought a minute. "It was very shady in the woods. The sunlight was behind him. I . . ." She drifted to silence.

"Tell me, step by step, everything. I believe you, but we have to find out what really happened."

She nodded in agreement. "I went out to the shed to search while you finished in the house. I was worried about Dawson. I was afraid someone had hurt him. I looked around the yard and then I heard someone in the shed. I called out to Dawson. No one answered, but the back door of the shed slammed shut. When I ran around the building to see what was happening, I saw a figure disappearing over the fence. I gave chase. I thought I was gaining on the running person, but I lost him in the undergrowth of those woods. I sprinted deeper into the woods, hoping to catch sight of the fleeing person again, and I went around a big tree. He was hiding there. He hit me on the head." She sighed. "I didn't get a good look. But I swear, I thought it was Dawson. Same build, same shoes. And his voice. But, as you say, he can't be in two different places at once. So, who was it that attacked me? And why?"

"I don't know, but we're going to find out. That's a promise."

"Right now, though, we're going to Mace's property, right?"

Tinkie was determined, and I didn't have another plan of action.

Before I could pull away from the curb, my cell phone rang and, since it was Coleman, I put it on speaker for Tinkie to hear.

"What's up?" I asked.

"The witness who saw Dawson going to Rutherford's wrestling empire may not be totally reliable," Coleman said. "DeWayne is talking to him now."

An interesting twist. "Tinkie feels it was Dawson who hit her, but she isn't positive, either." Coleman needed the truth to find the answers we all wanted. "Who is the witness?"

"Jason Lomus."

Oh, my gut feeling kicked in hard. "He's not a good guy. I don't trust him."

"He's an employee of the Nixville water department. He's unhappy with Fenway and Garwool, and claims they're into illegal activities. He said he's willing to swear in court that Dawson was going into Mace's property, but I have some doubts about the accuracy of this. He could simply be carrying a grudge against Dawson and trying to get him in trouble."

"Or he may be right. That might be exactly what he saw," Tinkie said. "I can't swear that it was Dawson who attacked me."

"We need to talk to this witness," I added. "Is DeWayne still in contact with him?"

"Not sure. Bear in mind, Lomus could be making this up, trying to stack the deck against Dawson. There's bad blood there. Lomus and Ellis hang out together, and I'm looking into the possibility that it was Lomus who stole Cupcake."

Ellis was nobody's concept of a truthful man. Was this city employee deliberately trying to mislead Coleman's investigation?

"Let's go." Tinkie drew me out of my thoughts. She pointed down the road. "Pedal to the metal, Sarah Booth."

"Impatient, some?" I asked.

"Go, now! Time's a-wasting."

I wasn't one hundred percent behind this plan, but I didn't have anything else to offer. I put the vehicle in motion and we were on the way to Mace's wrestling emporium. Only this time I wasn't going in through the front entrance. Budgie and DeWayne had that covered. At least the deputy was on the premises if Tinkie and I got in a lot of trouble. And Coleman was on the way.

Tinkie had printed out a topographical map of the Mace estate. The former wrestling star owned nearly fifty acres of land, and his home and office were located in the center of it. There were areas I'd already searched in the past, but most of it I'd never looked over.

The main entrance was on the south side, but we were approaching from the north. I texted Coleman, Budgie, and DeWayne to let them know we'd parked the car in a brake beside the property. We'd have to walk in—Sweetie Pie and Avalon were having a fit to take off into the woods. Luckily, we had them on leashes still. I didn't trust Rutherford or his employees not to hurt the dogs if they caught them. And I needed Sweetie's refined nose.

We'd infiltrated the property from the north side because there wasn't easy access there and from the map it seemed there was an area of densely wooded ground. Coleman had access to some aerial maps, but the forest growth was so thick none of us could tell if there were buildings hidden among the woods. That was my goal—to find out and to be sure no dogs were being held on the property. The idea of dogfighting niggled at me. If I could save just one dog I was ready to do whatever was necessary.

We plunged into the woods after I made sure the car wasn't easily visible from the road. We'd plotted out the route we needed to take to check for a kennel area far enough from the house that folks visiting wouldn't see or hear it. And we had to be very careful because if there were dogs being held there, we didn't want to set them off. Stealth was our only real advantage.

We trudged through the brambles and small bushes. While the fields had been cleared because the Delta soil was so rich and fertile, the areas left wild were tough to navigate. This brake was dense with thickets and brambles. Several wild crows, almost as big as that rascal Poe, fussed at me from an overgrown sycamore tree. Otherwise, the brake was in stillness. I could only reflect on how glad I was that it was winter and not summer, or we would be carried off by huge mosquitos.

Tinkie forged ahead of me, and I unleashed Sweetie Pie. "Be quiet, but find the dogs," I told my big hound. She looked back at me, whined softly, and took off down the little deer trail we'd been following. Avalon was eager to trail Sweetie, but she was being well-behaved and quiet, as if she understood the mission.

I worked up a sweat as I chased after Tinkie. For such a tiny little woman, she was fast! I was focused on following her when she abruptly stopped and held up her fist—as if she were in some covert operation. And in a sense, she was. I froze in place and listened, immediately hearing what caused her to halt. Dogs! We could hear a number of them, barking and howling. It was time to employ our best surveillance skills and figure out exactly what was happening on the property.

Avalon sat at my feet when I stopped, and I searched the

area for any sign of Sweetie Pie. The hound dog had disappeared, and that made me anxious. Sweetie was plenty smart and she'd survived several bad, bad men, but she was not invincible and plenty of people would shoot a stray dog. Just ahead, through the thick growth, I could see a clearing.

"I'm going in," Tinkie said when I shifted beside her.

"Let's call Coleman. He's probably already on the way, but we can make sure."

"Can you hear those dogs? They sound like they're being hurt. We don't have time to wait for him to come."

She wasn't wrong, but we didn't have the force to break up a dogfighting ring and likely drug cartel. Tinkie had her gun—which I honestly didn't know about until I saw her pull it from the waistband of her pants. She was developing some real outlaw behavior, carrying guns like a gangster.

I put a hand on her shoulder and held her in place. "Easy, Tinkie. We can't give up the advantage of surprise." If she went charging in like a bull in a china shop, we'd all pay the price.

She nodded and crouched down in the dense privet. I knelt beside her. "Do you see Sweetie Pie?" I was worried.

"No. Not a sign of her. And Avalon seems perfectly happy to wait it out here." She petted the gray dog and gave her a kiss on the nose.

Just as I was about to stand up, I saw a red blur of dog. Sweetie Pie was in the clearing and headed like a torpedo directly for a long red shed.

Two men, both carrying automatic weapons, came out of the shed door. They looked at Sweetie Pie and then scanned the area for other intruders. I held Tinkie back. She wanted to rush in, gun blazing, but that was not the game plan we needed. The dogs had to be our first priority. And since we knew they were there, getting them out safely to good vet care had to be our goal. I pulled out my phone to text Karl to let him know we might be arriving with a number of dogs.

"Good idea," Tinkie said. "We have to have a safe place for them, and the vet clinic is the best idea. You know Coleman and the deputies will defend them if necessary."

I did know that. But first we needed to find out if the dogs were in a bad situation. "Look, don't rush to judgment. We can't make any mistakes or else we're the ones who will need medical attention."

"Copy that," Tinkie said.

I had talked her out of it, but when the dogs began to cry out and scream, trying to stop Tinkie was a lost cause.

"Now I'm going in," she said. "You'll be two minutes behind me, and I have to stop whatever they're doing to the dogs."

"I'm right here. I'll give you a small lead, and then I'll be behind you." I didn't want her to do it, but I had to acquiesce. Her action was foolish, but I didn't have the power to dissuade her.

She stood up straight and tall and stepped through the last of the undergrowth into the clearing. With her head held high, she walked toward the long red shed. She'd put the gun back in her waistband and her coat covered it. I could only pray that she wouldn't be hurt.

Tinkie made it to the red building and slipped inside. I kept expecting to hear gunshots. Since Avalon had spent so much of her life chained up, I hated to tie her to a tree, but I couldn't risk her barking and creating more turmoil. Sadly, she was accustomed to being tied. I fastened her leash securely to a tree and followed after Tinkie.

At the door to the long shed, I stopped to listen. The dogs were barking inside, some howling. There had to be at least three dozen animals in there. I would need help getting them all to the vet. I was writing a text to Karl, asking if he had any employees who might want to make some extra cash by helping me transport. I didn't get a chance to send the text because I heard a shrill scream. A woman's scream. What the hell was happening to Tinkie?

38

Caution was thrown to the wind as I pushed the door open and stepped into the gloom of the long shed. The stench was overwhelming. Cages with dogs of all breeds and varieties stretched down the length of the shed. The dogs were frantic, and I could only guess at how horrid their lives were on a daily basis. But there was no sign of my partner. And no sign of Sweetie Pie. Both had simply disappeared.

I started to call Coleman and beg for him to hurry up, but before I could do so, I heard the back door slam shut and two men talking. They were coming toward me. I ducked into a tiny space between a kenneled pit bull and a terrified poodle. The poodle crept as close to me as she could and the pit bull only looked at me with the saddest doggy eyes I'd ever seen. There were scars all over her body. She was one of the most docile dogs I'd ever met, and she came to the kennel wall and licked my fingers. It was all I could do not to cry, thinking about the life she'd likely led up until this time.

I made up my mind right there: Mace was going down. Way down. Hard and fast. And if I could testify against him, I would beg that he served the harshest prison term ever handed down.

Hunkered down in the crevice between kennels, I listened to the men talking. When I could catch a glimpse of them, I realized they both looked like professional wrestlers, meaning they had bulging muscles and a swagger. And what they were talking about instantly captured my interest.

"What's he going to do with that little blond bit of nosiness?" one asked.

"She's tiny, but she put up a good fight." He laughed hard. "Lordy, she's scrappy. She throat chopped me, and for a minute I thought she'd kill me."

"He's not going to like her being here, poking into this business."

"She won't be able to tell anyone. He'll see to that."

I was dying to know who the "he" they referenced meant. Was it Mace? Zotto? Who? It was all I could do to restrain myself from jumping out and demanding answers. I had to be very careful, though. They had Tinkie!

"Really, what's he going to do with her?" the taller one asked. "She's married to the president of the bank. If she doesn't show up at home, they'll tear the county apart looking for her."

"True. That's why he wants us to start moving these dogs out. And there can't be a trace they were ever here. The next fight has been moved to Largo. We'll take the fighting dogs there. The bait dogs will have to be disposed of."

These were brutal men with no compassion. They wouldn't hesitate to hurt me or Tinkie if they were told to do so. But who was issuing all the orders? Garwool? Fenway? Dawson?

Mace? Zotto? Lomus? It could be any or all of those men. Or it could also be a player I hadn't uncovered yet. And they had Tinkie and maybe Sweetie Pie. I couldn't just cower behind kennels. I had to think of something to free Tinkie.

The men walked through the shed, counting the dogs, determining which ones would be taken to the new location and which would be destroyed. The two men were unmoved by the prospect of killing the dogs. They didn't care. But I damn sure did.

When the two men finally left the shed, I eased out of my hiding place and hurried to a window to check outside. The men would be coming back to "take care" of the dogs. Time was running out.

There was no movement outside the shed that I could see. No sign of the cavalry arriving. It was time to make an escape. But first I searched the whole place quickly. No Tinkie to be found, just three dozen dogs living a life of misery in kennels. At least the shed had some heat to ward off the winter chill. As I checked each dog, I felt my desperation grow. I had to save them. Whatever it cost.

I texted Coleman my location and some photos of the dogs. That way he could find me on the property. I eased out of the shed and headed south toward the main house. They had to have taken Tinkie—and maybe Sweetie—there. My path was clear—save my partner and my dog, then bring the wrath of hell down upon this crew of miscreants.

Coleman texted that he was on the way with several K-9 units. He was coming in the front door with guns blazing, so to speak. He was also bringing trained help to clear the dogs out and get them to Karl at the vet clinic.

I'd lost all concept of time, but my phone told me it was

after lunch. The day was slipping away from me. I gave a low whistle to see if Sweetie Pie would respond. Nothing. My stomach knotted. Where was my big hound? I had to find both of my missing partners, canine and human. But first, Avalon needed to be retrieved. I untied her and ducked back into the woods, using the cover of the trees and underbrush to circle around the shed and head toward Mace's home. If I could catch him unprepared . . . oh, the things I wanted to do to him.

Avalon was good as gold as we hustled through the woods. We were quiet, and I listened for any indication there was anyone watching or aware of us. So far, so good.

As Avalon and I kept moving, I came upon another building, a fitness center where four or five men were lifting weights in the winter cold. They talked and laughed, challenging each other. I listened to see if I could learn anything about the occupants of the property. The men talked, but it was about coming performances, workout tools, and things that weren't pertinent to my situation.

They were busy with their fitness program and I slipped past. Before I left the area, I checked the windows and looked inside. Four men were practicing falls and drops as a tag-team routine. Wrestling was scripted—something a lot of people refuse to believe—but the participants were still accomplished athletes. They could snap my neck if they decided to do it.

Behind me I heard the soft snuffle of a dog. Avalon and I both turned to find Sweetie Pie sitting beside us, tail wagging. She caught the hem of my shirt and tugged at me. I didn't hesitate. I just followed her back into the woods and down a trail that continued in a southward direction.

I pulled up the topographical map on my phone and tried to figure out where I was on Mace's property, but my map skills were sorely lacking. Sweetie Pie was my best bet. She knew things. And she was smart. We came upon another building, this one packed into a densely wooded area. I signaled Sweetie back over to me. I had a real sense of danger involving the large cabin. I was about to step forward when I noticed the camera. This building had security. Which meant that something was within that needed protecting. I intended to find out what.

I didn't have a gun, but I found a big tree limb that had fallen and I swatted the camera so hard I smashed it to bits. Someone would come to check on it, but I hoped to be gone before they arrived. Sweetie led the way and Avalon and I followed. Instead of the door, I went to the windows to check. The first thing I saw was Tinkie tied to a chair. She was gagged, too. But she seemed alone. Just as I was about to raise the window and slip inside, a man walked into the room. Mace. He pulled up a chair in front of Tinkie. He leaned his elbows on his knees and talked to her. I couldn't hear what he was saying, but he looked uncomfortable. He kept looking behind him as if he, too, were a prisoner of sorts. Which didn't make any sense, because this was his place. He was captain of the ship. Or was he?

He looked over his shoulder and spoke. This I could hear—at least most of it.

"You can't hurt this woman," he said. "There will be hell to pay."

"And they will blame you, not me. That's why I kept you around, Rutherford. You're the perfect scapegoat."

This was not what I anticipated. Rutherford wasn't the mastermind. He was a victim. But who was the man behind Mace? I couldn't see him, and I didn't recognize his voice. If I was going to break up the dogfighting ring, I needed to see this person's face so I could identify him to Coleman. It was interesting that I knew it wasn't Fenway or Garwool. So who, then? And when would Coleman get here? He would come in the front, so it might take him a bit of time to work his way deep into the property to find me. He could track my phone, though, so I knew he'd get to me as quickly as he could.

I eased around the outside of the cabin and went to another window, hoping to see the man behind the curtain, so to speak. I had to find out who was running this show. I used my hand to block the glare on the window and stared into the room. It was almost completely dark, except for the light that came from the window. I couldn't make out anyone, until a man shifted. Gradually, I was able to discern that he was tall, lean, and wearing a suit. Not one of the wrestlers. At least Gertrude Stromm wasn't in the room with him. I realized I'd been dreading the possibility that I would have to confront her. Ultimately, I knew she was behind the attempts to hurt me. She was implicated in the theft of the dogs. But why was she involved in this business?

Once I got Tinkie free and had Sweetie Pie on a leash, I was going to get some answers from Garwool and Fenway.

I eased around the cabin, trying other windows, but I couldn't see anything. The interior was dark except for the room where Tinkie was being held. And the man in the suit never gave me a clear view. He was always in the shadows. I couldn't identify him, which was frustrating.

I ended up back at the window where I could see Tinkie still tied to the chair. The cabin appeared empty, but I knew the man in the suit was in there somewhere. He hadn't come out, as far as I knew. And Mace was still in there, too. I didn't have time to procrastinate. I had to take action. I tapped lightly on the window, hoping to get Tinkie's attention.

She looked over quickly, and from the fear in her eyes, I knew she'd seen me. She tried to look over her shoulder and I realized someone was behind her. I couldn't see them, but if they looked, they could easily see me. I bent down and unhooked Avalon from her leash. If I were captured, I wanted her to be free to run and get away. If they caught her, they would likely kill her. My friends would find her and take care of her and also rescue me if I got in too deep.

I hurried away from the window, and just in time. The front door flew open and Mace came out to look around. He walked right past where I was hiding with Avalon in a clump of bushes. When he slowed, my heart began to really pound. Was he onto me?

He stopped not four feet from me, but he was looking deeper into the woods. "Sarah Booth, I know you're right there. Don't move. Get out of here. You're in danger and so is your partner."

Since he knew I was there, it seemed pointless to continue to hide. I didn't move, but I spoke up. "Untie Tinkie and let her go."

"If I do, he'll kill me."

"I don't care." The words came out hot and angry. I didn't care what happened to him, but I cared about Tinkie. "Let her go and I'll get help for you."

"This guy is crazy. He has no boundaries."

"Who?"

There was a commotion at the front of the cabin. Mace

turned abruptly and walked away. He appeared to be looking for someone. Was it a ruse? Or was he really as scared as
he looked? I leaned out of the bushes for a better view. The
hand on my shoulder gripped me like an iron claw. My knees
turned to rubber.

39

Mace turned around and the expression on his face told me we were both in big trouble.

"Let her go," Mace said to the person who had hold of me.

"I can't. And neither can you."

I recognized the voice and turned to face Zotto. He didn't look happy, but he did look determined.

"Zotto, let her go," Mace said. "It'll only be worse for everyone if anything happens to the sheriff's main squeeze."

"We have our orders," Zotto said.

"And I am going to disobey." Mace stood taller. "This has gone too far. I had a wonderful business here, teaching people how to perform. I loved my work. I made excellent money, and then—" He turned away. "Just let her go. This is over. I should have stopped this when they ordered us to do the dog-fights. That's not a sport. That's just cruelty and brutality."

"None of us liked it, but the consequences are deadly. Once you borrowed that money . . . they owned us." Zotto pulled me out of the shrubs. "You have no idea how you've complicated things for us."

I shook off his hand, and he let me go. I still had Avalon's leash, and she came out of the bushes to stand beside me, heeling perfectly. "I'm not leaving her, and I'm taking Tinkie with me. Law enforcement is coming for all the dogs in the shed. If a hair on them is harmed, I will make you pay in ways you've never dreamed of." It was pretty much an empty threat, but I had to make it. My pride demanded that I stand up and fight.

"You're not—" Zotto started.

"Let her go," Mace said. He looked at me. "Get out of here."

"Who is forcing you to do these things?" I asked. I needed a name. Someone to blame. Someone to pay the consequences.

"Get out of here before I change my mind," Mace said. "Get your partner and scram. Now!"

I didn't wait for a second invitation. I whistled Avalon to follow me, called up Sweetie Pie, and rushed into the cabin to release Tinkie. She leaped from the chair and grabbed me in a hug. "I knew you'd save me."

"Did you see the other man? The one calling the shots?"

"I didn't," she said. "I did find out Dawson isn't involved in this in a bad way, though. He's been trying to get the information on where the dogs were being held so he could help them. They were talking about having him capped because he brings so much attention to this place."

"I found the dogs. Coleman is on his way. But right now, let's vamoose. I don't want Mace to change his mind and hold both of us."

"Good plan." Tinkie rubbed her wrists for a minute to bring the circulation back. "Are we going back to the car or what?" she asked.

"We should try to find that man who is running this nightmare."

"Or the woman," Tinkie threw in. "Gertrude is in this up to her eyebrows."

"But how does she fit in with dogfighting and stealing dogs?" I didn't doubt Tinkie's assessment, I just didn't see how it all connected.

"Once we finish here, that's exactly what we're going to find out."

I wanted to ask how, but for the moment I felt the focus should be on searching for the man and then clearing out of the way for Coleman and the dog rescuers to arrive. If we could hem the kingpin up, we'd help Coleman and the dogs.

When we got to the shed with the dogs, Tinkie's eyes filled with tears. The conditions were deplorable. She rushed to kennel after kennel, talking softly to the dogs, winning them over so she could pet them and give them comfort. She put her hand lightly on my forearm. "You go look for the man. I'm staying here with the dogs." She reached into the back of her jeans and brought her gun out. "They didn't even search me. Mace and Zotto are totally ineffective as criminals."

"And that's a good thing." I took the gun. Tinkie would soon have help with the pups, and this plan allowed me to pursue the person I most wanted to punish. "You sure you're going to be okay here alone?"

Tinkie pulled out her phone. "Coleman is on his way and so is Oscar. I got Zotto to text him for me. He's picking up Chablis and coming straight here. I'll be fine. You be careful."

That was my plan. "When we take the doggos to Karl, while we're there, I'll pick up Pumpkin."

Tinkie rolled her eyes. "That dog is a demon."

"And you love her." I gave my partner a side hug and then hurried out the front door.

Zotto and Mace were aware Coleman and a rescue crew were on the way. I didn't think they'd warn the person forcing them to break laws. But I couldn't guarantee it. The best thing for me to do was find this mystery man and restrain him. He wouldn't get the jump on me. I'd make certain of that.

"Find the weirdo," I told Sweetie Pie, because I didn't know what else to call the criminal. To my surprise, Sweetie gave a little burble of a howl and then she and Avalon headed into the woods. I was left to follow at a slower pace.

The day was brisk and cold, but running through the woods made me work up a sweat. We were heading to what I hoped would be Mace's home. That's where there were more buildings and more likely hiding places for the unknown criminal. I followed as fast as I could, slowly peeling out of my jacket and tying it around my waist.

When Mace's home came into view, I called the dogs back to me and hunkered down in the edge of the woods until I could get the lay of the land. Just in time, too. The front door swung open and Mace and Zotto came out. They were carrying duffle bags. They threw them into the back of a truck and climbed in. Their plan was to make a speedy escape. I didn't try to stop them. Coleman would get them at the front gate.

The truck roared out of the driveway and disappeared around a curve. I cautioned the dogs to be quiet, and I ran up to the front door of the house. Without hesitating, I slipped inside. Sweetie Pie and Avalon would act as lookouts. If someone came up, I felt certain they would bark and howl and let me know.

I'd been in Mace's home once before so I knew the layout. I headed for the kitchen. The foyer was empty and silent as I passed through. I couldn't hear anything in any of the other rooms. I tiptoed down the hall, through the dining room, and to the kitchen door. I was about to push it open when it flew open on its own and I found myself face-to-face with Gertrude Stromm. I gasped.

"Sarah Booth, I knew you'd come. You can't resist sticking your nose in everyone's business."

I reached behind me to pull the gun from the back of my pants, but my jacket, which I'd tied around my waist, was in the way. Before I could free the gun, Gertrude rushed me. She had a blackjack in her hand and she swung with the intention of killing me.

I dodged the blow and ran. Behind me the front door burst open. Sweetie Pie and Avalon rushed into the house and Sweetie leaped across the room, landing on Gertrude's chest. She knocked her flat to the floor. For a brief moment, Gertrude had the wind knocked out of her. She writhed on the floor, gasping. But I was paralyzed. Gertrude had tormented me for nearly two years. She'd tried to kill me, harmed my friends, threatened those I loved and cared about, and stolen my dogs! And she was helpless on the floor, but I couldn't move. Sweetie Pie flopped across her, effectively pinning her to the floor. Avalon joined in. That was nearly two hundred pounds of hound holding her down.

"Get them off me!" Gertrude was furious. "I will kill you and that big hound of yours, too!"

"Sounding a little like the Wicked Witch of the West, aren't we?" I was finally able to talk and I imitated the witch from my favorite movie: "I'll get you, my pretty, and your little dog, too!"

"I can't breathe," Gertrude said.

"Too freaking bad."

I found a cord to a lamp and ripped it loose. With the dogs' help, I managed to get her on her stomach and tie her hands behind her back. It was one of the most satisfying things I'd done in years. As soon as Coleman got there, he could take her to the jail. I would happily sign papers against her or do whatever else it took to put her away for a long time.

"I will make you suffer." Gertrude was far from defeated. She was cornered and trapped, but she hadn't given up.

"Why, Gertrude? Why do you hate me so?"

If she had an answer, she wasn't willing to give it. Tinkie was going to be very surprised to see Gertrude. As for me, I felt like John Walsh on an episode of *America's Most Wanted*. I wanted to pump my fist, but there was no one to see it—and I didn't want to overplay my hand until Gertrude was behind bars.

"Who is helping you, Gertrude?"

Silence.

"Coleman is on the way, and you're going to jail. You'll be charged, tried, and convicted."

She completely ignored me.

I had dreamed about this moment, when she would be my helpless prisoner, for months now. I had her. She was caught. And yet, I didn't feel the satisfaction I'd anticipated. Lying on the floor of Rutherford Mace's home, Gertrude looked a little frail. I swallowed and stepped back.

"Who is working with you?" I tried one more time. Looking at Gertrude, I realized she wasn't the shadowy person I'd seen in the cabin. That person was still unidentified. And somewhere on the premises.

I heard a vehicle outside and I walked to the front door

to see who was arriving. But there was no sign of anyone. Sweetie Pie and Avalon had disappeared. They weren't far, but their absence worried me. I went back to the dining room, where I'd left Gertrude. The electrical cord I'd tied her with was cut in pieces and lying on the floor.

She was gone.

40

I searched the house from top to bottom. Gertrude had vanished, along with everyone else. My heart fluttered as I thought of Tinkie, alone and unaware that Gertrude was on the premises. Gertrude hated her almost as much as she hated me. What was scarier was that Gertrude had help here on the property. Someone, I didn't know who or why, was assisting Gertrude in her nefarious plans.

There was no time to waste. I had to get back to Tinkie and make sure she was safe. My cell phone buzzed in my pocket. It was Coleman, telling me they were ten minutes out. Relief slipped through my entire body. I was afraid of Gertrude. I could acknowledge that fact. She was mean and more than a little bit insane, and now she was once again free because I'd failed to watch her. Still, I had to stop kicking myself and focus.

Sweetie Pie and Avalon came bounding out of the woods when I crossed the yard. I was on red alert, but I was far from safe. Anyone could shoot me—there was no real cover between the house and one of the wrestling buildings. The hairs on my arms stood on end. At any minute I expected to hear a gunshot, and to feel the bullet piercing me. When I couldn't take it anymore, I started running toward the woods. Behind me was the sound of female laughter.

Gertrude was gloating. She'd been hiding in the house all along.

I was panting when I arrived at the cabin. Using the building as cover, I hurried toward the shed with the dogs and found her waiting by a kennel and talking to the terrified pit bull. He trembled in fear when she reached in to pet him. His life as a fighter was over. Too many grievous injuries, abuses, and cruelties; his spirit was totally broken. Now he was a bait dog, and his body showed the horror of what his life had been.

"Gertrude is here. I had her, but she got away." I was so relieved to see my partner safe and unharmed that I confessed my failure.

"Coleman will get her." She shook her head slightly. "You didn't do anything wrong. Now, listen. The cavalry is here."

She was right. We went outside to find several big vans pulling up. Men and women from several rescue groups got out and came toward us.

"The dogs are traumatized," Tinkie said, about to cry. "They've been so abused."

"They'll have a good life now," one man said. "We'll take them straight to Doc Smith and get help for them."

"Promise you won't put them to sleep." Tinkie knew the

score. Too often dogs from fighting situations were put down because people feared the abuse they suffered had permanently damaged them.

To my surprise, Dawson Reed walked over with more volunteer workers who'd arrived in his van. "You have my word that we will do everything in our power to heal them and find them loving homes."

Dawson started leading the fighting dogs out first. They came out docilely and made no attempt to harm each other, though the volunteers were careful to keep them safely apart. Dog by dog, the nightmare of the shed was emptied. When they began moving out the bait dogs, Tinkie planted herself in front of the kennel where the poor old beaten-up pittie waited. The dog's eyes were hopeless. To him, it must have seemed as if he were being pulled out of the kennel to meet his fate. A bad fate.

"This one is mine," Tinkie said to Dawson. "I'm taking him home with me."

"He could be dangerous. He's been so badly mistreated . . ." Dawson's voice faded when he saw the determination in her eyes. When Tinkie had that look on her face, there was no arguing with her. Her mind was made up. "Okay, I'll load him in Sarah Booth's car, but what about Sweetie Pie and Avalon? There isn't a way to keep them apart."

"I'll take Sarah Booth's girls home," Coleman said. "Put that dog in the back seat of her vehicle."

"What's his name?" Tinkie asked.

Dawson looked at a tag on the far side of his kennel. "Gun Metal."

"He's getting a new name. I'll let you know." She took his leash and walked out without looking backward.

"She bonded to that dog," Dawson said.

I walked out to watch Tinkie gently help the dog into the back. The poor baby fell heavily onto the soft seat with a sigh. His eyes closed almost instantly. With the vehicle parked in the sun, he would be plenty warm while we continued to work.

When the last dog was loaded, I pulled Coleman aside and told him everything that had happened. When I brought up Gertrude and her threats, his blue eyes turned glassy and his generous mouth thinned. "That bitch is going to jail."

"I had her, and she got away from me." I continued to beat myself up over that.

"Someone let Gertrude loose. You said the bonds were cut. It's good you weren't in that room or you could be dead. Now, I've brought the deputies and ten deputized volunteers. We're going to search this property and find Gertrude and whoever is assisting her."

Tinkie and I huddled with Coleman and the deputies. It was decided that we would help with the search in the woods. Coleman had enough volunteers that we could tackle the property with the hope of flushing out Gertrude and her un-named helper. I learned that Mace and Zotto were being held in the back of a patrol car. They'd turned themselves in and seemed content to wait for Gertrude to be found. They did confirm she was on the premises, but they denied knowing any other person—except the wrestling staff and trainees. Now they were Coleman's problem. He could sort them out when he got them back to Zinnia.

I gave Tinkie back her gun—she was the better shot—and we whistled up the dogs before we stepped into the woods in the section Coleman assigned us to search. He'd been reluctant to let us do it, but we were determined.

"Be careful," he said. He leaned down to Tinkie. "If you shoot Gertrude, don't miss."

Tinkie nodded. "I'll do my best."

The sunlight slanted through the trees as we stepped into the woods. In the dense shade the temperature dropped a good ten degrees, and it had already been cold. We could walk fast to stay warm. We set out at a brisk pace. I was very glad not to be alone in the woods with Gertrude. She'd proven more than once that she'd shoot me or Tinkie without hesitation. With both of us looking out and listening, we would be safer.

Though there were ten deputized volunteers—all with guns—searching the woods, there was still a lot of territory to cover. The brake where Tinkie and I had come onto the property was large. It covered most of the acreage that Mace owned, and the contours of the land made the going slow and difficult. There were bogs and springs and plenty of brambles and vines to slow us down.

Walking side by side with the dogs only a few yards in front of us, we set about our search. Only ten minutes into it, I felt as if the woods had swallowed me.

"I really want to shoot Gertrude," Tinkie confessed.

"Me, too." Why deny it? I wanted her dead.

"I've never wanted to kill another person, but she is . . ."

The words I would use to describe her were better left unsaid.

Raucous barking made us both jump. Sweetie and Avalon had hit a trail. Gertrude was possibly within our grasp! We leaped into action and were hot on the heels of the dogs.

41

The path in the woods widened a bit. When we came to a fork, Tinkie and Avalon took a left and Sweetie Pie and I set off down a deer trail to the right. Based on the topo map, these two paths would converge about fifty yards farther on. If my plan worked, I would get ahead of Tinkie and Avalon—and our culprit. But that was a big *if.*

Brambles and briars tugged at my feet and ankles; limbs slapped me in the face as I rushed forward. If we could trap Gertrude between Tinkie and me, then we'd have her. I didn't have a gun, but I picked up a limb. It was better than nothing. I put on a burst of speed, catching up to Sweetie Pie and running beside her. When I came to the place where the paths rejoined, I ducked down in a clump of ferns and weeds. If Tinkie flushed Gertrude ahead of her, I'd be perfectly set up to put my woody weapon to good use—I would knock her legs out from under her.

Sweetie Pie dashed down the trail toward Tinkie, and I held

my breath to listen. A few minutes later both dogs came out of the woods, followed closely by Tinkie. No Gertrude.

"Well, damn," Tinkie said. "She got by us somehow."

I wasn't surprised. Gertrude was slippery, and she'd proven herself to be a master of eluding capture. We followed the trail to the perimeter of the property and stopped on the verge. Looking north down the road, I could see the place where I'd parked my car before one of Coleman's volunteers had fetched it and taken it back to Mace's house. But there was no sign of Gertrude or her helper.

"What should we do?" Tinkie asked.

"Let's head back, get the car and your new dog, and head over to Karl's clinic. We can't do anything else here, but they'll start taking the fighting dogs there. Maybe we can help make them comfortable."

I stepped back into the dense foliage and stopped when I heard Sweetie Pie's vicious growl. Sweetie came rushing down the path and Avalon joined her. The dogs stopped, then looked south toward Mace's home. Their hackles were raised as they both growled deep in their throats. Something was going on and they didn't like it, but I didn't see anyone on the trail.

We came to the place where the paths diverged. I headed down one and Tinkie took the other. We were rushing back to Mace's home. Gertrude had to be there with the person helping her. Somehow we'd missed them.

Up ahead Sweetie Pie saw or smelled something. She gave a long, deep bay that ended in a guttural growl, and she was gone. I went after her, determined not to let her get too far ahead. I was almost to the juncture of the paths when Gertrude stepped into the center of the trail. She had a gun, and it was pointed at my chest. I stopped in my tracks.

"At last, Sarah Booth, we can have a chat. I really don't want to kill you. At least not yet. It's more fun to make you suffer. But I have places to go and things to do, and you're beginning to annoy me."

On the opposite side of the path, a man stepped out. He, too, had a gun. "Ms. Delaney," he said. "You have a talent for poking your nose where it doesn't belong."

"Who are you?" The question made me feel stupid, but I didn't recognize the man. He was vaguely familiar, and then I remembered I had seen a much younger version of him in the high school yearbook.

"Julian Dickerson, Esquire." He smiled and I was reminded of the cold, dead eyes of Hannibal Lecter. I'd be willing to bet he had a fetish for Chianti and fava beans.

"Julian Dickerson, the lawyer?" Another stupid question.

"Yes. Lawyer and so much more," Gertrude said. "Julian runs the largest dogfighting operation in the Southeast."

He was a well-dressed man, some would even say handsome. He had fine, dark hair, a scruff that some women would find attractive, and the palest blue eyes I'd ever seen. "Why?" I addressed the question to Dickerson. "You're a lawyer with a fine reputation. Why are you involved in any of this?"

Gertrude spoke up. "The money is good. The risks are negligible. The overhead is low, especially when you can blackmail your enemies into doing the dirty work for you. The dogs never live long enough to worry about vet care or their diet, just whatever crappy food is the cheapest."

She was taking far too much pleasure in this. My expression must have told her how I loathed her and how distraught her comments made me. "Dog murderer," I said. "How many are dead because of you?"

"Hundreds." She grinned. "And there's nothing you can do about it. Pretty soon I'm going to add that big hound dog of yours to the list. And that little Yorkie creature that belongs to your partner. I never should have let them loose, but I figured they were too far from home to make it back. Who knew they'd figure out how to return to Zinnia."

"I'm going to make you pay." I wasn't bragging, just stating a fact.

Gertrude cocked her gun and pointed it right at my chest. There was no way she could miss me. "Come on, Sarah Booth. Make me pay."

Not with a gun trained on me. But the evildoers hadn't counted on Tinkie. I just had to make certain she didn't walk into the trap. "Run, Tinkie, run!" I screamed at the top of my lungs.

"Shut up or I'll shoot the dog." Dickerson wasn't messing around. He whipped his gun around to point it at Sweetie Pie.

I could only hope Tinkie had heard me and was scoping out the situation. My best chance for rescue came by keeping them talking, hoping that Coleman would arrive. "Why dogfighting? How much money could be in it? I would think poker games or some high-class gambling, like in Monaco, would be more up your alley."

"There's plenty of money in dogfighting. Plenty," Dickerson said. "I never have to leave Mississippi to rake in the profits. When you appeal to the baser nature of men, there's always money to be made."

"How did you get involved in all of this?" I asked Gertrude, waving my hand around to indicate Mace's property, the dogs, everything. "You were away from here. You'd escaped apprehension. You were free. No one was chasing after you in Arkansas. Why did you ever want to come back?"

"Unfinished business. You thought you'd escaped me. I couldn't let you get away scot-free."

I shook my head. "You're an idiot. I never believed I was free of you. I would have looked over my shoulder for the rest of my life, wondering when you'd turn up again. Now, I'm going to have to kill you." My only tactic was to psyche her out and see if I could force her into an error. "Take the shot, Tinkie!" I screamed.

Gertrude flinched and ducked, as did Dickerson. That was my cue to make a break for it. Just as I dove into the woods, I heard a gunshot. I expected to feel the bite of steel in my body, but I felt nothing. Instead, there was a low curse from Dickerson. He came crashing into the oak trees, then spun and fell into the center of the path. He was bleeding profusely from a gunshot wound in his shoulder.

Tinkie rushed out of the woods into the path, but Gertrude was gone.

Dickerson tried to crawl toward me, but he fell to his side. I had no choice. I went to him, kicked his gun deep into the briars, and tried to staunch the bleeding. I looked down the trail, but Gertrude had gotten the drop on us. The path was empty. If I left Dickerson, he might bleed to death before anyone else found him. "Tinkie, go after Avalon and Sweetie Pie, please. If you see Gertrude, hide. Don't corner her."

"Are you sure you're okay?"

"I'm fine. Go!"

She disappeared in a flash, and I was left with Dickerson. I got him to lie down in the path so I could put pressure on his shoulder. It gave me pleasure to press hard on the gunshot wound. He winced, but didn't complain. So, I pressed even harder. I was trying to staunch the blood flow—or so I told myself.

"Why in the world would you get mixed up with dogfighters?" I asked Dickerson.

He tried to sit up, but I pushed him back down. He wasn't able to resist me. "It's a long story."

"I have time." I wanted to hear his side of things. Why in the world would a successful defense attorney get involved in dogfighting, or in any other activity with Gertrude? Why risk losing his law license over something like this?

"I represented one of the dogfighters in a domestic dispute. We became friends. I attended a fight. It was exciting. The money changing hands—it was as if it were falling from the sky."

"Watching helpless animals get mauled and brutalized was exciting?" I wanted to punch him in the face with everything I had.

"You can't view the dogs as having feelings," he said. "It's like watching boxing. You can't think about whether it hurts the fighters or not."

I ground my elbow into the bullet wound. When he cried out in pain, I laughed. "Sorry, does that hurt? I'm not about to view you as someone who has feelings."

"I'm going to press charges against you."

"Try it. See how far you get." I didn't care if he reported me to Coleman—or the Mississippi judiciary. He could do his worst. "Settle back and relax until Tinkie returns. Or the sheriff. Either way, you're going to jail."

I picked his gun up out of the weeds on the side of the path and sat down cross-legged in the dirt to wait. He wasn't in danger of bleeding to death—drat it.

*   *   *

A few minutes later, Tinkie returned with both dogs following. I stood up and pointed at Dickerson. "Tinkie, keep your gun on him until Coleman arrests him."

"Where are you going?" Tinkie asked.

"To Mace's house. Gertrude is probably there."

"Maybe. I didn't see her near the dog shed. But you should wait for Coleman and the deputies. Gertrude will kill you. You know she'll try."

I did know, but I wasn't about to let her get away. She was on the property and on foot, as far as I knew. I was younger and quicker. "I'll be careful."

"Take her down, Sarah Booth."

"I intend to." I leaned down to Dickerson. "What is Gertrude to you?"

He looked down into the dirt and sighed. "She's my business partner."

"And Fenway?"

He shook his head. "Fenway is a fool. His daughter runs the show."

"Penelope?"

"She's the one who introduced me to Gertrude. She got involved with that Jason Lomus and he had her over a barrel."

"You're a smart man, Dickerson. How much money do you need?"

Dickerson sighed. "It was the excitement at first. The dogs, the crowds, the gambling. And Penelope loved it. She ran the betting and she was making money hand over fist. We'd go to a fight and it really turned her on."

"Money." I was disgusted by the greed and depravity. "All of that suffering for a few dollars."

"More than a few." Dickerson took a deep breath. "I did

try to get out, but I was in too deep. That's why I got Ellis to steal those dogs. I thought if I turned up the heat on the dog-fighters, then I could get out of it."

"Explain that to us like we're five," Tinkie said. She was clearly furious.

"Steal a few dogs from some old ladies in town. For the last ten years Tilly had raised untold hell in Nixville, going to board meetings and trying to hold Fenway and Garwool accountable. She gets the locals stirred up, so she needed to learn a lesson. Tilly and Squatty were the perfect dog own-ers to pick on, too. They hired you to find the missing dogs, which was exactly what I'd hoped. You come along, start pok-ing into things, the fights had to be cancelled. Folks talked about going into hiding for a while. I was going to take that opportunity to break ties with Penelope and get clear of the whole business. I planned to move my law practice to Ocean Springs."

Great. So, he'd had a plan. Whoopee. It hadn't gone very well for him. But I had a few more questions. "Was Garwool involved in the dogfighting?"

Dickerson snorted. "Not on your life. Garwool is an idiot. Penelope can barely stand to talk to him, but he's been a ter-rific beard for the fighting rink. If she told him the grass was purple, he'd believe her."

"He never suspected?"

"Not Penelope. Or me. Penelope fed him people like Ellis Adams and Lomus. She sent him chasing down a rabbit trail after Zotto and Mace."

"Then they weren't involved?"

"No," Dickerson said. "Some of the wrestlers were, but not Mace or Zotto."

"But the dogs were all on Mace's property," Tinkie pointed out. "He had to know."

"Mace never left the house. He left it up to Zotto to run the schools, teach the classes, help the wannabe wrestlers hook up for matches and things. Mace and Zotto may have suspected, but neither of them wanted to look. The setup was too convenient for them to want to tip over the apple cart."

"Willful ignorance," I said.

"Plausible deniability," Dickerson replied.

"You're going to jail," was my response.

"I wouldn't be so sure." Dickerson, for all of the fact that he'd lost considerable blood, was undisturbed by getting caught. "No one really prosecutes animal-cruelty cases. There's not a jury in Sunflower County that will take dogfighting as a serious crime."

"That's where you're wrong. Sheriff Peters is going to put you under the jail," I told him. "Now, where is Gertrude? Tell me."

"Even if I knew, I wouldn't tell."

That was fine with me. I looked at my partner, who was sitting on a stump on the side of the road. She had a clear view of Dickerson and she had her gun trained on him. "Go ahead and see if you can track Gertrude, Sarah Booth. He won't get away from me. Catch her, and let's put an end to all of this. I want to make sure all the dogs are safe with Karl and then I want to go home and hug Chablis."

42

Coleman was at Mace's house when I got there, winded and sweaty. Even in the cold, brisk day, I was overheated. Sweetie Pie and Avalon rushed to greet Coleman, and he bent to pull the dogs close. "I was worried," he said. "These people have no compunction about killing dogs. Or private investigators."

"I know. Let's search the house. Gertrude has to be here."

Coleman didn't say anything, but he fell into step beside me. "Where did you get the gun?"

"It's Julian Dickerson's. He's been shot, and Tinkie is holding him prisoner down the path toward the dog shed."

"Who shot him?" Coleman asked. He was amused, not angry.

"It could have been Tinkie." I wasn't going to rat out my partner, but ballistics would tell the story, anyway.

"Good for Tinkie." Coleman put a hand on my back in a gesture of support. "Now, let's find that crazy old bat."

Coleman sent the deputies to find Tinkie and Dickerson,

and we went into Mace's mansion. It was a big place, with lots of hiding nooks and crannies. "Should we separate?" I asked him.

He shook his head. "Gertrude intends to kill you. I intend to stop her. You shoot first, okay? Don't give her any kind of an opening to hurt you."

We opened the door and went inside. Mace and Zotto had already been rounded up by the law officers on their first sweep. If Mace was running drugs, the deputies had found no evidence. The house had an abandoned air. Completely silent. Only I wasn't sure it was empty. Gertrude was devious. And she'd proven to be very effective at hiding in plain sight. She'd also demonstrated a proclivity for ruthlessness and a desire to cause pain for those she hated. Namely, me and Coleman and my pups.

Inside the door we stopped and listened intently. Sweetie Pie hung back beside my leg until I gave her a signal to search. My heart was in my throat as the dogs took off in different directions. Avalon went up the stairs and Sweetie headed for the kitchen. I would never forgive myself if something happened to them, but they were far stealthier than I could be. I had to hang on to that reality.

Coleman went up the stairs behind Avalon. For a big, well-muscled man, he was amazingly quiet. Not a floorboard creaked beneath his weight. When he disappeared on the landing, I went to the kitchen. The back door was locked, and I started in the mudroom and made my way forward. I was at the front of the house when I heard a motor start. I rushed to the sidelight near the front door and began to curse. My car was roaring out of the yard—with Gertrude behind the wheel.

She'd stolen my nearly new vehicle. And Tinkie's new dog!

Coleman came down the stairs at warp speed. We gathered the dogs, hopped into his truck—with newly replaced windows, thanks to Gertrude—and gave chase. But Gertrude was too far ahead of us. I couldn't be certain if she hid in the woods, camouflaging my car, or if she beat a trail to the main road and took off to parts unknown from there. Whatever the reality, she lost us.

I leaned against the cold window in the truck and swallowed back tears. I was so certain we were going to catch her, that the long months of being stalked by Gertrude were over. I'd allowed myself to believe she was going to get the Karma she so justly deserved.

Coleman and the deputies retrieved Tinkie and Dickerson. He was definitely going to jail, and he'd never practice law again. The fallout from his involvement with the dogfighting ring would ricochet all over Mississippi.

Coleman supervised the search of the property, leaving me in Mace's home with my dogs and my partner. I searched through some paperwork and records, but there really wasn't anything there to incriminate Mace and Zotto. Apparently, they'd been telling the truth. They weren't involved in the dogfighting ring.

Zotto and Mace had already agreed to testify against Dickerson, Garwool, Penelope, and Fenway. They'd also held firm to their belief that Dawson Reed was a good guy. Tinkie and I discussed that bit of good news as we waited for Coleman and his men to find my vehicle. It chafed me to wait, doing nothing but worrying about the abused dog in the back seat, but we had plenty of good news to keep us upbeat. The Fenways' and Garwool's rule of the small town was coming to an end. A whole new regime would be elected in

Nixville. Whatever Garwool's role in the dogfighting, he was done in law enforcement. Fenway had a ticket to Parchman state prison, and I hoped his daughter would end up in the women's prison near Jackson. The deputies and volunteers were picking up the wrestlers who had been actively involved in the dogfighting ring. They, too, would serve time.

That was all good news, but the best good news was that Karl Smith had found a rescue in Virginia that would take the fighting dogs and work to rehabilitate them. Peter O'Neil, the highly regarded dog trainer, would stop by regularly to work with them and their rescuers to make sure they were completely safe before placing them in a loving home. It was the best possible outcome for the dogs.

The bait dogs were doing great at Karl's, and he'd lined up several people who had already committed to adopting some of them. He would keep them until they were healthy and ready for love. Not a single dog would have to be put down. All in all, it was a miraculous turn of events.

Except that Gertrude had my new vehicle and Tinkie's dog, and she'd disappeared off the face of the planet.

Tinkie, the rest of the dogs, and I rode back to Zinnia with Coleman. Several of the wrestlers had been apprehended and they were being held in the Nixville jail so their statements could be taken and evaluated. The very helpful Deputy Tom Terrell was in charge of them, and he made it clear he'd share any pertinent information with me. Later, the men would be transferred to Zinnia for easy access for Coleman to question them.

When we got to Dahlia House, Coleman idled in the front yard. Millie was on the way with some food for all of us. Cece was at the courthouse photographing the wounded Dickerson, who was telling outrageous lies about me and my dog. I could only hope the fool would go on camera. It was going to be a huge story that Mississippi's most prominent defense lawyer was losing his license and going to jail for dogfighting. And in the midst of his whanging about how awfully I attacked him, he let it slip that his intention was to kill Jezebel. It seems that the hero police dog had sniffed out his drug empire in Jackson. He'd evaded connection to the drugs—so far. But Dawson had been closing the gap on those facts. Jezebel had played a key role in shutting down the drug supply. When Dickerson learned she was in Nixville, he was determined to finish her off for good.

Now that would never happen.

Fenway had resigned as mayor and was begging Coleman not to send him to prison. He claimed not to know what his daughter and Gertrude had been up to, along with Dickerson's help. Fenway spilled his guts with little prodding. "That lawyer. I thought he was a decent man," Fenway said. "He was sleeping with my daughter when she was engaged to Garwool. The police chief and I are the victims here," he insisted.

Coleman wasn't exactly buying that line, but like all smart lawmen, he kept his lips zipped and hoped the building pressure would force Fenway to reveal even more.

As for me, I took the dogs inside, made some coffee, and waited for the food. Millie arrived shortly, and Tinkie and I were soon filling her in—while stuffing our faces with fried chicken, turnips, and corn bread. Oscar arrived, and my eyes misted over when Tinkie collapsed against him and began to cry. It had been a hard, traumatic time for all of us.

Tilly and Squatty showed up at Dahlia House, Tilly with a seven-layer chocolate Dobash cake. Squatty had ice cream. Even though I was full as a tick, I couldn't resist that cake. As the stress and tension slowly unwound in my gut, I breathed deeply. The dogs were safe. That was what I needed to hang on to. I couldn't undo the cruelty they'd suffered, but I would do my best to make sure the rest of their days were filled with love and treats. As to Dickerson, Fenway, Penelope, and the rest of the evildoers, I would not rest until the harshest sentences had been handed to them.

And Gertrude remained to be apprehended. But she, too, would be punished. Eventually.

When Coleman got the call from South Haven that the highway patrol had found my car abandoned at the Mississippi River, I had to accept that Gertrude had well and truly evaded me yet again. The good news was that Tinkie's big red pittie baby was in the car, alive and unharmed. It was bitterly disappointing that Gertrude had eluded us, but she'd lost her source of income, and deputies in Arkansas had raided the bed-and-breakfast where she'd worked for the Fenways. She wouldn't be going back there—not even for her possessions. They had been confiscated by the police.

I'd failed to capture Gertrude, but I'd made her life very complicated, at least for the immediate future.

Oscar brought Chablis with him, and she was excited to see my dogs and Pluto the cat. Poe, the raven, liked to devil the little pampered beast, but on this occasion, everyone was on their best behavior. We settled onto the front porch to wait for news from Coleman.

One of the volunteers had driven to South Haven to pick up my car and bring it back. Before he returned it, Coleman had ordered the crime scene techs to go over every inch of it to be sure Gertrude hadn't planted a bug or anything so she could track me. That was Coleman's big concern—that Gertrude would somehow be able to follow me and catch me alone. Gertrude would not be happy until I'd paid the ultimate price, and Tinkie, too. That it made zero sense didn't matter. With each passing month, Gertrude had slipped further and further off the rails.

When the deputies brought my car back—complete with the pittie dog Tinkie had named Zelda—DeWayne looked worried. He pulled Coleman aside and handed him something. Coleman glanced over at me and then approached, a piece of paper in his hand. My heart lurched at the expression on his face.

"What is it?" I asked him.

He sighed and handed me the paper. Tinkie gathered close to read it over my shoulder, along with Millie and Cece, who had just arrived.

The note, in block letters, read THIS IS FAR FROM OVER. YOUR PARENTS SUFFERED THE ULTIMATE PRICE FOR THEIR SINS, AND SO WILL YOU.

I gasped and the paper was whipped from my fingers by a sudden burst of cold wind. Sweetie Pie chased it down and put a paw on it until Coleman could retrieve it.

"Do you know what this means?" Coleman asked me.

"No." I didn't. And I didn't want to. Every single cell in my body rebelled against thinking about this. "Gertrude is insane. That's all it is."

"I'll make us a drink," Tinkie said. Millie and Cece followed her into the house.

Coleman pulled me from the chair and into his arms. He

held me tightly. "What happened the night your parents were killed, Sarah Booth?" He spoke so gently, but his words were ice picks in my chest.

"Nothing happened. They were coming home from a party. The men who worked the wreck said a deer or something ran out in front of the car and Daddy swerved. The car flipped in a cotton field. They were killed instantly." I went over the story I'd been told numerous times—and had tried just as often to forget. That night was deeply etched into my soul. Aunt Loulane was there, spending the night with me while my folks went to a party. She had come into my bedroom and sat down on the bed. Her featherlight touch stroked my forehead. And she'd told me the news that had changed the trajectory of my life. My parents were dead.

"Did you ever have reason to believe it wasn't an accident?" Coleman asked me.

The truth of the matter was that I'd never, ever entertained the possibility. Because if it was . . .

"Don't even say it." I whispered the words against Coleman's chest.

"Gertrude knows something," Coleman said. "And she is going to tell us, one way or another."

"Maybe I don't want to hear it."

He pulled me closer. "Come inside with your friends."

He didn't give me a chance to object. He ushered me in the front door and into the kitchen, where coffee was brewing. Tinkie was making drinks, and Millie and Cece were putting away the remainder of the food. Tilly and Squatty had fallen asleep in the spare bedrooms with their pups.

"I can't do this," I told Coleman.

"It's okay," he said. "It's all okay. I'll handle everything,

Sarah Booth. All that matters is that you're safe. The pets are safe. Your friends are safe. We'll worry about this later if we have to. For now, let's put this aside. Tomorrow is another day, as your aunt used to say. By the way, I got a call from Harold."

"And?" Coleman was grinning, but I didn't understand why.

"He wants to keep Pumpkin. He says Roscoe is in love with her and has been frantic all day looking for her. I also heard from Jody Holm, and she loves that terrible canine. It's up to Jody whether Harold keeps Pumpkin or not."

That was good news indeed. Harold would be the perfect home if Jody was certain she could let the pupster go. "That's fabulous." I was happy for Harold and Pumpkin, but my heart was still heavy.

"Do you think we'll ever really stop Gertrude?" I asked.

"We will. I promise you." He tilted my chin up to give me a kiss. "Whatever needs to be done, I'll make sure it happens."

And one thing about Coleman, I could count on his word.

After everyone had gone home, I went into the parlor to look for the note, but it was gone. Sweetie Pie, Avalon, Pluto, the devil dog Pumpkin, and Poe were all with me. Coleman snoozed in the bedroom upstairs. Tilly and Squatty were also asleep. Tomorrow they'd go home and help organize placement for the dogs we'd rescued. Dawson Reed had offered to help, too.

Coleman had removed the note to spare me, and I was glad. But Gertrude had succeeded in the cruelest of all of her efforts. She'd stolen the peace of believing my parents' death had been an accident. She'd opened the door on the horrible possibility that someone had killed them deliberately. My father had had enemies. He was an officer of the court. And my mother had spent her life sticking up for the underdog. That got under people's skin. But it had never occurred to me that they could be so hated that someone would kill them. Until now.

"Hate isn't so hard to understand."

The woman who stood in front of me was obviously from another century. Her center-parted hair fell into ringlets on either side of her face, and her dress was demure and looked constricting to me. There were mobility issues, too. But now wasn't the time for any company, spectral or otherwise. I had my hands full.

"I don't know who you are or why you're here, but I'm not in the mood." The truth of the matter was that my pain was so intense I didn't think I could breathe.

"The world is cruel and hard, Sarah Booth. Your parents protected you from this for as long as they could. Every living creature should know safety and love."

"Please, leave me alone." I stared at the apparition, feeling the anger rise up in me. I wasn't in the mood for lectures or even pleasant conversations. I wanted to be left alone.

"You did everything you could do—"

I picked up a glass candy dish and hurled it at her. Of course, it went straight through her and fell on the carpet. I knew I was dealing with Jitty, but I wanted only to be left alone. "Go away. Just go away."

"I can't. We fight to protect others. That's what we do. What your folks did. We fight, even when it seems we'll never win. You are so lucky to be born into a time when you can fight with all the weapons that men use to win. In my day, I had only my pen and a desire to tell the whole story of one good horse."

"Who are you?" I didn't want to know. I only wanted her to leave me alone. But it was Jitty, and Jitty never took no for an answer.

"I'm just a woman who loves animals. Horses, in particular. And I'm a storyteller. I even published a book. Only one, but you can still read it if you like."

Now she had piqued my interest. Horses and books—two things I loved beyond reason. "What book?"

"*Black Beauty*. Perhaps you know it."

Oh, did I know it. I'd shed many a tear over the pages of a book that told the story of a horse's life from the horse's point of view. It was filled with love and cruelty, and it forced people to think about the topic of how horses were treated at a time when they were the primary source of transportation and heavy work in the United Kingdom and around the world. Beauty and Ginger, her friend. Such a hard reality for me, who read the book when I was a child. The good news, though, was this one book had helped to shape me into the person I had become. It had helped make me an advocate for all animals.

"How did you know so much about horses?" I asked her. "Do you ride?"

"No, never on horseback. But I was injured, as you can see, in a terrible accident. I became reliant on horses to get me where I needed to be. I watched and I learned. I listened to the horses, some of whom were greatly loved and others who suffered every day of their lives. I knew humans could do better. I needed to tell a story to make people think."

"And you did. You really did."

"Then I can rest knowing my efforts were successful. I died shortly after the book was published."

"It was a huge and raging success. And still is. There's even a new edition now."

Her smile was both sad and tender. "I only hope it makes people understand that animals feel. We must do better. No one should suffer, Sarah Booth. And I know right now you are missing your parents."

"Do you know my parents?" I had to ask someone. Maybe she would tell me. "Were they murdered?"

"This isn't my story to tell. Or Jitty's." Anna Sewell began to morph into my beautiful Jitty. "I'm so sorry, Sarah Booth. I never wanted you to know. I never did. Neither did your parents."

"Know what? That they were murdered?" I could feel my temper igniting again. "Of course I want to know. I deserve to know. And I am going to find out what happened and I swear to you the person responsible will pay. If it was Gertrude . . ." I'd never considered Gertrude might have been the person who destroyed my life even when I was a child. It was intolerable. Unacceptable.

I started up the stairs.

"Where are you going?" Jitty was suddenly in front of me, blocking the way.

"To get my clothes. Gertrude was headed north. I'm going to find her and kill her." I meant it, too.

"Sarah Booth, this is why I've protected you all these years. This is not what your parents would want. You know that."

"Today, I live my life for me. For what *I* want. What *I* need. And I need justice."

Jitty sat down on the top step. She was still blocking my way, and her expression was so sad. "I've failed you and your parents."

I wanted to ignore her, but I couldn't. In the time I'd been home, Jitty had been my constant. She'd show up when I needed a nudge or bit of advice. She'd tormented me and also given me comfort. "You haven't failed. Gertrude has just overplayed her hand."

"I can't stop you from pursuing her. You've known this all along. But I can ask you one thing: wait until you talk this over with Coleman. Do what you can for the dogs, for the animals. Bide your time. I promise you, the opportunity for justice will arrive. And you will be ready."

I felt my energy slowly depleting. I was exhausted. Instantly, I felt like Dorothy trying to run through the poppy fields on the way to the Emerald City. I slumped down on the stairs and leaned against the banister. I was too tired to keep my eyes open another minute.

"Go to bed." Anna had returned and she stood up and stepped aside. When I gained my feet, she walked with me to the bedroom. Coleman had lit a fire for me, and I climbed beneath the covers fully dressed. It was just too much effort to change into pajamas.

"Will you stay with me?" I asked Anna, who was taking on the golden mocha tone of my haint. "Maybe tell me a story."

"I'm always with you, Sarah Booth. Even when you don't think you need me."

"Did Gertrude kill my parents?"

"Search for the truth. You'll find it."

Her voice had begun to grow dim and wavery, and when I looked at her, she was transparent. She did a little twirl at the foot of the bed, and a shower of hay rained down on her. Before the hay hit the floor, I was fast asleep.

A bit later, I heard footsteps. Coleman had gotten up to stoke the fire, and now he slipped across the floor and eased into bed beside me. He pulled me tight against him and held me.

"We'll find the truth, Sarah Booth. I promise."

"I know," I whispered. "In the morning we'll start looking for Gertrude."

"And we'll find her."

Sweetie Pie and Avalon jumped up onto the bed, with Pluto right behind them. It was the safest place in the world for me, at least for the remainder of the night.

Acknowledgments

Each book is special to the author, but this book explores a subject very close to my heart—animal rights. For the past thirty-plus years I've worked with a handful of dedicated friends to support Good Fortune Farm Refuge, a nonprofit devoted to animal welfare. We are tiny, but for the animals we've been able to help, it has changed their world. Currently, I have cats, dogs, and horses here. It's my honor to take care of them. Please urge your lawmakers to pass protection laws and mandatory spay/neuter laws wherever you live. It can change everything for animals who have no one to make sure they are safe or even fed.

It takes a ton of people to get a book from the writer's brain to the bookstore, and I have some of the very best folks in the business helping me. My agent, Marian Young; my editors Hannah O'Grady and Madeline Alsup; the St. Martin's production team, John Morrone, Alisa Trager, and Lisa Davis; the art department at St. Martin's that creates the very clever covers, Rowen Davis and David Rotstein; the cover artist, Allen Douglas; and Sara LaCotti and Sara Eslami in the marketing and publicity departments.

I also want to thank the booksellers and librarians who have long supported this series and my other books.

And a very special thanks to the readers who have stuck with me and Sarah Booth for nearly three decades! Who knew when I came up with the characters of Sarah Booth and Jitty that I would have the joy of spending so much time in their company.